WHETHER

VIOLENT

OR

NATURAL

WHETHER

VIOLENT

OR

NATURAL

a novel

NATASHA CALDER

THE OVERLOOK PRESS

First published in the United Kingdom in 2023 by Bloomsbury Publishing

Library of Congress Control Number: 2022950046

ISBN: 978-1-4197-6466-0
eISBN: 978-1-64700-831-4

Printed and bound in the United States
10 9 8 7 6 5 4 3 2 1

ABRAMS The Art of Books
195 Broadway, New York, NY 10007
abramsbooks.com

CONTENTS

WE ARE FITTED FOR
WORKS OF DARKNESS

As far as I'm concerned, it begins like this: me and Crevan become sliding silhouettes in the night, we two stepping out together across the star-washed courtyard of the castle with my hand in his hand, he ahead and I trailing along behind, me playing the part of reluctant child so as to be sure that he won't let go, me like a wave-rider facing a rolling breaker and suddenly glad of being tethered to the board. There's nothing in the night but us, us and the thale cress that lines the path, us and the eagle-owl that circles high, high above the crumbling parapets of the old keep. Even the stars are still and silent, not singing to me like they sometimes do on a cloudless night, not twinkling out their astral boasts for all to read and weep. I don't mind. Stars don't stay quiet for long, not if they can help it, swanking vanities that they are.

Besides, I'm busy being baby. Sometimes it's Crevan who needs comforting, but for now it's my turn and I want to savor every moment, every second of ceded control, of not having to think or decide what to do next, where to go, how to behave. I let him lead me past the greenhouse, the glass panes silvered with night. When we slip by the door there's a gasp of humidity on my skin, unexpected in the chill air. A stench of rotting flesh rides upon it, plant-born, stemming from one or other of the *Stapelia gigantea* that flourish in the arid heat. They are carrion plants, florid tricksters that pass themselves off as rotting corpses in the hopes of attracting the calliphorids upon which they rely to disseminate their seed.

I want to stop and say hello properly, to do what I can to purify the plants' habitual rancor with pleasantries, but I've barely begun when Crevan gives me a stern look and I catch the words dead between my teeth.

"Yes, daddy, I'll be quiet now. No, I know. No games. No fooling. Let's go."

We go. Though we quickly leave the greenhouse behind, the foul odor lingers for a long time after, coated on my tongue, the roof of my mouth, the back of my throat. Every taste of it is telling me to gag, to wretch, to purge. *Wrong*, it says. *Throw it up*, it says. I know I'm being tricked. Better still; I know what the trick is and I know how it works. But that doesn't make it any less effective. Part of my brain—the part that keeps me safe, keeps me breathing, flinches me away from pain—is most definitely duped. No smoke without fire, it thinks. No putrefaction without a corpse.

But stay, we have reached the far wall. There are walls in every direction here, on all sides of the courtyard; walls too high to jump or see over. You could climb, though. There are lots of places where the brick has crumbled—worn in, worn away—leaving little nooks and niches where you can grip with your fingers, dig in with your toes. Before Crevan came, I climbed the walls whenever the fancy took me. I would sit on the top and kick my heels or lay down to laze in the sun. I would walk their length and pretend they were much narrower than they really were, the width of one finger instead of two spread hands. I would flail my arms as though I was losing my balance, a tightrope walker swaying precariously on a line stretched between the upper limbs of giant redwoods. But Crevan doesn't like to play those sorts of games. He goes in and out through the postern and he never thinks of the walls as anything but an extra layer of defense.

Now he stops; head tilted, one ear cocked. He's listening for invaders, for the knifemen lying in wait, for the trespassers and vagrants who want to steal the island from him, from us, from me. But they aren't there. They never are. There's no one on the island but for us, me and Crevan. I try to say as much but he won't be told, won't have the plain facts pointed out to him. It's a habit, I guess, this tedious precaution of his, this need to check that the silence of no breath is everything it seems: an absence and not a stifling. But then he's been on edge ever since he came here. *A moment's inattention can be lethal.* That's what he tells me sometimes. Perhaps it's even true, I don't know. I have passed several thousand moments of inattention and come to no particular harm, but I suppose that doesn't account for all possible eventualities. Suffice to say only that I am happy to humor him, and so I try very, very hard not to tut impatiently or tap my foot as Crevan listens at the postern gate.

Finally deciding that he hears nothing because there is nothing to hear, he tugs on the latch and the gate opens like a mouth. Crevan pulls my arm and we pass together through that narrow throat and out into the belly of the island.

The land beyond the courtyard is wilderness and all the richer for it, for having been let alone, for having been allowed to grow, flex, and twist; a hundred, hundred hungry plants battling to eat the sun, to suck the sweet mulching goodness from the earth. I like to think of the island as mine—ours—but only a small part of it truly falls into our dominion. The rest belongs to the trees, to the briar and bramble, to the wasp, horntail, and honeybee, to the hawk-moth and cinnabar, to the vole, mouse, and shrew. I used to be welcome here, a cherished guest with the freedom to come and go as I pleased. But ever since Crevan came, the wilderness has taken more and more against me. The trees turn their backs upon me, the shrubs and thickets knot their branches together to bar me from wandering where I am not wanted. My presence is tolerated at best and I can hardly stand it, can hardly stand their spiteful glances and whispers. I tell myself it won't be forever, that they'll come back around before long, that we'll be fast friends once more. It's not much consolation.

A half-muttered reproach flies my mouth like a breath and makes Crevan click his tongue at me. So I hush like I'm supposed to,

ridiculous though it seems to continue playing along with his delusions like this, with his strange penchant for counterfactuals. Even
now, when we have kept watch and listened, when the causeway is
buried deep beneath the brine, he believes there might be others
on the island, creep-crawling unseen and set on slitting our throats,
snapping our necks, cracking open our skulls like soft-boiled eggs
that seep out rich ooze, thick and fragrant. Playing along only
encourages him and I know I shouldn't do it, I know, I know. But
I can't help it. For one thing, it's probably not doing him any real
harm. For another, well, he seems so invested in his little balloon-
ing fantasy, so dependent upon it, that I just can't bring myself to
undermine the illusion, no matter how tempted I may sometimes
be, no matter how curious I am about how he'll respond, how he'll
behave when the dam is broken. I hum instead; better to put my
energy into that, better to draw his displeasure than to degrade his
delusions.

Another click of the tongue from Crevan.

"Yes, yes. Silent as the grave, mustn't alert the bad men that lurk,
the creeping nasties twisting their garottes taut, good and ready.
Sorry, daddy."

But my apology only elicits a further click. I can tell that Crevan
doesn't approve, doesn't think much of my fooling. Letting go of
my hand—no more baby for me, that says, no more playing, not if
I won't behave—he slinks on ahead, reflexively adjusting his gait as
he goes, crouching low and rolling his bare feet from toe to heel to
pick his silent way through the understory, through the moss and
the celandine and the dogwood and more besides, more than even
I can name. A full moon is shine-shining above, and all the gnarling
branches of the elms are bathed ghost white, becoming phantom
trees as unreal as the imagined maneaters that Crevan spies at every
twist and bend.

We are on the southern face of the island—the far side from
the causeway—and it is covered in its entirety with the same
dense shrubland that claimed us the moment we set foot beyond

the courtyard. Our only route through it—now that I am on poor terms with the trees—is a dirt track that cuts down sharp as a card through the bracken, steep and uneven, the earth underfoot gnarled with exposed roots, rocks, hummocks of moss, a hundred niggling traps the wilderness has laid to snag at us, to trip us up, to frustrate and hinder. One day I'll bring an ax and turn it all to kindling.

"Help!"

I plant my foot edgewise and the treacherous ground shifts beneath me, turning my ankle exactly how it shouldn't, throwing my whole weight, my balance, sending me staggering off the track and wildly off kilter. I fumble and flail, grabbing out at the lower branches of a nearby yew to steady myself, hoping for safety, not expecting to catch a fistful of hawthorn as well, not prepared for the spine like a knitting needle that impales the web of skin between my finger and thumb. Seeing Crevan's eyes upon me, I make a simpering whimper and sulkily pout my lip.

"It *hurts*," I tell him. "It hurts and it's all your fault. All your fault that we have to come down this way when there are plenty of paths on the island that you can walk down easy as anything without practically dying."

What I say is true in every word. There are many paths on the island that lead from castle to shore and, of these, several are broad walkways of paved stone that meander around and across and down in slow, decorous manner. You can race along them with your eyes shut tight and never once fret about twisting an ankle or breaking a wrist. I often have. Leastways, I often did before Crevan came.

Crevan, for his part, is unperturbed by my childish complaints. He gives me a level look and sets about reminding me that I know very well why we mustn't use any of the other island paths. And, of course, I do know. We can't use any of the other paths because Crevan is paranoid—delusional, deranged—but that's not nice to say, so I don't. It's not polite to point. Besides, I suppose it's not really paranoia if the fear is warranted. And Crevan really believes it is. That has to count for something.

Crevan is not so kind. He never is. He has no qualms about taking my silence and turning it against me, informing me in no uncertain terms that I need to be more careful, that the problem with me is I don't take things seriously, that I'm not nearly cautious or frightened enough, that I would fear for my life if I knew what was good for me.

"Come on. This is the only track that can't be seen from the mainland," he says. "You know that. And——"

On and on he goes, as though I am even remotely interested, as though I haven't heard it all before, as though I have any desire to hear the same old arguments rehearsed all over again. He is really very tiresome sometimes.

I'm starting to regret my largesse, my magnanimous gifting of silence, my gracious offering of the benefit of the doubt when really none is deserved—none at all, not in any way, shape, or form—and finally it pays off. Crevan, plainly seeing that I am implacable, unmollified, unyielding, comes to stand close beside me. The moonlight limns his brow, the high arches of his cheekbones, the curved bridge of his nose, and makes his pale, pale eyes glow-flicker phosphorescent. He is nearly a head taller than me and has to crook his neck to speak directly into my ear, his lips barely only just brushing against the soft vellus hairs that fur the lobe. It's delicious. With every whispered syllable comes shivering delight.

"Do you want to die? Because that's what will happen if we're seen." His hand grasps my jaw, his gaze becomes severe; he is a man possessed, hell-bent intent on making me understand. "I knew you were here before I reached the island," he tells me. "I saw you from the shore. It's why I came. There you were, proof there would be food and shelter for the taking. I could have killed you. Anyone else would have; would have cut your throat as soon as look at you."

Promises, promises.

"Is that the case?" I ask, keeping my voice so low it barely reaches my lips, so low I can feel it more than hear it, a gentle reverberation in my ribs, my throat, the back of my mouth.

Crevan doesn't usually like to speak about the day he came to the island, however much I have tried to make him, however much I myself have lingered over those few and precious moments when I watched him walk down the causeway, the sand flats already gleaming electroplated as the tide seeped in. He seemed entirely untroubled by the encroaching sea, but then perhaps he did not yet know how quickly the causeway can become submerged, how deep the water gets. I should have been afraid, should have realized then the trouble he would bring—a flint of ice on a hot summer day; dangerously fragile, portending nothing good. But his beauty strode out with him, plain for all to see, and it held my every thought. It bent my eye to the red and gold of his burnished copper hair, to the skin as pale as sun-bleached bone. He moved with vulpine grace and, in my heart, I was already prepared to forgive him anything, everything, whatever he might do, whatever untold horrors he might unleash.

And in return, he—he gives me nothing. He will not even speak of that first day, can't seem to do it without invoking the phantom trace of torments past, the tortures and agonies about which I am eager to know but on which subject he refuses absolutely to be drawn, never offering much more than the occasional grunt in response to my careful questions. I want more than that. I want to hear about the keen eyes that might even yet be looking hungrily toward us from across the sea. I want to scratch out and scrape up every last bit of the time before; of the time when Crevan walked the world without me, of the time about which I know so tantalizingly, excruciatingly little. It's selfish, the way he keeps this part of himself from me. Not sportsmanlike, expecting me to take so much on trust alone. And now he's finally broached the topic, I'm at a loss for what to say; desperate to keep him talking, yet anxious about steering him astray. Before I can so much as twist my tongue into the shape of a single word, he smiles, a flash of teeth in the night.

"I would never hurt you," he says. "You know that."

Do I? I wonder. Perhaps he has no idea how his silence kills me. Anyway, it doesn't matter now. I've let him slip off course. More fool me. There will be no talking him back around, not tonight, not ever, not knowing my luck. I pluck the hawthorn spine from my hand and push Crevan aside, my forearm to his stomach, my fingers to his chest. I shove and he stumbles backward but, ever sure-footed, does not lose his balance.

"Are we doing this or what?" I ask. "I thought you wanted to go. So let's go."

"Come on then."

We go once more. I do not seek his hand again.

Hot-faced, we scramble down slope's end and drop at last onto the sea wall. Crevan lands on all fours like a cat but I, as ever, am far less dignified, compromised into inelegance by hips, knees, shoulders, wrists that all have ideas of their own about the right way for a joint to move and roll, to lock, and not one of them in agreement with any of the others—or with me, for that matter. I twist from side to side, letting my arms fly and flop as if they are only two steel spikes that have been pegged into my shoulders with string. Twist and swing, twist and swing. The momentum catches, builds, and I wonder whether perhaps—if I am lucky, if I am good, if I eat my greens, my crusts—my arms might fly loose of their own accord, tugged free from the lump of my flesh by their own speeding weight. I catch Crevan smirking and stop. My arms flump down to hang limp at my sides, flaccid and pendulous, as though they have forgotten what they are for, as though they really believed my little flight of fancy just then, as though they dreamt themselves into being all chromium steel and have been sorely disappointed to wake and find that they are not, that they are nothing but meat and bone. Their despondent lethargy becomes quickly unbearable. When Crevan isn't looking, I jiggle about and am relieved when the limbs seem more like themselves again; two perfectly ordinary arms, thank you very much. One right, one left. Check and check.

I am indiscreet in my delight. Crevan spies me again and his brow furrows in the middle, two neat grooves graven side by side. I stick out my tongue and tell him to mind his own business. Then, for want of anything better to do—and because it seems as though something *must* be done—I crouch down to whisper my hellos to the broad back of the old sea wall. It hugs the shore of the island for—oh, miles and miles, I'm sure—like a dirty big wyrming serpentine dragon coiled around its hoard of treasure, concrete flanks all armored with scales of jagged quartzite. I pat at them with my palms flat, making tentative, soothing strokes.

"Good evening, Mr. Dragon sir, and how do you do and what fine weather we've been having and, yes, I daresay you are right in that regard but I don't suppose it can be helped. Well, quite. Marvelous, yes. Simply sublime."

"Kit."

It is a moment before I place the sound, though of course it is just Crevan, calling me by name—or rather, by what he thinks of as my name, but which in actual fact has nothing to do with me whatsoever, a terse monosyllable of entirely no significance. He may as well call me *knife* or *shell* or *thread* for all the natal correspondence there is between such words and the thing that I call myself. On Crevan's behalf, though, I must admit that his persistent use of this misnomer is not entirely his fault. He calls me Kit because it's the first thing that happened to spring from my tongue the day he arrived, sprang out of me like everything else always does, welling up out of who knows where or what: the funny old words I find for them things that I see and them things that I don't. Kit. I'm stuck with it now, I suppose, for I can't divine any way of righting him without making him embarrassed and ashamed. Knowing my luck, I'll be stuck with it forever.

But I won't be made to take all the blame. Crevan has his own contemptible part to play in this—for it was him who came to the island in the first place, and it was him who started it, telling me his own precious name and then asking for mine in exchange, as though that was fair, as though it was right to weight the scales like that, to make himself vulnerable as a means of insisting that I make myself vulnerable too. He should never have done that. Certainly, I never would the same, for it is not right and meet so to do, as I'd have thought any-old-anyone could see. And that's supposing Crevan was telling the truth, though I'll bet—my bottom dollar, a fiver, the house—that he wasn't. After all, I have only his say-so. And in the reverse instance, whereby he has only *my* say-so as to what my name is, I know with absolute certainty that I am lying, that my name is not and never was Kit. On the basis of this one test case, I am forced to conclude that, in all probability and out of it, Crevan was lying at least as much as me. Probably Crevan is no more his name than Kit is mine. That would be just like him, giving a lie so as to make me give up a truth. He's sly like that, is Crevan. But he doesn't fool me, not for one second, not for a single moment. I know his game and his type and I know the score and I know that I'm winning. Though perhaps not for much longer, not if I'm careless, not if Crevan can help it.

"Kit."

I can't deny there's a pleasure to hearing that name in his mouth. It might not be *my* name, but Crevan believes it is, and every time he shapes his lips around it, every time his voice carries it out into the island air, the word sounds more and more like it might really mean me, or at least some part of myself, or at even less-least a part of someone akin to myself. Kitty Kit Kitty. Perhaps that is my name after all, a true name lurking beneath the one I was given at birth, only waiting for a chance to come out, the right stranger to tell.

"Kit."

Crevan's voice is soft as chalk above the waves that lap and break against the stone. I stare out to the Vantablack expanse of the sea stretching beyond and up into the night. Then I give the sea wall a final pat—*good dragon*—and, straightening, turn to the man who asks for me.

Already he is stripped to the waist. Scars cable his chest and stomach, his back, his shoulders, his arms; every one of them a little puckering mouth healed shut into a compressed white line. Suddenly I am baby again, pliable and oh-so-easily impressed. I skip eagerly along the wall to his side and brush my lips to as many of the little scar mouths as I can reach, bobbing my head like a pecking bird. And here a kiss and here a kiss and here a kiss. Crevan brushes a smoothing palm over my hair, kneading my scalp with the pads of his fingers until I am still and spinning, kissing frenzy forgotten, eyes closed, head leaning into his chest. I wind my arms about his waist and let loose my every muscle, collapsing into him rag-doll-wise, knowing he will take my weight, trusting he will not argue or question but only stand straight and true, holding fast so I need not.

Then he asks if everything is all right and I snap away, joints clicking back into place, every motion an abrupt jolt that articulates—I hope, I swear—my disappointment. I shake my head when he asks again what the matter is, dismayed that he doesn't know, that he can't simply tell, that he has to ask, that he could think there is anything wrong with me when obviously the fault lies with him. But then a moth flit-flitters by, etiolated wings pale against the night, and I am lost to its stuttering, faltering dance. I make my hands to match and flutter—thumbs laced, fingers spread, a moth of flesh and bone—and turn and step as best I can, following the lead of my unknowing, unwitting dance partner. Crevan does not tell me to stop, only watches me with that funny half-laughing, half-fretting look of his. Dear, dear Crevan. Poor, silly Crevan. I am back at his side in a rush of affection, willing to forget the matter, to let it drop entirely, extending my hand in olive-branch fashion and white-flag manner, running my fingers along the worst of the scars, the one that slices from rib to hip; a fibrous, serrated strip.

"Tell me about this one," I say, then laugh to show I don't mean it, not really.

Because I don't ask about the scars and Crevan doesn't tell, I know that. It's just how things are. But he accepts my peace offering all the same and then, by way of return, holds out his left arm, turning it so I can examine the patterns inked on the inside of his wrist. There are seven in all, a neat line of stamps prettily arrayed and running from the base of his palm to the crook of his elbow, no two the same, each one bearing a different symbol in exquisite miniature: one a rose, one a pike, one a red-billed chough. Chee-ow! Chee-ow, chee-ow! Here are stories of the before-times that Crevan is willing to share. I circle my fingers around his wrist and lightly touch the image that looks like a twisting, twirling eel.

"This one," I say. "Tell me this one."

"You've heard it before."

"So? Tell me again."

"Maybe you can tell it for me."

Maybe I can. I've certainly heard it enough times before, but stories have a way of mulching into strange shapes when you aren't looking, when you leave them unattended in the back of your mind, in the pit of your heart. And besides, I tell stories differently from Crevan. Better, I would say. More rambling, he might counter. But then he's not the sort to speak at length, not the kind to let himself go or get carried away. Well fiddlesticks to that. After all, what's a little embellishment between friends? Maybe how I tell it isn't quite how it happened, not exactly, but it's as good as—at least, as far as I'm concerned, as far as I can know or remember. So sit down and stay awhile, sit still and listen.

Crevan is far, far away from here and it's long, long ago—before ever he came to the island. He is on the mainland, somewhere under the watercolor-wash skies of the east, where the land is fen and marsh, moss and carr, slop and tar, mud and yet more mud. He wades slow through the still water, trying not to make a sound, trying not to mind that his legs and feet are soaking wet, trying to keep wary and on-guard, knowing that the waters here are shallow but here so deep he'll be in over his head if he's not careful, if he slips his foot or chooses wrong. Growing all around are the bulrushes and sedges that lured him into the fen in the first place: a living screen, a living cloak to hide and conceal, to keep him safe from the party of backbiters that has been spied here or hereabouts, at least according to the whispers, the irritant rumors that urgent-spread upon the wind like so much ragweed pollen. Already he has two souvenirs from encounters with parties of this kind and he knows he's lucky to have escaped with so little, to have been allowed to keep his life, his breath, his body, and his blood. He does not think his luck will stand another test, another capture.

Crevan is frightened. Crevan is always frightened. He doesn't know, like I do, that everything is going to be fine, that he will survive not merely this but a further four such encounters. He doesn't know that the end is coming, that before long he will reach the island and everything will be better. He is alone and afraid, trying not to drown, trying not to get caught. But the backbiters are better at this than he is. They are not your common or garden sinners, mind; they are not the sort that speak unkindnesses about you when your back is turned. No. They are far, far worse than that; sinners older and crueler still, the sort that creep up upon you when you least expect it, the sort that attack you only ever from behind, the sort that wait until you are on the back foot, backed into a corner; trapped, run to ground, ambushed, the sort that—just when you think you've escaped—come to bite you back.

Come to bite Crevan.

Working in perfect silence, they surround him on all sides and he knows nothing about it until it's too late, until their visors leer out of the reeds to reflect his own horror-struck face back at him, until the stun batons crack and the gloved hands grip. He never had a chance, poor baby, no more than a spindle-legged fawn against the hungry, hungry wolves. Crevan gets restraints, gets lifted up and carried bodily from out of the fen, crash-crashing through the spike-rush, few-flowered and creeping, crash-crashing through the sweet-grass and sedge. Crevan is all moans and complaint: making protests that go unheard, promises that he cannot keep even if they would be agreed to—and they are not because the backbiters never listen, because the backbiters have one purpose only and they don't care what you think or what you want or whether you were going to pray tonight to no one at all or if your favorite color is blue. Backbiters only want to hurt you, only want to draw your blood and taste it, to see whether you're ripe yet, to see whether you're ready to be ate. Or so the old stories used to go, the stories I heard once, as a child, long before I came to the island. Really backbiters are just a-hunting infection, infestation— bacteria—though there's no *just* about it, not really, for therein lies a sport more injurious and deadly than any other you might, as of yet, have had cause to endure.

This is for your own good. For everyone's good. That's what the backbiters tell Crevan as they take blood, samples, run numbers. Tests. They don't tell him what they're looking for and, even if they did, it wouldn't matter because all he can do is hope against hope that he doesn't have it, hope that it's not too late for him, that he won't be counted as a lost cause; a reservoir, a vector, a threat that needs to be cut off—culled—as soon as possible, before it's too late for everyone else. He can see the backbiter with the needle that will do it, waiting, waiting, patient as anything, waiting for the results that will dictate the command to put that needle in Crevan's arm and plunge, to inject the venomous bane that will seize the muscles and stop the heart. *There, there, painless as anything, better for us all to put the poor thing down, put it out of its misery.* Such sweet compassion. Or that's what would happen, only all the tests come back as big no-nos, uh-uhs, no-ways, nothings-doing-here. Crevan is clean, at least of this particular species of bacteria, whatever it is the backbiters are looking for. The first he knows of it is the slump in the shoulders of the one holding the culling needle. *Ah well, can't be helped. We'll get 'em next time. Just you wait and see.*

Then it's time for the patch. The purpose of which, as Crevan explained to me the very first time I asked after the pretty pictures on his skin, is exactly what it sounds like: to correct, reinforce, repair. To stop Crevan from fraying, from running ragged, to protect those parts of him that are already worn out and threadbare. *Imagine a square*, is what he told me. Imagine a square of something that's thin and clear and so flexible that it could be folded up without breaking, even rolled up if you had the dexterity to do it. On one side are all these tiny, tiny needles, so small that you can hardly see them but enough for the skin to know when the square gets laid down on the inside of your arm. And some of those needles contain prophylactic—medicine to protect, to defend against the specific bacteria the backbiters are a-hunting—and some of them have the dye that makes the picture that shows the dose was given, that the bearer is protected. Crevan says there's other information held in those images too, things that can only be seen under a special light, like the day and the time and the name of the medicine. But Crevan says all sorts of things and there's no sense in believing them all. Either way, it doesn't sound like anything to fret about, right? Crevan will get patched up good and proper, be protected from bacterial infection. Lucky him.

But there are hitches. For one thing, have you ever seen the back-biters? I mean, I haven't, but Crevan has and maybe you have too. Maybe you've glimpsed the rubber suits that are supposed to keep them clean and safe but that are invariably in some late stage of decay, cracked and worn. Maybe you've seen the minute perfora-tions in the protective wrappers that hold the patches, ragged holes from where itsy-bitsy microbial mouths have chomped away at the plastic, creating inlets for every kind of nasty you can think of. *If the bacteria don't get you,* says Crevan, *then the backbiters will.* They cull more by mistake than on purpose, inadvertently introducing all manner of secondary infections with their rotting equipment. It's just the way it is. How it will always be. Apart from not here, not on the island, because the backbiters don't know it. Or if they do know it, they don't know anyone is here. Or if they do know anyone is here, they don't care whether we get sick or not, die or not. I have never seen their kind, have never had no patch, have never got no pretty pictures of my own to show off and admire, all neatly stamped along my arm. All I have is Crevan's word. Still, seven patches. He's lucky to be alive at all. But now he's safe. Nothing can get at us here, here where there is only us: him, me, and the wide, wide sea. But I refrain from mentioning this to Crevan. I know he'll only cry black swan, I know he'll only say that just because it hasn't happened yet doesn't mean it never will. *Paradise doesn't last forever, Kit.* Blah, blah, blah.

So here we are, together and safe upon the sea wall. There's a flash-flick of movement; the entirely explicable surprise of a bleached tooth in a rotted head. It catches Crevan's eye and makes him look. A night heron, perched a little way farther down the wall to fish. It casts us a scornful look over its sharp bill then stretches its wings and takes to the sky, cutting a sweeping arc through the air and then coming down light and delicate as a falling leaf, settling at a new perch safely out of reach of either one of us, where it can continue undisturbed to hunt for its dinner among the hushing waves. Crevan clicks his tongue and sets about the rest of his undressing, sliding off his fearing and his mawkismo along with his trousers. He turns—all rationality and pragmatism, all naked and unabashed—to ask if I'm coming in, to tell me the longer I wait, the worse it will be.

"Yes, yes," I say. "I know. You go on ahead. Splish, splash, splosh."

Crevan obliges because it's what he was going to do anyway and because he can hold it off no longer. I watch him sink into a low crouch and then launch himself in one wild leap from the wall, pressing his hands together above his head and straightening out his legs into a neat point so that the whole of him becomes a perfectly crafted dart, poised and balanced, elegant in ways I will never begin to know how to emulate. He flies into the waves without a sound, without a splash, and disappears into the sea; not so much as a ripple to mark the course of his passage. It is only a moment before he reappears, but long enough for me to wonder—for me to seriously consider and entertain the notion—that perhaps there is no Crevan, that perhaps there never was, that the Crevan I know is nothing more than a figment of my imagination, a delusion I have been happily indulging myself in and have now—for reasons beyond my grasp or understanding—decided to release myself from, letting this fiction, this fabulous apparition, to disappear at last; to return entirely to the nothingness of unreality. Goodbye, Crevan. Farewell, adieu, so long. It was fun while it lasted, for me if not for you.

Then he breaks the surface, head and shoulders cresting high above the waves, seeming almost stubborn in his physicality, in his undeniable there-ness.

"I made you up," I say with as much sternness as I can muster, hands on hips, brow creased. "I made you up and it's extremely rude of you to ignore that fact."

Crevan laugh-coughs in the cold of the sea. "Come on," he says. "The water's fine. You'll feel better for the exercise."

So says Crevan, so always says Crevan. He is a man obsessed. If he can't find some ice water and plunge into it, he's not a happy *Oryctolagus cuniculus*. Which, I suppose, is the point. Or at least, the point that he is always trying to tell to me. *Good for the body, good for the mind*, that's his view; that if I had a dog, I'd walk it every day and that I should treat myself with the same pragmatic respect. Me, I'm not so sure. For one thing, I don't think I *would* have a dog. If there were a dog here on the island, I'd let it get on with . . . well, whatever it is that dogs do. And if that involves a lot of running about or—unbelievably—sea swimming, then fine. It is a dog and may do as it pleases. I am not a dog. Different rules apply. Woof.

But it seems to please Crevan whenever I make a show of taking him seriously and this, in turn, brings me no small amount of amusement. It is with this in mind that I strip down to my skin. Goodbye, gray gaberdine windbreaker; goodbye, gray woolen sweater. I let them drop crumpled at my feet and they are quickly followed by the rest: my gray gaberdine trousers and my gray silk thermals, my thick woolen socks all ribbed and ridged with the bamboo liners sewn in. I dive into the sea. The raw no-heat shock of it seizes me at once, clamps over my mouth and nose, hammers the air from my lungs, sucks every last bit of warmth from my body. The brusque, brisk fright of it is enough to paralyze, only I am expecting it and I know just what to do, hanging still in the depths like a floating weed, waiting for my heart to relax, to slow-adjust, to get over the startling hell of being plunged into arctic night water. Then I kick out hard, propelling myself up to break the surface. The brine bites and snaps, snarls, brushes my skin with what feels like fire—with what feels like acid—and then at last comes the dizzying rush. I yelp, baring my teeth in a wide, gleeful howl. Treading water nearby, Crevan laughs and gives a howl of his own, crying up at the full moon above like some kind of mythic beast, a sea wolf with red fur; a sea fox. We swim a few clockwise circuits, kelp fronds licking lazily at our hands and feet, and then return to the part of the sea wall where we left our clothes.

I haul myself up and out of the water. My arms are already feeble, weak, frail after even so brief a swim, all the good blood in me shunting to the core of my body to keep heart, lungs, liver warm and never mind the extremities, so it's as much as I can do just to slither onto my belly and lie panting. A few minutes longer and I might not have made the climb back out, might have been dead in the water. Crevan, who seems to feel the cold in the same way as a salmon shark or lamprey doesn't, helps me up, holding out a hand and pulling me roughly to my feet.

"Here," he says, throwing me a flannel shirt from his own discarded pile of clothing. I use it to towel off and then dress as quickly as my stumbling-numb fingers allow. By the time I am done, Crevan is dry and dressed too, and what's more, he is back at my side, his arms tight about me, insulating, sharing the heat of his blood. I shiver and draw close, close as I can, making us a pathetic huddle of two.

"We should get back," says Crevan. "We need to eat. Get warm."

"Yes and yes and yes."

Yet we neither of us move. Perhaps we know already; have already guessed that it is about to happen, that it is about to begin. Or perhaps we are just reluctant to leave the sea, to break the serene clarity that comes after immersion within the gelid waves, a full-body baptism by moon ice. Even shiveringly-shudderingly cold as I am, it is oh-so-pleasant to be held fast in Crevan's arms, to look aimlessly out across the night sea and to know with complete and rare certainty that this is what it is to be alive; nothing more, nothing less than this, this shared fluttering beat of a slow-thawing heart.

And then Crevan takes a sharp breath, a gasp like a curled fist slamming into a glass mirror, one that shatter-scatters out a fine haze of glittering splinters and sand. He points outward, far beyond the bounds of my sight, and asks in trembling tones whether I too see what he sees.

Despite his apparent alarm, despite the warning pulse of dread in my wrists, my throat, I think perhaps he has only spotted one of the blubbery fat seals that sometimes come to explore the rockier outcrops of the island, out for a nighttime swim, just like we are. I follow the line of Crevan's finger as best I can, squinting, peering, eyes narrow. I see nothing, nothing at all, nothing unexpected. Beyond the breakers, the sea is clear as distilled gin. Or so it seems to be.

Another second of staring and there it is: a sharp-lined mass floating among the waves, aimless as driftwood. The moonlight— serenely in on the secret—teases us, shows a hand with the fingers splayed, shows an upturned face; eyes closed, mouth open. A body in the water. *No.* I don't want it. Not right, not right at all.

"A woman," says Crevan.

I turn, pressing my face into his shoulder. "*Make it go away,*" I whimper, not daring to voice my prayer entire: *Make a cross-current to catch the body and carry it back out to sea.* Instead, I give only word-less, whining plea.

"Quiet."

The tide is against me, every wave driving the body closer and closer still. When next I look, it is only a few feet away. A wave-wanderer, an Oceanid, a Potamoi; sea-kin of some kind or other. How Crevan can be so sure the body is that of a woman, I do not know; not from so far away, not with how the long brine-swept hair shrouds the face, not without asking first. But fine, let him decide. I don't want to look. I don't want to see, don't want to know who this sea-kin is, what she looks like. Why is she here? What does she want with us? What could she possibly want? Because she can't come here. She *can't*, she simply can't. It's not fair, not allowed. She'll ruin everything, I can feel it in the thrash and twitch of my stomach, and I don't want that, don't want *her*.

I scream.

"Be *quiet*, Kit."

For the first time, I notice how tense Crevan is beside me, how his muscles are all wound up—coiled tight, ready to snap—and for a moment I think *oh, poor baby* and wonder how I could have been so foolish, so careless as to forget how frightened he is, how scared he is of all the backbiters and all the other creeping-crawling nasties from the mainland like the ones that gave him his scars. Of course he's upset, of course he's afraid. I should look after him, tell him it will be all right. But then I look again and wonder to see that he does not look so much disquieted as he does concerned, his face lined with worrisome care, his green, green eyes fixed upon the water.

There is a sudden snap of movement. A flailing limb, perhaps, though it could just as easily be a cresting wave or a trick of the light. Yes, that must be it. Only Crevan sees different.

"She's alive," he says and jumps to his feet.

"Don't," I say, understanding. "Don't, please. I don't want it. You can't—"

It's too late. Crevan doesn't listen to me. Crevan *never* listens to me. Before I can think how to stop him, how to persuade him against it, he is diving into the water, fully clothed and nowhere so neat or graceful this time around. Splash-plash-crash, the waves churn to foamy delight. In a few powerful strokes, he reaches the floating woman. I watch through my fingers, not daring to believe what is happening. This is *my* island, mine. I don't want another body here. The ones we've got are plenty, enough to be getting on with, themselves already far, far too much to bear.

Not stopping to check whether she lives or dies—and which is worse I cannot say—Crevan hooks his hands under the woman's armpits from behind and begins to tow her to safety, legs whip-whipping together to propel him backward through the water. When he reaches the wall, he has to shift his grip, heaving himself up with one arm and dragging the woman along behind him with the other. I do not help, cannot, cannot bring myself to move an inch from where I sit, hands over my eyes, fingers spread wide. An ill-timed wave tugs at the woman's limp body, jolting her from Crevan's grasp. For a heart-stopping moment, it seems that she will slip away and be pulled to the depths. I bite my lip and hope. But Crevan catches her just in time, damn him, damn the day that first I saw him, damn the freak twists of chance that turned his eyes to *my* island and brought him here. I choke and cough and gasp for the words to tell him to put her back where she came from, to say that the sea can have her if it wants her so bad, to ask who are we to intervene with what the fates have so commanded? This woman was meant to drown, let her drown. But the words do not come, only stay stuck in my maw like a scritchy-scratchy bone swallowed wrong-wise. Crevan doesn't hear the words I cannot say, only tightens his hold on the woman and makes one final push. Then they are out, him panting on hands and knees, her flat on her back.

"What have you done? Why are you doing this to me? I don't like it, make it stop. Now, Crevan. Please. You have to."

But he ignores me, his every attention bent on the woman. He is looking at her in a way I cannot fathom, in a way like he is afraid, in a way like he knows who this lost soul might be and fears it. But come, stay. That is impossible. She is a stranger, a woman—nothing more, nothing less.

He pushes aside a tangle of her hair and I see a face, striking in the moonlight, strong and lantern-jawed. There is a gap, a line of parted flesh running from her right nostril and down to her mouth, dividing her top lip completely in two—a deft bisection but with no blood and no scarring to be seen, so I guess it was something given to her by the womb rather than by any knife or scalpel; an unexpected felicity of her creation, a loose end that was never tied up, an absence as loud and proprietorial as a thumbprint on a lump of clay. What is *not* womb-given is the nasty bruise on her forehead, just below the hairline.

"Hit her head," says Crevan, surmising. "Got knocked out and fell in the water. Lucky we saw her."

I think of screaming again, of throwing myself into the sea, of cracking my own head against the stony spine of the sea wall, crack and crack and crack until Crevan leaves her and comes to get me, comes back to himself, comes to see that I am still here and that he has betrayed me, crossed me, left me out in the cold. But I do not and he does not either, does not flick his eyes away from the woman for so much as a moment. Lowering himself down, he awkwardly hover-leans with his left cheek poised just above the woman's nose and mouth. Nods when he feels the rush-brush of air against his skin. She's alive, alive-o; alive, alive-o. Oh god. Oh *hell*.

He sits back on his heels and takes up the woman's hand, seeking her pulse with his fingers. Let it be dimming, I pray, let it be erratic and fading and soon to die down. But it is hopeless. I know that even before Crevan sighs his relief, even before he turns to me at last, his lips as white and pressed as any of the scars knitted across his skin. He tells me the woman is all right, that her pulse is faint but steady, that she has a good chance if only we can get her warm and dry, if we can get her back to safety. His own sodden clothes are clinging to his skin and already he is beginning to shake with the cold. If we stay here much longer, he'll be in danger; every passing second bringing him closer still to the slurred confusion of hypothermia, to the fatal drop in pulse, pressure, breath. My heart aches, breaks. I can't do nothing. I can't leave him here. And he won't come without the woman, that much is clear.

Should have let her drown, Crevan, should have let her drown.

I look out across the water to where the moon drops slowly through the sky. For one maddened moment, I see myself shoving

Crevan aside, I see myself determinedly rolling the woman off the wall and back into the sea like so much waste to be flushed away with the tide. Should have let her drown. It would have been kinder by far.

"We can't keep her," I croak. "It's strictly no pets."

But Crevan doesn't hear. He is hoisting the woman from off the ground, looping his arms around her chest so as to take the bulk of her weight.

"Help."

He is desperate in a way I have never seen; in a way I cannot ignore or argue against.

"Please, Kit."

I demur for a moment longer and then concede. "This is no good," I say, grabbing hold of the woman's ankles. "You'll have tired of her in a fortnight and then we'll still be stuck with her. Or worse, you'll get attached and she'll get better and want to leave or she'll stay sick and die and either way it will destroy you. And I'll be the one stuck taking her for walkies. Bet you anything."

Crevan makes no answer to my grumbled complaints, does not gratify me with response or notice. Not so much as a smirk or a wink. There's no being baby now, no way to raise even the faintest glimmer of happiness. I can see his attention is snapped, straining as he is against the weight of the woman, no doubt already thinking of the steep path ahead and how easy it will be to slip and fall, to send us all flying, to leave us all with broken necks. I wonder that his instinct isn't screaming against our every step like mine is, but then I suppose that it's too late; far, far too late for instinct. Crevan left his behind the moment he dived in the water. Before that, even: the moment he saw and pointed, the moment he made the body a real thing, a thing that we both saw and acknowledged, a thing we had to decide about one way or another. He could have said nothing. Could have rubbed his eyes and said: *Funny, I thought I saw something, but I must just be tired.* But he did not and as a result we have already ventured so far beyond the waymarker of no return that I can barely believe it; already we are stumbling blindly past the border posts of a now where all possibilities lie open and into the determined hell of the future, the way ahead laid out for us more surely than we can dread or guess. It has begun, that is the long and the short of it. Even though we none of us quite know it yet, quite know it then, it has begun. The way is set.

Should have let her drown, I think again. *Should have let her drown*.

JOSEPH'S GUMS AND SPICES

There is a castle, but most of it is phantom now, most of it is spectral: an echo of what was once raised up out of the island's rock and is now, stone by stone, storm by storm, being razed back down to the ground as surely and steadily as the sun burns away the water of a salt-lake to leave behind nothing more than a mineral crust, a white shadow of an ancient body long-since evaporated.

There is a castle, but you can only see it now if you squint, if you know where to look and how, if you can take the suggestion of bare fossilized bones and knit them out with flesh to see the true form of whatever forgotten lumbering creature it was that once did stroll the same earth it later came to be entombed within; buried for centuries, for millennia, before being rude-rough excavated by some well-intentioned hobbyist with a spade and everything to prove.

There is a castle, but it's mine now—just like everything else on the island—and I'm not interested in sharing, not interested in guests. It's *my* home, mine. It's where *I* live. And you can't come in, not to have a look around, not to rest your feet, not to use the facilities. No cold callers or junk mail. Trespassers Will. Please and thank you and goodnight.

Of course, there's not really any living to be had in the castle itself. It's more absence than substance, more decay than matter, more abstract than not. What little stonework remains is either roughly pitted after eons of being beaten by the driving wind that blows in on all sides from across the sea, or—in those few, more sheltered parts, the soft underbelly—swaddled and swathed in densely growing moss and lichen. Entire structures have entirely collapsed, leaving nothing in their wake but a few forlorn stumps of granite to mark where once there were pillars, corridors, cloisters. Stone arches loom against the sky, portentous doorways that lead through to nowhere and nothing, as though some two-ton brat of a giant—ignoring his mother's express instruction—stretched open his ogreish mouth as wide as it would go and was caught out by a change of the wind or the rise of the sun and got stuck that way, turned to stone and then slowly eroded so now all that remains is that dreadful, gaping maw. Serves him right, I say, making a nasty face like that when he *knew* what would happen, when his mummy had already said.

Of all the things that once upon a time really did use to be there—here—in the castle, of all the discrete buildings and parts that made up the whole of it, only the walled courtyard and the keep are still more or less intact, the latter glowering disapprovingly over the rubble, keeping watch over the island and now clad all in solar panels like a medieval knight in plate armor. Only the keep has held strong against the vagaries of weather and circumstance, against the almighty macerating power of the second hand, tick, tick, tick. It's only the keep that has, in fact, kept. (Thank you, thank you, I'll be here all week. All month. All year. Until I die and, in all likelihood, probably for quite some time after that, at least until *I've* been properly macerated too.) The keep is taller than anything here or hereabouts and I bet you can see all the way to the mainland from up on its roof, though I don't know for sure because I've never been up there. Not as far as I can recall, anyway. Certainly, the last time I checked, the last time I stuck my head in, there wasn't any way up: the stairs that lead up from the only entrance have caved in, crumbled, rotted away. There is a way down—or was once—for there is a heavy trapdoor set into the stone floor. But it is locked and I cannot open it to explore, so it may as well not be there at all. As far as I'm concerned, the keep stands hollow, a discarded carapace, an empty straitjacket, a shell without a snail. Probably it's been that way since before there was a me to worry about it. I'm not sure. I don't remember, all right? I've been here a long time and I can't possibly be expected to remember everything. And it doesn't matter anyway, because the keep belongs to the realm of the sky and that is not my concern. My concern lies elsewhere, below the ground along with the better part of my dominion. My concern is the den: a ten-by-fifty-foot steel bunker, cased in poured concrete and embedded deep among the foundations of the castle like witch-weed clinging tight to the fine roots of some poor, unwitting host crop. It is a keep as sure and as sturdy as the other, a buried keep, a keep-safe, a keep-out. It is where I live, and where Crevan lives too—or has done ever since he came to the island and found me. No one else has set so much as a foot inside it, not for so long as I can remember. And now we are bringing this stranger, this blow-in, this washed-up piece of flotsam of a woman right into our sanctuary. Ho-hum. On our own heads be it and all that.

In fairness—not that there's much of *that* going around—I, we, Crevan and me, can't lay complete claim to the den any more than we can to the rest of the castle. It's older than we are. It was divined by minds other from ours, built by other hands, lived in and cared for and cleaned by other people, other bodies. I mean, in all probability anyway. Things like this don't just grow up out of the soil, do they? You can't plant the right seed or tuber and expect it to grow into a fully furnished steel box. That's not the way these things work. Den and castle both are artificial, man-made, handmade, homemade. Homespun? Homegrown? No, that can't be right. I'm getting carried away, carrying this dead weight of a woman. And on we march, hup, two, three, four; onward, onward, marching as to war.

No, I didn't make the den. I didn't command for it to be made or fabricated or driven into the earth. But whoever did isn't using it anymore, doesn't need it anymore, is long-gone, long-dead. So it can't be stealing, can it? To live there, I mean, to claim it as

mine—ours. It hardly belongs to anyone else, because the dead
don't own anything, do they? Saving their graves. Although I
suppose maybe it's the grave that owns the dead and not the other
way around, leastways it must be if a grave robber ever made his
name—his fortune, his bread and butter—by snatching a body
from out of a tomb. There, that settles it. The dead are commodities
that may be owned and are therefore not themselves owners, not
themselves owed anything at all. Yes, that seems right. So why do I
still have this nasty, niggling feeling that I'm forgetting something
important? Never mind, never mind, I expect it will come back to
me before long.

So here we are, Crevan and me, a lifeless body strung out
between us, hell-bent on sharing all of a sudden, on opening our
doors to the waifs and strays, to the freeloaders that wash up on
our shore, the stragglers and vagabonds, the penniless and pitiful.
More fool us, more fool us. If we didn't show her the way, if we
didn't forcibly manhandle her into our den, the woman would
never have found it; not working under her own steam. For one
thing, she's unconscious. For another, you have to know that the
den is there, you have to know where to go. To start with, you
have to get into the walled courtyard. Then you have to find the
wooden wicket gate, all unassuming and drab in its gray stone
architrave, curly iron hinge-fronts braced across its width, and
think to yourself: *What might be behind that, then?* You have to
decide to open it up and climb down the spiraling stairs that wind
down into the underearth, steps all narrow and worn, slippery
with age; no lights, no railing, no nothing at all.

And that's the easy part. Because once you get to the bottom,
then you're in the old catacombs, a sprawling network of hollows,
cavities, chambers: a foundation of abandoned honeycomb with the
glooping syrup all sucked out and the bees all flown, an ancient
smoked-out warren. What's more, it looks like a catacomb should,
the way you fear it would, the way you would be disappointed if
it didn't. At every corner there is another tomb or sepulchre or

sarcophagi or monument, many bearing grave engravings in ornamental copperplate. Some walls are icon-painted, others are lined
with pit-eyed skulls. If it weren't so old, it would be gruesome.
Even now, Crevan assures me, it is not for the faint of heart, though
personally I am fond of it, of every kitschy nook and cranny of it,
with all those lovely old bones hugging themselves tight in their
coffins, not a care in eternity, snoozing eternally, dozy with dreaming and dust. It would be easy to lose yourself in here, easy to get
turned upside down, inside out, around and around, to forget the
way out. Then you'd be stuck. You'd keep wandering around for a
long time, probably, no doubt getting more and more hopelessly
lost. Maybe you'd stumble at last across the stairs to the overground
and cry with relief, staggering out into the sunlight. Then again,
maybe you wouldn't. Maybe you'd grow tired and sit down to rest,
despairing, and have a little sleep. Maybe you'd sleep away the hunger
and the loneliness along with your last breaths, your last heart-
beats, your last thoughts. Maybe you'd sleep until you were nothing
but your own bones. Now wouldn't that be something?

For those of us that know our way as sure as eggs is eggs is eggs,
the catacombs hold no terrors. I'm sure I could navigate them blind-
folded, both hands tied behind my back. Set me down anywhere,
spin me around three times fast and just time how long it doesn't
take me to find the den. Watch and wonder. I'm a migrating salmon,
a little glass elver. I just know where to go. It's magnetic. I don't
miss once, not ever, not never. And here it is at last, the heavy blast
door that leads to the den, shining plate steel oh-so conspicuous
against the surrounding dusty stone. Usually, I'd be relieved to
see it. It means home, it means sturdy walls all around and peace
and warmth and my own dear bed. But today I am worry-wort,
today I am fretting, today I am holding an unconscious woman by
the ankles.

It's a miracle we've made it so far, a miracle that she's still in
one piece. Climbing the twisty dirt track up the steep southern
face of the island with the old deadweight in tow was every bit as

treacherous-troublesome as you would imagine. Our balance was all off-kilter, mine and Crevan's both, and every step from one foothold to the next a struggle more fitting to a giant or a hero than to little old me. The worst part came when I caught my toe on a loose rock and wibbled and wobbled and teetered and tottered and wavered and quavered before finally crashing down into the bracken to land jarred-hard on all fours, the skin on my palms and knees ripped, gritted with dirt. It *hurt*. It still hurts. And I never wanted to carry the stupid woman up-down here anyway.

Now, reaching the blast door, I can feel the dread washing through my stomach like bile purging an ill-considered meal of rotted fish. Wrong, wrong. Shouldn't be here, shouldn't be doing this. Not allowed. Forbidden. Stop. Do not pass go, do not collect two hundred pounds, whatever pounds are. I try to tell as much to Crevan, stuttering-stumbling over the words, and he shakes his head, all impatience and disapproval.

"You have to trust me, Kit. This is the right thing to do. Please."

What can I possibly say to that? He shifts his hold on the woman to relieve me of her weight and I move for the handle, but the raw grazes on my palms make it hard to grip the spokes without wincing, without crying out. I have to use my elbow and wrist instead, every turn of the wheel making my nerves twist uselessly, like an ill-fitting screw cap that won't settle into the threads of a glass jar. I slump and give up. *Should have let her drown.*

"I *can't*. This is no good, Crevan. No good at all."

"Come on," he says. "It'll be all right. She's hardly a threat. Look, she's half-dead."

Which is not nearly dead enough, not according to me, not according to anyone. You ask and see. What if she wakes up? What then? So I make no move but simply stay standing where I am, frozen, suspended between two conflicting instincts, two equal but opposite forces, two compelling voices shouting in my ears. One says obey, the other says keep outsiders *out*.

"You let *me* in, Kit."

"That's different. *You're* different. You're you. You're my you."

Crevan looks at me in that askance way he does sometimes, all gnawing lip and furrowing brow. He will not give in, will not give up, no matter how long we stand here and argue. So very well and damn him, so very well and damn us all to hell.

"All right, all right. We'll do it your way, if that's what you want, if it matters so much to you, if it's so damn, damn important."

I turn the spoked handle again. The locking bolts clunk back so that I can open the blast door, which I do, grunting against the tombstone weight of it. And then we are in, safe and home, home and dry. The gnarly snarly knots in my neck, in my shoulders, begin to loosen. There's no place like home. Click, click, click.

I stand for a moment, enjoying the exquisite solidity of the patterned linoleum beneath my feet, a perfect tessellation of squares and stars in a warm array of terracottas, fawns, and granite grays, all washing aglow in the soft light of the brass-caged lamps ensconced along every wall. Home. What I would most like to do is put on one of the CDs from the rack, lie down on the furry rug beside the sofa and thumb through one of the illustrated encyclopedias from the bookshelf, or perhaps one of the comics. I've read them all a thousand, thousand times and know each one at least as well as myself and somewhat better than Crevan; well enough that I only have to run my hand past the neat row of spines and it will stop automatic at the right one, at the one that I need to read right now, at the only one that fits the caprices and whims of that precise moment. I don't even have to think about it. It's the same story with the CDs. My hands know the right jewel case by touch alone.

It frequently astonishes me how well mapped these stories and songs are to every part of my mood and matter. I mean, they don't even belong to me. I didn't choose them. I didn't put them here. That was someone else, whoever built the den in the first place, our unknown benefactors. I can imagine them riffling through their personal collections and deciding: yes, these are the ones we want to preserve, these are the things we must have on hand when we

finally descend and close the blast door behind us, these will be our
companions in the chaos that follows the disintegration of civilization and the collapse of mankind's dominion over the Earth. And
what a selection. It's almost as though our benefactors had me in
mind, saw me coming—although I know, of course, that such a
thing would have been impossible. Still, I remain grateful. *Blessed*
would probably be the right word if I believed in divine favor, but
I don't so it isn't. Just a quirk of luck, the way the cards fell. And
thank goodness for that, because I don't think there was ever such a
fine way to pass the time as visiting a cherished book, a heart-book,
with a good song for company—an old reliable, one you know all
the words to, one you know all the notes. I like to lie on my stomach as I read, swinging my legs in idle arcs: heel to backside, toe to
ground, over and over and over. I am halfway to it, halfway across
the room when Crevan stops me with a click of his tongue.

"Come on, Kit. Help me carry her to a bunk."

I oblige, because I am ever so good and ever so nice don't you
know and always well behaved, resuming my hold of the woman's
ankles to help take her weight. We shuffle across the floor with the
woman hanging between us to where the rank of cedar bunks stands
behind a lattice screen, concertinaed open in wide folds to divide the
sleeping area from the living. There are four berths in all (all aboard!)
and three of these are quite empty, stripped bare but for the foam
mattresses that still lie recumbent on the slats, ivory padded covers
starting to yellow beneath protective layers of translucent plastic.
Only my bunk—the best bunk, the top one that's farthest from the
blast door—looks at all inviting. I made it up fresh only this morning, tucking a crisp cotton sheet tight around the mattress, neatly
folding the tartan blankets and carefully brush-brushing the weave
free of lint and bobbling pile. I can hear it calling to me, its voice soft
and woolly, making little murmuring suggestions about how I could
climb up and crawl under the covers right now if I wanted, pull the
blankets around me and let myself be nestled close in the warm and
the dark, let myself be comforted to sleep.

"She can't go on my bunk," I say to Crevan. "See-ay-en-tee can't."

"Right," he says, in a weary tone that means I'm a fool for believing such a thing had even crossed his mind.

We sling the woman unceremoniously into the bunk down and across from mine, and then Crevan straightens, one hand on his hip, the other on his brow. There's that look on his face again, like maybe he knows this woman but can't quite bring himself to believe it. And neither can I—neither *will* I. Long-lost companions do not simply wash up in the one place you just happen to be living. That's not how it works. So it must be something else that's troubling him, something I cannot quite get at. I'd puzzle it out further, but that's when Crevan frowns and reaches over the woman's body to feel down the side of the mattress, fingers in search of something his eyes have inadvertently glimpsed. Honestly. As though this were the time for a bit of domestic archaeology.

He gives a small grunt of surprise and pulls free what he has found, holding it up to show me. It's a slim paperback, corners burring soft, yellowed pages falling loose from where the glue has lost its stick. I know it straightway, without barely even looking, without squinting to read the faded lettering on the spine: *The Swiss Family Robinson*. I loved it in years gone by—long before ever I knew Crevan—loved the adventures it held, the children so like and unlike, so familiar and yet unknown: four brothers vying for the attentions and affections of mother and father dearest.

I should have burnt it long ago.

"Did you know this was there?" Crevan asks, teasing. Probing.

I shrug and hope that will be enough for him to take the hint, but today I am resolutely out of fortune's favor and he does not.

"Come on, then," he says. "Why don't you put it on the shelf with the rest of the books?"

"No," I snap, with no choice now but to protest, no choice but to let him see. "No, no, no. Not allowed. I don't want. Don't want *it*. Please."

Crevan's frown deepens along with his confusion. "It's just a story, Kit."

"No, it isn't. It's wrong. It's bad. It *hurts* and I can't stand it, not to see it, not to have it looking back. I hate it. Hate how nothing bad that happens in it ever stays bad. Hate that everyone always survives. And they always do, without fail, like it's easy, like it's simple—the whole cast, family, kit and caboodle. Even the damn dogs. And they shouldn't. They don't deserve, they don't—"

"All right," says Crevan, his tone all sorry-I-even-asked, all this-is-way-out-of-my-remit. "It's all right," he says again. "Look, I'll put it back. You don't need to worry."

Good and true to his word, he reaches over the woman and slides the book in place, wedging it into the tight gap between mattress's edge and the cedar frame of the bunk. Then, at last, it is gone from sight. I let it fall out of my head as well. *Forget-get it, Kitty Kat. Come back to the here, come back to the now.* I focus hard, staring at Crevan. His clothes are hanging from him in sodden folds, water drip-trickling onto the linoleum. Of course. I touch his arm oh-so lightly and the netted moisture seeps over my fingers in minute droplets that I then brush to my lips. I wonder if he is cold. He isn't shivering so much now, but then that's hardly surprising after the effort of the climb from the shore. The heat of that won't last him long, won't keep hypothermia at bay.

"Better change," he says, as though reading my thoughts and clearly as keen to move on as I am. "She needs to dry off too. Come on."

He strides through to the master bedroom and I follow behind, tentative as ever, as always, mistrustful of stepping within the one part of the den that is Crevan's, even though I am allowed, even though I am well within my rights. This is where our clothes reside, after all, and I have never yet been denied the pleasure, small and occasional though it may be, of picking out for myself what to wear. But my being there always feels razor-edged—with promise, with threat—for the room is still his and he might choose to bar the way whenever he so pleases or, otherwise, to invite me in when there is no apparel-apparent need, when there can be no excuse relating to the practicalities of habiliment. Not that he ever has, not that he's ever asked—though I think he did try to once; his fingers twisting through mine, his eyes fixed upon my lips. But then he thought better of it, catching himself—his breath—and snatching the words between his teeth to swallow down unsaid.

It's not that I mind the room being his. I like my bunk—preferred it from the first, from the moment I came to the island—and wouldn't trade it, not forever so, not for anything, and definitely not for Crevan's double bed. It's not like there's anything special about this room of his. It's decorated in the same manner as the rest of the den and his bed isn't made up nearly as nicely as mine, his blankets all boring and brown. The only thing I really like about the room, the only thing I do a little bit wish was mine and not Crevan's, is the wardrobe, and perhaps that's because it's one of the few things for which we have a rule that is explicit rather than implied, namely that I must not open its left-most door, must not look at what's inside. That's what Crevan said—no, asked. No, commanded. Whatever's there is his and his alone, and I must not pry because it isn't good or nice. I must simply let him keep himself to himself, his cards close to his chest—his secrets in the wardrobe— and try not to mind, which is not so hard in the end, not so hard as I thought it would be, not when you take into account that probably there is nothing there worth knowing about, that probably Crevan is only trying to seem mysterious. Besides, there's plenty more wardrobe to go around. It takes up the entire length of the right-hand wall, polished cedarwood doors stretching from floor to ceiling and inlaid with ornamental carvings of spiraling vines, branches, and fruited boughs, impish goblin faces peering out from among the curling leaves, some foreboding and others enticing, smiling secrets and winsome profanities and deadly maledictions.

Now, standing once more in Crevan's room, I catch the eye of one such charming fiend, his hair all branching oak leaves and acorns. His grin is wide, like he's happy to see me, like he's missed me, like he would much rather *I* lived here in this room than Crevan did. Well, thank you fiend-y, that's so terribly sweet of you, but you don't understand. I can't live in here. For one thing, I can't abandon my bunk because that wouldn't be very considerate or nice. For another, Crevan is older than me, so he *should* get the bigger bedroom—or, in this case, the only bedroom—because that's how these things work, isn't it? Grown-ups get master bedrooms. Grown-ups get to sit in the front. Grown-ups get to prise charred crusts out of the toaster with a knife and no one can shout at them or tell them not to. And I might be twenty-seven or twenty-eight, but I'm hardly a grown-up. Not like Crevan is, with all his careful consideration and serious we-need-to-think-about-this-properly shtick. I don't see that I'll ever be like him, not really, no matter how old I get. In fact, I can't see how I'll ever become a proper grown-up even if I live to be a hundred and one. Although maybe you don't have to be a grown-up anymore if you get that old. Probably it's much worse to be forty-nine or fifty-three or sixty-two. Definitely old but not entertainingly so. Needfully responsible. Who wants that? Certainly not me. I think I'll skip those years if I can, go straight on to doddery and decrepit as soon as possible. Yes, that sounds like far more fun.

"Come on."

"Yes, Crevan. Sorry, Crevan."

I open one of the wardrobe doors (not the left-most one, never the left-most one) and fill my lungs with the smell of the cedar, an occult collusion of citrus and sawdust. The deep shelves are lined more richly than any treasure chest. There are pillowcases and quilt covers; bath mats, flannels, and facecloths; muslins, tea towels, and napkins; clothes of all kinds and sizes, many too impractical to be bothered with: slips, camisoles, and leotards; lightweight tops in halterneck and handkerchief and spaghetti strap; tight pencil skirts and floating tulle dresses; pinstriped blazers and satin-backed waistcoats. I have seen more colors among these fabrics than I ever did in the island's wildflower meadows: jewels and metallics, pastels and stones, bold primaries and subtle

shades. Some are plain and others patterned in houndstooth, ging-
ham, and polka dot; brocade, check, and chinoiserie; prints both
animal and botanical; camouflage, damask, harlequin. Confections
enough to rival any sweetshop, a kaleidoscope of fashions past. But
what makes them truly, startlingly dizzying to behold is their fragile
inutility. Synthetics all—more kinds of nylon, acrylic, elastane, and
polyester fabrics than I can name—and each one prone to several
different varieties of plastic-eating bacteria. Though they are safe
enough within the cool, dark confines of the cedar wardrobe, itself
protected by the den's steel and concrete walls, it wouldn't take
much for the entire lot to become contaminated. A leak, perhaps,
bearing waterborne microbes. Or the insertion of a single infected
item—worn out in the island's wilds and hastily put back into the
wardrobe without first being boiled. I do not wear them, do not
bother with them. It's simply not worth it, not worth putting on a
sweater in the morning that can so easily become threadbare and
chalky with decay by the late afternoon. I saw it happen once, you
know, and see it still sometimes in my dreams: a bright red T-shirt
running to ruin, the fabric suppurating and dissolving; withering
before my eyes like a petal in a flame. Crevan says it was not always
like this, says there was a time when you could expect a thin polyester fleece to last a lifetime at least and longer still than that—an
age, an epoch, an era, perhaps even as much as an Earthtime. But
not anymore.

So much to say that Crevan and me, we stick to the fabrics made
of natural fibers that—so far, anyway, so we hope—seem resistant
to microbial rot: wools and silkworm-silk, a wide array of cottons.
There are not so many items of these as there are of artificial
fabric, and they are nearly all brutally functional with regard to
color and cut, however gentle on the skin. But there are enough
to keep both Crevan and me comfortable, clean, protected. Now,
as Crevan dries off and gets changed, I rummage through what
remains until I find some things that might be suitable for the half-
drowned woman: a woolen tracksuit, a long-sleeved T-shirt made

of bamboo. They are a little too large but better than nothing, better than the waterlogged clothes she has on. I hold them up to show to Crevan, himself half-dressed.

"They'll do, Kit. Please get her changed."

I nod and scamper back out to the bunks, shooting the little leaf-haired imps on the wardrobe door a silent farewell. I go to where the woman lies passed out, unconscious still, unmoving still. I put the dry clothes on the top bunk and then kneel down to start peeling off her wet ones, throwing each sodden garment down onto the floor with a satisfying slap-slop. They are not good quality, I can see it now in the light. Some sort of poly-blend, no doubt, already ragged, already worn thin, though not exactly eaten away in the manner I expect, in the manner I remember. That doesn't mean they are clean. The only thing to be done is take the whole lot back outside and let the bacterial microfauna already infesting the weave to get on with it, to chow down and chomp until the fabric ferments into mulch. Tut, tut. We should have stripped this one down before we ever brought her inside. I think fleetingly of my CDs in their nice shiny jewel cases, of the laminate wrapping on my illustrated encyclopedias. The bacteria are inside the den now, no doubt about it. Do they know? Can they smell the feast that waits for them? Or perhaps the kinds that eat polyester sweaters don't also go in for rigid polystyrene. Even if they did, there's nothing to say they could make it that far, unaided, past the dividing screen and all the way to the CD rack. Then again, there's nothing to say they couldn't, nothing to say the contamination hasn't already spread. What will happen? I wonder. How long would it take to eat through the plastic cases, to start rotting the discs themselves, to devour the Mylar film and polycarbonate, to gobble up every single last song and melody? It doesn't bear thinking about. And that's the problem. We weren't thinking straight when we brought the woman inside. Or, you know, at all.

Still, I suppose it can't be helped. Not now, anyway. The bed's been made, the horse bolted, the milk spilt. I let the clothes sit in their wet pile and set about toweling the woman dry as best I can, chafing roughly at her skin to encourage the circulation and trying not to mind too much when I catch the grazes on my hand. She is in good condition—apart from being half-dead of course—and certainly well nourished: her face is enviably plump, her stomach round, her legs and arms amply covered, her reserves evenly spread across her body.

I pat the fat that bands my hips and thighs, trying to reassure myself that my own stores are perfectly sufficient, but it's hard not to feel the lack, being otherwise scrawny as I am. At least I'm not as bad as Crevan. He is thin-thin, nearly all muscle and sinew with only a fine layer of fat across his stomach that can't withstand more than a couple of hungry days. I thought he was going to die the winter the heating failed—he had nothing to draw on, no backup or anything. Nothing spare. He simply started melting away. We got the heating fixed and it was all right in the end, but still, it was something of a shock to find that Crevan's body doesn't much care for him, that it doesn't want him to live, that it has made no plans for hardship, no plans for his continued existence. Really, it's a wonder he's lived as long as he has—particularly considering those long years out on the mainland where everything is harder, least the way Crevan tells it. What food there is must be fought for, and there's no counting on it either, no guarantee that it won't go rotten, that it isn't carrying some disease, that it won't be snatched right back off you before it's so much as halfway to your lips. Not that you'd guess as much from looking at the woman. Wherever she's drifted in from, it's not the land of the hungry, the deprived and the desperate, the diseased and the dying. Although I suppose sometimes there's no telling with sickness. But she looks healthy enough.

If it is strange to see the woman's naked body, then it is only because it makes my own body strange to me. I am not ashamed of nakedness, do not find it indecent. I spent long days unclothed before Crevan came to the island and would do still in temperate weather if he hadn't asked me not to, if he hadn't blushed and spoken of his embarrassment, of his discomfort. I suppose he never had the benefit of being entirely alone, of not having to see himself reflected back to him in the eyes of others, of not being matched up and measured against the expectations of anyone else. Whereas I, I had the island all to myself for ever such a long time. There was no one to affront, no one to offend. No one to map me out and say: *You are like this, you should be like that.* No one to say: *But you are a woman and I am a man, it is improper.* To tell the truth, I'd forgotten there were such things as men and women before Crevan arrived, forgotten there were such divisions and categories to know and learn. I still struggle to remember it now—or rather, struggle to remember how they apply to me. I am just myself. I have always been just myself. Only Crevan makes me think otherwise, reminds me there may be more to it than that.

He is easier with me now than he once was, easier with himself too. But I remember what he was like when he first arrived and I don't doubt that he will see this woman's naked body as a stark indecency too, don't doubt the reason he delegated the task of undressing and drying her to me. He sees her nakedness as something to be ashamed of, something to fear. God knows why. Wary that he will be done soon, I hastily manhandle her into the dry clothes. She doesn't so much as stir. I would mistake her for dead if it weren't for the shallow rise and fall of her ribs. That said, she isn't stiff like a body would be by now. Her limbs flop and flail and flex uncontrolled when I jolt her about. There's no risk that I might snap a bone when I force her arm into the sleeve of the tracksuit.

"There, there, isn't that better? Aren't you more comfortable now?" I tilt my head to one side, half-cocked, like I can't quite hear the woman's answer, though of course her lips do not move, though of course she says nothing at all. "What's that?" I say, playing still. "Cold, are you? Well, you should have thought about that before going sea swimming in the middle of winter. What did you expect would happen? I mean, I ask you. Don't come running to me when you die of pneumonia."

I take one of the blankets from off my bunk and drape it across the woman, then I perch on the edge of her mattress and slide my warm hands around her cold one, willing the heat of my blood to spread into her skin and sinew. *Wake up, wake up, wake up.* I wonder what she will look like awake, what color are her eyes, whether they habitually glint amusement or excoriatingly glare, or whether her preference is a stare as blank and as null as white noise flick-flickering across a cathode ray screen, humming with static. I can only wait and see.

In the meantime, I can't stop staring at the gap in her top lip. It's like nothing and no one I've ever known, a detail of her being that is simply uncharted in every single one of the books and illustrations and pictures that are all I have to piece together an entire world. What else have they left out? What else do I have wrong? Because it's certainly not *her* who is wrong, not in this regard at least, that much is obvious. It's me who's at fault, me who doesn't know an ass from an elbow, a face from a face. What is it like to have such a gap, I wonder—and is it even a gap at all? Gap implies absence, gap implies partial, incomplete. Gap implies something that was there and now isn't, or something that should be and never was. But maybe this woman's lip is the way lips are supposed to be, the model for all others that may only claim to be poor copies, a natural aperture as exquisite as any nostril or mouth. An opening can be very useful. What is the pupil of the eye if not a hole? What is a pore, an ear, a gill? They are beautiful all of them, beautiful in their exquisite functionality. Perhaps the matter of this woman's lip is another such as these, and I simply don't know the right name to call it by. Well, there are many things I don't know. It's useful to be reminded of it every now and then. Probably the woman knows the right word, probably she could tell me—if she ever wakes up, if she ever deigns to grace us with her conscious presence.

I squeeze her hand with mine, clear my throat all purposeful-wise and set myself to business, such as it is. See if I can't coax her from her sleeping, can't persuade her out of it.

"It's going to be all right," I tell her, making my beginning as best I can. "You'll see. We've gone to all this effort to bring you here—even though we shouldn't have, even though we should have let you drown—and now the least you can do is wake up, the least you can do is recover. It will mean ever such a lot to Crevan. Probably. I'm not sure why, but I get that sense off of him, don't you? Certainly, he'll be unbearable if you die. He'll do that mournful, rueful thing he does sometimes, closing in on himself for days. I think it's because he doesn't like being made to look a fool, doesn't like showing himself up. He risked his skin for you. And mine too, you know. Because you could be anyone, couldn't you? You could be dangerous. And still he dived into the water and brought you back. It *can't* have been all for nothing. It just can't. Crevan will hate it. And then maybe he'll hate me for not warning him or doubting him or for looking like I'm thinking that I *told* him what would happen, what it would be like, how it would all come out in the wash. Please don't do that to me. Please. Don't make me regret what I didn't do, don't make me regret not forcing Crevan to tip you back into the sea, to let you drown. It isn't kind."

Absently nosing, I move aside the blankets to peer at the inside of her left wrist, curious to see whether she shares any patches with Crevan. But the skin is clear, untouched, unsullied, saving for one sole hairband—navy elastic with a pretty red ribbon bow. I snap it off her wrist and slide it onto mine, pausing to admire the fetching trinket. Very nice. Then I check the inside of the woman's right arm but this too is bare. Well, what do you know? The woman is like me. Certainly, more like me than like Crevan. She's never been caught by no backbiters, never been given any patch against anything or nothing. Perhaps she too has been living on an island of her own, somewhere out of sight, somewhere down the shore from my own. Or perhaps she has some hideaway on the mainland. Perhaps there is a whole group of them, good at avoiding the back-biters, at killing any who do hunt them down, who do cross their path; a commune of cutthroat anarchists. I wonder. It has to be one or the other, doesn't it? For her to have lived so long, to be well fed, to be unpatched by any backbiter. From what Crevan tells me, this is not the way of things. Then again, I too am just as long-lived, similarly well fed and equally unpatched. Judging by my experience alone, there is nothing at all out of the ordinary about this woman. And yet, and yet. Crevan says *I* am not of the ordinary, and who am I to contradict him? What do I know? I'm just a good-for-nothing dum-dum-dummy.

A touch on the blade of my shoulder, half-caress, half-nudge, fingers firm and light. It's Crevan, dry now, warmer now, wearing a pair of waxed hiking trousers belted at the waist and a long-sleeved thermal of merino wool in a glass-bottle green that makes his eyes fizz luminous. His red hair is damp and wild from being brine-tipped, sea-tousled, and his face is still pinched with cold. But what little color usually resides in his cheeks is beginning to return, the faintest wash of damask rose. Sometimes he is so beautiful it makes me want to weep. Sometimes he is so beautiful I want to paint the contours of his finely-boned face onto the walls. Sometimes he is so beautiful I want to take a scalpel and dissect him, to turn him into a living diagram like the ones in my illustrated encyclopedias.

"You should have something hot to drink," I say. "You should have some honeyed tea. Whisky with lemon. An infusion of flowers and spices. Cinnamon and star anise. Cardamom and cloves."

"Later. Let's deal with her first. What's the damage?"

"Besides being half-drowned, you mean?"

"Come on, Kit. Let me look at her."

Still determined to be ever-so-obliging, mister, I shuffle out of the way and watch as Crevan makes his inspection with slow method. The woman has few visible injuries. There is the swollen bruise on the forehead that looks as sore as anything. And then there is a series of angry red welts lashed around her left ankle. That's it, that's all she wrote. Saving, of course, whatever internal damage she may have sustained while being carried on the back of the sea. Her lungs could be half-full of water. Her organs could be ripped,

bruised, bleeding. Who can say? After wrestling her into a new set
of clothes, I don't *think* any of her bones are broken. Anything else
and we'd have to cut her open to find out. Or, you know, she could
wake up and tell us how it hurts and where. That would do nicely.

Crevan points to the red welts. "Looks like a jellyfish sting. We'll
need the first-aid kit. Could you get it?"

"Am *I* a first-aid Kit?"

"No."

"But—"

"Not now, Kit."

"Oh, so I'm a not-now Kit?"

"Kit!"

"All right, all right, I'm going. I'm practically gone already. Won't
be two ticks, two minutes, two shakes of a lamb's tail."

I skip past the dividing screen and along to the bathroom at the
other end of the den, a marble affair behind a glass door, cream
tiles rippling with gray and flecks of quartz. It might be the most
luxurious part of the den. Fully half of it is dedicated to a glorious
walk-in shower with a brushed-aluminum rain head the size of a
dinner plate. There is a heated towel rack. There is a marble sink
with a mirrored cabinet above, little lights studded along the edge
that flatter and glow soft. I turn a silvered tap and let the water
run warm to rinse the crusted blood from my palms. The water is
clear, good enough to drink. There is a well behind the den, there
is a septic tank and purifier—and all in fine working order, thank
you very much. I pick up the heavy bar of soap from where it sits in
the dish and work it between my hands until it lathers, scenting the
air with citrus, red basil, and lime. It makes my grazes sting bright,
but it is bearable, a nice clean pain. I open the cabinet and pull out
the metal basket that contains our ready supply of pill bottles and
ointments, bandages, and Band-Aids. There's plenty more in the
storeroom and a few other select pieces of medical equipment, but
I figure this'll do for the woman. At least for the time being. First,
though, I dig out two large bandages and patch them over my raw

skin. There, see? Good as new. Then I hurry back to Crevan, basket in hand.

"Get the tweezers," he says.

I rummage in the basket until I find them, a pair of slim silver pincers, nasty and long. Crevan tells me what to do, directs my attention to the woman's ankle, points my eyes to where a few thin, translucent spines stand proud of the wet red welts where she got stung.

"Pluck them out," he says. "Or scrape them out with the edge of the tweezers if you can't get a grip."

"Get a grip. Get a hold. Get a grasp. Get a read. Of yourself. On the situation. Get real. Get with it. Get—"

"You're doing it again, Kit."

"Sorry."

I work swift-swift then, plucking out the spines one, two, three without any more fussing or fretting. Honest. Then Crevan nudges me to one side. There's a little brown glass bottle of antiseptic in his hands, which may or may not be entirely ineffective. Who knows? It's the fun of the game, the luck of the draw, the unfortunate consequences of microbial adaptation. He twists off the metal cap and upends it, dousing the welts to clean them out. Or so we hope.

"No bandages for now," he rules. "She should heal better in the open air."

I look around. Ventilated it might be, but there's no part of this den that could be described as open air. Still, I suppose Crevan knows what he's doing. He better had, because it seems like a whole lot of not-any-help, the equivalent of fixing a backed-up toilet by spritzing perfume. I mean, it might be just the way to treat a jellyfish sting, I don't know. I'm prepared to trust Crevan on that one. But it does look to be the least of the woman's trouble. She's still unconscious after all, and there's even less we can do for that nasty-looking bruise. Crevan digs out an aluminum tube of a thick yellow unguent that he smears all over the swelling.

"To bring the inflammation down," he says, but not like he believes for a second it will work. "Not much else we can do."

"She'll wake," I say confidently, sorry to see his spirits brought so low. "I had a little talk with her and I mean it's not like she could promise anything, could she? But I think she was listening and I think it will be OK. She'll get better."

But Crevan does not look convinced, so I take a deep, deep breath and press on, pressing my point. "You've put on the magic ointment," I say, nice and slow, "and I took out the stingers. So now there's nothing to stop her. She's probably already on the mend. Just a bit more rest and she'll be back to full health, good as new, perfectly restored. She'll wake up and you won't ever never guess that we found her bobbing along in the sea like a lost rubber ducky or a glassy man-of-war. She'll wake up and then we'll talk to her and she'll talk to us and probably she'll be very frightened not knowing where she is or why or who we are, but that's OK because we'll calm her down and explain what happened and then she'll see that we're all right, that everything's all right, that we've got this lovely den and who wouldn't want to be tucked safely away in a place like this?" I pause and consider. "I hope she doesn't like it *too* much, though, because I don't know if we can keep her, I don't know if we should. It would be good if she wanted to leave. It would be good if she didn't want to take the den from us, because she might, you know. And she looks pretty harmless now, she looks like we could take her easy, take her no problem, but that's just because she's unconscious, sliding around in the land of nod."

"Kit—"

"No, Crevan!" I won't be put off, not now, not when it matters so. He has to *see*. "Look at her properly, *look*. She's got proper heft and she's a survivor, for sure. She could hurt us. She could kill us. She could certainly try to, anyway, and I don't think I want to see that, don't think I want to be on the other end of a murderous rage if it's all the same to you. The mess will be something else. And what if she's got people? Friends? Family? What if there's someone out there looking for her, looking for us? We should take her back, Crevan. Put her back in the sea. Take her to the mainland and leave her on the coast, in some cove or harbor where she could have easily been washed ashore. Throw them off, stop anyone from coming here. Because she'll be trouble," I mutter, the panic rising, half-wondering how I got to this point when I started off somewhere else entirely and half-certain that what I'm saying is deadly true. "She'll be trouble," I repeat. "When she wakes up. She will, you know. We can't tell what she's going to do, how she's going to behave. Even if she means us no harm, even if she's toothless, we'll still have to feed her and clothe her. We'll still have to share our air with her and the bathroom too. And we don't know anything about her. What she's like. If she eats with her mouth open. If she cracks her knuckles. If she tells terrible jokes. I don't want her here, Crevan. It's not good, not right, just you wait and see. I hope she never wakes up."

Crevan makes no reply to this, only lets the suggestion of my words sit in the silent air between us and build into something other than what it was that I said, transmuting, transforming, taking on a new body and substance until it becomes not *I hope she never wakes* but *make it so she never will*. Well, it's an option of sorts and one that takes care of some immediate worries if not all. I wonder if Crevan is seeing the same flashes of futures and possibilities as me: a hand over the mouth and nose, a rock to the head. That's all it would take, after all, when she's lying passed out, unable to retaliate or resist. She would go from being a breathing body to a dead one. Not much of a change, all things considered. We could carry her out to the trees and leave her to rot amid their thirsty hungry roots. There are scavengers aplenty on the island apart from us—there are burying beetles and calliphorid flies and herring gulls and carrion crows—and they would soon strip the bones clean, clean, clean. We could do it, I'm sure. If we really wanted to, if we put our minds to it. At least, Crevan could. He's killed before—not that he hardly ever admits to such.

"Do you think—"

"No," Crevan snaps, striking his palm against the cedar post of the bunk. It's abrupt, a sudden fit. "Come on!" He is shouting now. "This isn't a game, Kit. You need to stop. I know you're frightened—"

"Am not! Not frightened, not me. I swear. You don't know, you can't possibly—"

"Come *on*," he says once more but in different tone; quieter now, calmer now, not so stern. Like he's taking pity, like he regrets how he spoke before. "Come with me."

He takes me firmly by the wrist and leads me back past the dividing screen, back past the sofa and CD rack, past the bathroom and the galley kitchen on the other side of that and then to the final door that leads through to the storeroom, cool and dark, the walls lined with steel shelves and every one of these stacked high as can be with all manner of earthly goods: cans and packets wrapped in silver foil, racks of green-glass bottles, water drums and filters, fat canisters of kelp biofuel, endless boxes of soap, disinfectants, flares, radios. On one shelf a dismantled rifle and carton upon carton of ammunition, enough to hold back an invading horde. In short, everything a small family might need to survive the worst of calamities.

I don't know how long it took our faceless benefactors to amass such a reserve or what caused them to leave it behind. But whatever befell them—nothing good, for sure—their misfortune was to our lasting benefit. Shame that we have no way of thanking them, no way of even knowing their names—though there are initials stamped on many of the shelves, many of the containers, monogrammed on the towels in the bathroom: NBM. That's it, our only clue—but not one I am much interested in following. What would be the point? Why inquire after the dead? No, my concern is only for what was left behind, for what is now ours. Mine. And what isn't lurking here jarred or canned isn't worth having: honey and marmalade, lemon curd and raspberry jam, chutneys and pickles, stuffed olives and artichokes, sardines and mackerel and salmon—all smoked, brined, and canned—fermented cabbage and jalapeños, beetroot and sweet-corn and peas, chickpeas and lentils, more beans than you can invent or imagine or name: black-eyed and kidney, cannellini and butter, broad, and borlotti, adzuki and haricot. It is all ours now, our collateral against the future, our security against the villains and looters that might even now be creeping toward the island. All here, all kept safe together in the best room in the house, a place like magic, where the style is strictly utilitarian but the effect is giddying, like being let loose in a glittering apothecary, being handed the keys to a war chest. It's a pantry–larder–smokehouse all in one, a groaning harvest table, a confectioner's window display, a panoply of sugared almonds. It's a walled paradise concealed within the den's own barriers and so doubly protected, a garden of plenty, a wonder, an impossible dream. Just seeing the laden shelves makes me feel better, like there's still some magic left, like there are still some things that are good. But the instant hit of comfort they provide is not the entirety of Crevan's aim.

Striding to the middle of the floor, he kneels and presses with his fingertips at a faint dip in the linoleum. A hidden trapdoor springs open, revealing an empty hollow. The cavity is only a few feet deep and not very long and not very wide. Crevan slips himself into it like a foot into a shrunken sock and then I join him, curling my body around his, seeking out the crooks and crannies like water does, and then pulling the trapdoor shut over us with a ringing clack.

The darkness is total, far beyond that of night. We are embalmed in stone, hard concrete pressing in against us from nearly every side. I can feel its rough surface against the top of my skull, the edge of my spine, the base of my sit bones. Crevan extends his hands and feet around me, ramming them into the walls of the enclosure as though to test their solidity. His entire body is braced, every muscle tensed, every tendon taut and ready to snap. It shouldn't surprise but it does. After all, I'm the one getting worked up. He's the one in control. But maybe he is as frightened as I am, as disturbed and as put out. Maybe it's even worse for him than it is for me. Maybe when he says that I'm panicked, that I need to get a grip, I really should be the one saying it to him. Maybe taking care of me gives him a way to take care of himself too.

For a moment he stays like that, stays tense like that, holding himself perfectly rigid, perfectly motionless. Then, at last, he takes a long, steady breath and lets his body relax into me. I breathe. Remind myself that we are safe here, hidden as we are from all angles, all eyes. We don't have to worry about who might be watching, might be coming up at us from behind. Not when there's only one possible entrance and no one but us knows about the den or the trapdoor—no one who still lives, anyway. If Crevan and I spontaneously died, right here, right this very second, our bodies would never be found. There's a certain relief in knowing that, in feeling the cold embrace of this long-ago and future grave. It says that I am really truly safe, that we are safe, that everything is going to be just fine. And just like that, in just another moment, I am relaxed as ever I was and rather bored now as it happens, nice as it is to be held by Crevan, nice as it is to hold him back. I'm done with the foxhole, the bolthole, the dugout. Done for now, anyway. I'd quite like to get out, if it's all the same, quite like to go and do something else now please, something other than lie folded up in the dark, something fun, something that makes it worthwhile still having all these breaths to breathe, all this blood to beat. Let's *go* already.

But Crevan isn't done yet, isn't soothed, not him, not forever so. He's as serious as a storm warning, his forehead pressed to mine like he's trying to sap away all the bad good-for-nothingness out of me via skin-to-skin conduction, busy stilling a fear that I let float away long seconds ago. But he can't know that, can he? Poor baby. I play along and hope it makes him feel better, hope it helps him to believe that he's a-helping me. I do not snigger or yawn or chatter, just lie quiet and still, glad he can't see my face, glad he can't tell that I'm so over it, baby, and can't we move on now, can't we be done now? Still, he holds on to me, serious as a banana split isn't.

Heaven forfend we should deal with our sentiments in a timely fashion. Let's wrap it up, people; let's get this show on the road. I stifle my impatience and wait. Finally, Crevan makes a move, grasping my hand and making me wince silently at the sudden pressure on my palm, raw beneath the Band-Aid. Sometimes Crevan is the worst.

"I won't let anything happen to you," he says.

Tell me something I don't know, dummy, tell me something new. That's what I'd like to say, that's what I'm a-thinking. But I keep it to myself, every ungracious little bit of it, and only make a faint murmur by way of reply, purposefully indistinct. And then, because it still doesn't seem quite enough, I ever so carefully press my dry lips to his cheek, a kiss of gratitude in the dark. *There you go, baby.* He means well after all, the dear little thing. He really does. It's not his fault he can be such a terrible bore. (But goodness, can't he, a real champion—there should be prizes for it, there should be medals.)

At long, long last, the spell that binds him there (and so too me) is broken. I can feel it seeping away and out into the concrete, can feel the creeping discomfort that takes its place, the next-door-to-embarrassment prickling. And what are we doing here after all, folded up tight in this crevice, suspended together in stone, hiding from a woman half-dead? It's foolish, is what it is. Cowardly. Craven.

The hangdog shame getting the better of him, Crevan shifts, murmurs some pretext, some excuse, and reaches for the trapdoor. He climbs out ahead of me then stops. He turns, stoops, lends his hand like he always does, in that way you can set store by. He heaves and hauls and hahs and hums. He pulls me up and out, out into the light. He sets me on my feet, sets me up, straight, right, apart, going, loose, free. Ready for whatever comes next. Or, as it turns out, not. Not at all, not remotely, not even one little bit.

THE DISPOSITION AND MANNER
OF OUR DEATH

This is how it happens, how we come to the end of days: humanity gets seriously into plastic. We make it cheap, we make it quick, we make it by the yard. There are more kinds than you can remember or imagine. This stuff is versatile. Flexible when you want, rigid when you need. It ushers in a hundred, hundred quiet revolutions. It changes how we eat, how we shop, how we provide medical care, how we get from A to B and what we wear when we go. It changes the way we build. It endures like you wouldn't believe. It does not rot, does not decay, does not go bad after being left out in the sun. That's what makes it heaven-sent. That's what makes it hell.

It's a while before anyone notices, before anyone stops to think about the consequences, about what it means to pump a planet with discarded straws, bottles, cartons, cotton swabs, and wet wipes, about what it will be like to live swaddled in bubble wrap. It's a problem, a problem for everyone: for the birds in the sky and the fish in the sea as much as it is for the people on the land who make the plastic and wear it and build with it and eat it and sweat it out again. It is a problem and bacteria are the solution. A new kind of bacteria, one that can devour plastic by the ton; digest it, break it down into energy, and use it to live. It happens by chance at first, a species that develops out in the wild, a new kind of *Ideonella* that emerges, by some alchemy of nature, from the wastes of a bottle-recycling plant. Having been so miraculously discovered, the bacteria are tested, measured, assessed, and found capable of digesting polyethylene terephthalate—good old pee-ee-tee—which is a surprise for all concerned and one no less welcome than the unexpected corroboration of an alibi to a defendant. And although these particular bacteria are not particularly efficient or fast, are not in any kind of a rush, soon they are being developed in laboratories all over the world, there to be bred and enhanced with keen intent into new and wondrous strains—all bright, all beautiful—capable of degrading and assimilating more types of plastic, more quickly, those extravagant dinnertimes compressed down from six weeks to six days to six hours. Then, ready at last, ready or not, they are put to work and good use out in the waste centers and dumping grounds. For a time, everyone is happy, everyone wins.

And then, just like that, the new kind of bacteria becomes a new kind of problem, a problem of a different nature entirely: superbugs that slip out of the landfill refineries when no one is looking and spread, with their hungry, hungry mouths and their catholic appetites for synthetics of all kinds.

They eat everything, these plastiphages, these plastivores, destroy everything: bright red polyester T-shirts and far, far worse; miles and miles of water pipes, insulation diverse and various, the airbags out of cars and the casings off computers. Seals, gaskets; a thousand tiny critical plastic pieces that you didn't even know were there but which underpin every single piece of infrastructure on which you rely—all crumbling, all failing. Well, perhaps not all, but any. There are still a few stashes of clean plastics here and there, though these are dwindling and no less prone to corruption. Just not corrupt yet.

But stay, the worst is yet to come. Like all great survivors, the bacteria evolve away from their particular specialisms to appetites more general, more variated, more voracious. They become omnivores of a sort, adding a taste for the human along with their penchant for synthetics. How, I cannot say. Perhaps the bacteria direct their hunger along conceptual lines, taking the

idea of *man-made* to its serious and logical end. Perhaps we
have eaten and absorbed so much of the plastic we have been
churning out that we are more or less indistinguishable from
it. Perhaps it is simple chance that the one bacterium develops the dual capacity, the double appetite. The upshot is bad
news for us (isn't it always?): a microbe that thrives when introduced into a bloodstream, a microbe that infects and burns a
body up, a microbe that can kill. And it comes at a point when
so many bacterial infections have already become untreatable:
pneumonia, tuberculosis, septicemia. It is our fault, you know,
entirely our fault—we have been tempting fate for years; we
use our precious antibiotics recklessly, extravagantly, behaving
as though they are an endless panacea, a bottomless well of clean
water that may be dipped into as much and as often as we please.
We are profligate like you wouldn't believe. We overprescribe.
Antibiotics are doled out for any kind of infection—bacterial or
not, warranted or not—and we fail to complete our courses of
medication as directed, however imprecisely. Antibiotics are fed
in growth supplements to livestock, applying cure as prophylactic and so swiftly eroding its utility. Antibiotics leach and pool
into the soil, into the water that we drink. So exposed, the bacteria learn, transform, mature—the bad just as well as the good.
The list of drug-resistant bacteria grows fast, grows quick.
And then come the deadly adapted plastiphages. We waste our
last antibiotics fighting them—there is no time, no funding to
develop anything new, to develop anything effective—and it is
null, entirely null. The bacteria are audacious, tenacious, ahead
of the curve. They evolve too quickly; mutating, creating exquisite single-cell forms that cannot be countered or treated by any
medication, cannot even be eradicated by any disinfectant. In a
heartbeat, we are rendered defenseless.

And it's as simple as that; back we go to chaos, back we go to a
state of nature. Never mind that we no longer have reliable medical
apparatus with which to treat disease and infection; we don't have

the medication either. That's it. These are the end days, that's how we get here. Total bacterial resistance. There's no point complaining, no sense in blaming the microbes. After all, life will out if it possibly can, that's natural selection for you. It's just mutation, it's just the way it goes. For a while, we had an antibiotic of last resort. And then we didn't, and then there were none.

SWALLOWED IN EVERY
PUDDLE AND POND

I never really bothered with the greenhouse before Crevan arrived. Miraculous though it was to see the vintage glass still standing proud and uncracked in spite of everything, in spite of how old rip-roaring time had unleashed its tragedies and trialing tribulations on the surrounding castle, reducing it to ruins and scattering the rubble all about. Truth is, I hadn't seen much use in it. Structurally sound the greenhouse may have been, but to my ignorant eyes what grew within seemed an impossible mess, wild and sprawling with vines that coiled and pressed up against the glass, nettles that shot out from strange angles and reached as wide as the span of my two arms outstretched. It was feral, uncultivated. If the plants could be tamed—and I was not entirely convinced on that point—then it was quite simply beyond my knowledge and ken.

And that wasn't the worst of it, either. No, the worst of it was the smell, although *smell* certainly seems far too feeble a word to describe that particular olfactorial blight. Even *stench* or *reek* hardly cut it. It was a fetor, a disturbing funk experienced not so much in the nostrils as it was at the root of the tongue and in the pit of the belly, one that provoked the bile to rise and wash the back of the teeth. I couldn't catch it without retching; couldn't walk too close by the greenhouse door without battling the need to collapse to hands and knees, to throw up, to choke out the entire contents of my acridly quavering stomach. I didn't know what the cause was, didn't know what was hidden away in there, among the weeds, but I could guess and that was bad enough. I didn't know it was only the *Stapelia gigantea*, the carrion plants that grew just inside the door. How could I possibly have known or guessed? I'd never heard of them before. And to the uninitiated, you can imagine what seems more likely: an actual decomposing corpse or a plant that's just pretending. Anyway, I knew nothing and had no idea about the extent of my ignorance. I was convinced. A body, I told myself, a body among the weeds; a corpse, probably the flesh already half-sloughed off as it rots, rots, rots. And the very last thing I wanted to do was cut through the overgrowth and prove myself right, prove what I had known all along, but which, in the end, it transpired I hadn't known at all.

Then Crevan came. He looked at the greenhouse nestled where it was within the walled courtyard and saw not what was, but what could be. It helped, perhaps, that his sense of smell was not—is not—quite so keen as mine. He could stand at the door of the greenhouse without so much as grimacing or breaking into a panicked sweat. When I explained, when I told him what I could smell and what I thought was lying concealed within the tangled shrubbery, he only shrugged. The dead, it seemed, did not disturb him, were of no consequence to a man such as he. *It's the living you have to watch out for, Kit*, is what he said to me, and I suppose he was right enough about that—after a fashion, at any rate, after a kind.

There was certainly no arguing with him about the greenhouse. If he wanted to wade knee-deep into that particular grave of fetid foliage, then I wasn't going to stop him. I more or less left him to it, giving him a wide berth as he ripped out all the tough grasses, shrubs, and ferns that clamored together for space. He was bloody-minded about it, working at all hours, entirely untroubled by being out and above ground on sunlit days, what with the high walls of the courtyard standing guard all around, making certain that he could not be seen, that he could toil on unobserved by whatever alien spyglass he insisted, in that sweet deluded way of his, must even yet be turned to the island, watching and waiting; patient, greedy.

"The backbiters don't know we're here," I would chide. "Leastways that's what you told me, leastways that's what makes sense. Probably they don't know that our island even exists."

"The backbiters aren't what worry me."

He'd said that much before, of course, and never much more than that either. Personally, I think he just liked how it sounded, enjoyed coming across all mysterious and enigmatic, all worldly-wise and weary. He didn't realize that there were times it had quite the opposite effect, giving him the occasional air of a total and utter prat. But, like I say, there was no arguing with him. He had reason to believe there were mainlanders to be afraid of and he'd decided, somewhere along the way, that everything would go more smoothly for us all if he didn't trouble me with the details.

Perhaps he was right. Perhaps I really would have panicked if I'd known. Or perhaps the simple ordeal of transmitting the information would have been enough to trigger some sort of mental failure on his part, agitating brain's fractures until the mind judders to collapse. I have no way of telling. But he approached the greenhouse with the same set determination and there was no arguing with that either. And in those early days, it seemed no bad thing that he should have a distraction, something to occupy his hours and keep his mind off of the mainland ghoulies and bogeymen on which he seemed so fixed the rest of the time. The work acted on him like a lawn roller, flattening and leveling, compacting him into something sturdier, something civilized. Light returned to the greenhouse chink by chink and—slowly, surely—so too did it return to Crevan. Assuming, of course, that there had ever been light in him beforehand, that his grim glower had been borne of the unspoken trauma and distress of his mainland years and was not merely a peculiar detail of his DNA. Either way, the terrible gray he'd arrived with lifted, dispersed, went into retreat. There was light in the greenhouse and, for the first time since his arrival, I saw Crevan smile. A proper smile, I mean, not one of those tight-lipped grimaces I've seen from him plenty of times before and since, the sardonic kind that flutters somewhere between wryly superior cynicism and out-and-out disapproval. When Crevan smiles true, it's a thing to behold: a cloud of breath on the cold air, a perfect knot in a length of cord, a thick slab of chocolate being unexpectedly pressed into your open hand.

Of course, he found the cause of the smell almost at once. He showed me the carrion plants with their flowers like enormous corpulent stars, explained what their little trick was, their little game, their way of making it seem like they were a corpse when they were really nothing of the sort. How they'd come to be there or why, we could only guess. It was hard to believe anyone had planted them by choice, but it didn't seem likely that they'd have found their way to the island—and then to the courtyard and then to the greenhouse—by accident alone.

"It's a disguise," I said to Crevan after he explained. "It's a trick."

"Exactly."

"No, not like that, that's not what I mean. It's a trick, a decoy. Not the plants themselves, but putting them there. I bet there's a body buried beneath them, I bet there's a body in their sandy bed. That's where I'd hide one, anyway. That's what I'd do if I had to. Because how would anyone know? Even if they could smell it, even if they caught the rot of it, all they would think is: *My, but aren't those carrion plants convincing.*"

Crevan gave me one of his sidewise looks. "You're not much like other people."

"Thank you. I think. Or is that not meant as compliment? I can't tell. You know I can never tell."

"It's not meant as anything. Just the truth."

"Can't be truthing if it's only you that thinks it. And I bet you anything that you're the only one, that others would disagree."

"There aren't any others."

"Not so! Not so, but quite otherwise. There's me, for a start. And then there's all the people you've met, not to mention the ones that you haven't, and—"

"I didn't mean it like that."

"You said you didn't mean it as *anything*."

Better by far than the carrion plants—better by a long shot, a chalk, a mile—were the twelve fruit trees we found at the very back of the greenhouse. Admittedly, most of them were dead and dying. Crevan cut down the weaklings, the runts, and lavished his attention on the survivors. The reward that first autumn was a glut of ripe fruits, heavy and syrup-sweet, that we gorged upon until our stomachs ached and we could eat no more.

———

Autumn, autumn; one of four and the finest by far, though nothing—of course—without its sisters spring and summer before, without its brother winter after. Four in and as one. The world over it is the same—or was—for the world is split, the world is quartered. The globe has four corners, the compass four cardinal points. Four and four and four. There are four temperaments, four humors. Four evangelists and four gospels. Four suits in a deck of cards. Four movements in a symphony, strings on a cello, beats in a bar of common time. Four letters in all the best words. Four fingers on the hand, four chambers in the mammalian heart. Four horsemen of the apocalypse, a rare and rarefied quartet; quartered and so complete.

Four bunks in the den.

If I were a bacterium, it wouldn't matter. The one me could divide to become two, and then the two me could each divide again to become four. That would be the complement full, the set complete. It would be as easy as that. But I am only me. Only ever stupid, useless, good-for-nothing me.

———

The morning after the drowned woman arrives, the morning after Crevan pulls her limpet-like, life-sucking body from the sea, we are both of us toiling to clean the greenhouse. We should be sleeping, but neither of us can, even though we're dead tired, bone tired, dog tired. Crevan says he was living nocturnal for years before he even came to the island and, since he arrived, I have done my best to follow his cautious regime, shunning the sun, becoming a creature of the stars and the moon, a child of the night. Or so I like to tell myself when I am pretending, when I am making believe that it is fun to only ever be out after sundown. But the truth is we are more snuffling hedgehogs than sharp-clawed eagle-owls. There is no joy in fear, no delight in being constantly reminded that we are prey. In Crevan's mind, it seems that's all we are, all we can ever be, no matter how much I tell him that there are no apex predators here on the island, that no one's got a hope of finding us whether we venture out into the daylight or not.

Today, though, he cannot sleep and neither can I. We both try for a while, each of us turning fitfully in our separate beds while the drowned woman lies there on the bottom bunk, unconscious still, a grim unknown among the familiar furnishings of the den, one weird enough to warp the rest by contiguity alone, changing our cherished, well-kept home into a strange place overrun with disturbances and qualms and sneaking, whispering fears. We neither of us can stick it out for very long. I hear Crevan get out of bed, hear his footsteps cross the floor. His door opens and his head appears beyond the foot of my bunk, where he stands suspended in shadow: a half-starved beast scenting the air. His eyes hunt me out and then he blinks to see that I am awake, that I have been awake all this time.

"Are you going to eat me, Mr. Wolf?" I ask, hoping he will take the bait and play the game, take up his fairy-tale role—even if he is more *Vulpes vulpes* than *Canis lupus*. But his jaw set-clenches tight and I know he will not bend. Not today.

"No, Kit."

"Why not? Perhaps I'm delicious. Perhaps I'm the best meal you'll ever have."

"Don't tempt me," he says. It is warning, it is jest.

"So you *are* tempted?"

"No."

"Spoilsport."

He shakes his head like he's shaking away the last of the beast that prowled out with him to my bunk. "Come on," he says. "Let's . . . let's go up to the greenhouse."

After the dark of the den—of the tunnels, of the catacombs—the gray dimness of an overcast day is enough to make my eyes ache, but the dull pain soon eases. The air is apple-bite crisp and oh-so redolent with the musk of decaying leaves. The white-winged gulls are squalling noisily overhead, squabbling over fish scraps just like usual. And in the light I can see what we have clearly missed in the ventures of successive nights: the glass roof of the greenhouse is streaked with white, splattered with enough bird droppings to form a protective crust that stops the sunlight from penetrating through to the plants below.

Clicking his tongue against his teeth, Crevan goes to fetch a sponge and a basin of warm, soapy water. There's a short ladder propped up against the greenhouse and I hold it steady for him as he shimmies up to the roof and begins to tackle the mess. Even after he loosens the worst of the dirt, the glass is far from clear. I refill the basin and we swap places. It should be a real grind, a chore, a misery. Certainly, the work is slow and it stinks and there are any number of other things I could be doing right now, thank you very much. But there's a funny kind of pleasure in it as well; in the methodical application of sponge to spackled shit, in the absorbing mindlessness of wiping down panel after panel. Perhaps it's the courtyard walls being snuggled so secure about us, or perhaps it's the bracing freshness in every breath, or the soft breeze kiss-kissing my face and hands. A peace settles over me. I dip the sponge back into the water and let slip away all thoughts of the drowned woman in the den. Dirty water spills down my arms and the bandages on my palms loosen and become grubby. I'll need to give my hands a proper wash later. But, for now, for ten glorious minutes, I put the grazes and the woman from my mind. In a moment, and with a certain amount of effort, I'm convinced that she might not exist at all, might never have existed. And I know better than to blow a good thing, to look a gift horse in the mouth, to rap my knuckles on its wooden sides and shout taunts at the Greek soldiers lurking in its belly.

We clean the glass and let it dry. Then Crevan climbs back up the ladder to buff away the water streaks with a cloth. Despite the cover of cumulus and stratus, the panels gleam. I don't suppose they'll stay that way for long, not with the birds circling overhead, but there's nothing we can do about that. I follow Crevan into the greenhouse, where we push on past the putrid cloud of the carrion plants and are met by the nectar fragrance of ripening peaches, plums, apricots, and cherries. Reaching into the leaves of the nearest fruit tree, Crevan plucks a swollen fig from the branch. It yields readily to him, splitting beneath his thumbs to reveal pink flesh, fibrous and glistening. He holds out half and I eat from his hand, tonguing the rough seeds and hungrily sucking out the pulp. He smiles at me, beautiful in the sunlight, his red hair burnishing gold, his green eyes quickening bright.

"Better?"

"Better," I say and kiss his open palm.

He chews down the sweet rind of the fig and begins his inspection of the trees, stopping here and there to prune a browning leaf, to peer more closely at a new growth of moss across the bark. There's more besides: strawberries, tomatoes, and lettuces growing in shallow trays that we planted afresh with supplies and seedlings from the den after the greenhouse was first reclaimed. But it's still the fruit trees to which Crevan devotes the best part of his time. The darling man. Really, I know I shouldn't admit it, know what he would think of that, but the truth is that this astonishing outlay of effort is all for my sake, all in service of my sweet tooth, my fruit-bat tendencies. One bite of a ripe peach and I'm gone, pliable as clay, not caring one iota—one jot—what happens next, because

I'm done, finished, brought to silence by the rapture of fine-napped skin against my lips; of the clumsy click of my teeth as they meet together to cut apart a mouthful of syrup-wet flesh; of the juices that spill and trickle and grow sticky on my chin, my fingers, my wrists and forearms.

And to think of all those years when I let the greenhouse languish and the fruit trees along with it! I did not know what it was to eat until Crevan came to the island, what it meant to be truly sated. I have done my best to keep this from him, to stop him from getting an inflated sense of his own worth, but my efforts at disguise have been of limited effect. He knows. I can see it in the arch of his brow, in the flicker at the corner of his mouth. He knows and it brings him some kind of delight. Perhaps he thinks he matters to me, that he is important, that there will come a time when it will seem that I must decide against him and that he will be able to remind me of the fruit he has given me, that he has the secret to staying the hand of fate. Well, let him believe it, if it brings him comfort. Perhaps it is even true, I don't know. Only time and circumstance can tell.

Of all the trees, the fig is my favorite, the fig is the best, the only one that is truly, maddeningly absurd; a fair match for the carrion plants, as inexplicably strange as the eel. It is friends with a special type of wasp, but a tricksy friend, a dangerous friend. The tree puts out its first immature fruits, its fleshy syconia, each one hollow and lined with ovaries on curling pedicels. It's a tempting hidey-hole for a gravid wasp that cannot resist the offered shelter, the protection of the walls of the syconia circling all around. And look! There's a hole right here at the bottom of the fruit; a gap, an aperture, an opening. The wasp can crawl right inside. Only the hole isn't so wide as perhaps first it seemed and the wasp has to fight its way through, never minding when its wings get shredded and torn away, or when it loses its antennae. It's too late to stop now and impossible to turn back. Perhaps the wasp already knows, perhaps it senses what will happen. It clambers at last into the hollow, bruised and nearly destroyed. It lays its eggs, depositing them along with the pollen it carries, fertilizing the ovaries of the fig so that they may grow and bear seeds.

Then, with little ceremony and less complaint, the wasp dies.

Around the corpse of their dead mother, the eggs hatch and become larvae, growing as the fig grows around them. Just as soon as they can, they mate, conducting what can only be a frenzied, frantic orgy in the hollow of the heavy fruit. Once they are sated, they dig their way out. The males—born wingless, born only for this—die almost at once. The females, carrying eggs, crawl to freedom, picking up more pollen along the way. They fly to another fig; to lay eggs, to die, to begin the cycle anew. And back in the mother fig—the crucible—the fruit is slowly digesting that first wasp, attacking its dead body with enzymes that will break it down into nutrients to be absorbed, energy to be consumed.

The wasp, so devoured, becomes the fig. It has no choice. It is dead. It would be almost as though the creature never existed, but the fig cannot fruit without it, cannot grow strong without it. The wasp lays its eggs in the flesh of the fig. The fig eats the wasp. There's a gruesome balance to it, a macabre justice. All fair, all proper, all horrid. Natural law at its most brilliantly depraved. And so I love the fig, and so the fig is my favorite.

In the long, long ago, there was a place called Rome and it was ruled by an emperor called Augustus. And he had a wife, Livia. This much I've read, this much is beyond doubt, this much bores me. There were wars and controversies, power plays and allegiances; hard-won, hard-lost. The usual thing, I expect, back when empires were commonplace and ordinary, back when there was time to care about more than mere survival, back when we welcomed leviathan and called it civilization. I don't know. I don't care much for politics. I can never get my head around the detail, around the intrigue and speculation, around the contortions and convolutions, around all that grandstanding. And without the detail, it's nothing. Just two men alternately weeping and screaming in separate rooms, for reasons that certainly surpass my limited and earthly understanding. It's something to do with hats and who's wearing them, I know that much. But it doesn't count for much these days. Hat-wearing, I mean. Not beyond the literal sense, anyway. So I am not interested in the life of Augustus or the things that he did. And yet, and yet. He sticks in my mind even now, unwelcome as a glass marble lodged in the nasal passage: august Augustus and Livia Drusilla. She's the one to watch, the one who is said to have helped him along to death by smearing poison onto fresh figs. Some say it was a trick, an evil work, a murder. Some say that Augustus was in pain, that it was assisted suicide, that it was mercy. Others say there was no poison and in fact no figs at all, just the old reliables: disease, age, ill chance. Still, poison on fresh figs. You'd never know.

"Tell me, tell me true—what would you do if I died?"

"Eat your rations," says Crevan, not so much as glancing around, not so much as allowing for even a moment that it might be a real question needing a real answer.

"You wouldn't even be a little-bit, tiny-bit sad? A little-bit, tiny-bit upset?"

"Don't be morbid."

"But I want to know! So you must tell me, Crevan, you must. Because sometimes, you see, it seems like you wouldn't miss me at all. And that's not very nice."

Crevan clicks his tongue and does not turn to face me. "It would be the end of the world," he says at last. He's not playing anymore; I can tell from his tone, I can tell even without looking him in the eyes to see for sure. He's as serious as the grave is deep—a proper one, that is, not the shallow, hasty kind favored by certain circumstances and criminals.

"That's done already, silly. That's past, that's prologue. Everyone knows that—not that there's many of us left to know anything at all. The world is over, the world is ended."

His answer comes quick then, his answer comes quiet and clear: "Not our world, Kit. And that's all that matters."

Do I dare believe him? Do I risk it? Do I let myself be bold, confident, certain? In short, can I trust this man at all? He is beautiful and I would like to, for his fine words entice, offering as they do near everything that I wish, desire. But perhaps they are not true—or, if they are true, perhaps they are only true right now, in this moment, and will not be in the next. Yes, that must be it. If Crevan's words were lasting true—truly true—he would never have brought the drowned woman from out of the waves; not when she might sink us, not when she jeopardizes everything. Pluck, pluck, pluck. I'm worrying the elastic of the hairband on my wrist, enjoying the wet smack-snap of it, sodden as it is from our hard work cleaning the excrement from the roof. I slip the band off and trail it through the soil of a nearby plant pot, making crude, looping patterns in the dirt.

"Then what are we ever-so-ever going to do, Crevan?"

He doesn't look up but I know he's heard because he stops dead still among the leaves of the cherry tree, one hand laid delicate on the bark of the trunk. I turn my attention to another plant pot, use the hairband to make different shapes, not minding overmuch as the ribbon tracks through mulch and muck. I'm sure I'll regret it later. But, for now, the slow rhythm is enough; hypnotic, soothing.

"Do about what?"

"Don't play dumb with me, it's not cute. And it's not your turn."

Click, click, click. His tongue tuts out his exasperation, buying time before he has to answer. Because of course he knows what the question is. There's only one thing I could be asking after, only one stranger lying unconscious and unattended in the den.

"We're going to wait and hope she recovers. That's all. We don't have much of a choice."

"Yes, baby, we do, baby."

"Meaning?"

"I *told* you already about not playing dumb."

"I wasn't playing, Kit."

"Just naturally dumb?"

"If you like."

"Well maybe that's your problem. Yes, yours and not mine, not mine at all."

"So what did you—"

"If you don't know, I'm not going to tell you."

It's a bold promise and one I can't keep. Crevan knows it as well as I do. No doubt that's why he's humming content and quiet to himself. He casually checks the underside of a low-hanging leaf, making it seem like he's just getting on with things, making it seem like he's not desperately hanging on for my very next word. I snap the hairband back onto my wrist and then, at last, I concede.

"Three minutes without air," I say. "Three days without water. Three weeks without food. That's all."

These are rules of thumb and thus needfully broad. I read them somewhere— oh, long ago now—and have since been at pains to confirm them by conducting my own experiments. Admittedly, they aren't very good experiments because I'm the only test subject and one alone doesn't make for a particularly useful sample size, not to mention the lack of control group. Then again, on the unfortunate occasion that I am deprived of air, water, or food, I'll probably only care about my personal limitations. It's not much good knowing that the average person can survive for three minutes without oxygen if it so happens that you expire within half that time through some quirk of your own biology—your lung capacity, your fitness, your lurking comorbidities. As it happens, I can hold my breath for four minutes and forty seconds, and I have high hopes that I'll be able to break the five-minute barrier if I keep practicing. And my current record without food is thirty-four days (yes, it was horrible; no, I won't be attempting to push that particular boundary again anytime soon). But I've never lasted more than two and a half days without water, and it's brutal like you wouldn't believe. The woman in the den—she's breathing all right and it will be a little while before the lack of food becomes critical. But she's getting more and more dehydrated by the minute. We don't even know how long she was in the sea for. At the very least, she's coming up on twenty-four hours without water, and it might be a great deal more than that.

Crevan passes a palm across his chin. "What's your point?"

"My point is that us sitting about and doing nothing at all but waiting for her to wake up might be killing her anyway."

"You want to intervene."

That's not at all what I mean, but he's telling, not asking, and I don't contradict. Don't dare. Let him work it out for himself.

A second slips by. Another. Crevan, deep in thought, dismisses each with a click of his tongue before pronouncing his conclusion: "It's hard to hydrate someone when they're unconscious."

"We could get a squishy squashy sponge," I say. "Run it under the tap. Squeeze it into her mouth."

He shakes his magnificent head. "Too dangerous. She could choke."

And what a crying shame that would be, I think to my lonesome self. Pity, I really hoped the suggestion would work. I guess Crevan doesn't have much sense today, won't be so easily led, won't be anything but obtuse when it comes to this particular subject.

"But there might be another way." He starts to explain and then cuts himself short. "Never mind. We might not have the equipment. I need to check first. Don't want to get your hopes up."

Fat bloody chance. I curl my bottom lip into my teeth and shrug. As far as I'm concerned, this discussion has run its course now. I've offered everything I've got. And yet Crevan is still staring at me, his face contorted into an expression of implied significance, like I should instinctively know what he intends by some kind of trans-cranial osmosis. It's maddening. I really hate him sometimes.

So here we are, not talking about the drowned woman or anything else really, not now. We're pretending like it's another ordinary day, although on an ordinary day we would never be here in the first place, on an ordinary day we'd both be fast asleep below ground, with nothing to fret about but whatever it is that trails us separately through our dreams and our nightmares. We stick to what we know, what's safe; going about our business in the greenhouse, dancing between the sweet sugar scent of the plums and the spreading rot of the carrion plants.

Beyond the glass, the skies alter and grow dim. For a moment, I think that the day has grown confused by our presence. That the world, habituated to seeing Crevan and me out on the island only at night, believes it has been caught on the back foot, believes that it should already be night and is trying its very best to make it so. A reality warp. But of course that is nonsense. Perhaps there is, instead, something wrong with *me*? An error in my vision, a clouding of the brain, a dissonance that my synapses are attempting, sudden and frantic, to resolve.

The true explanation is more prosaic. I look up and see dense clouds rolling in across the sky, each one spoiling, each one threatening. I frown. Changeable weather is only to be expected here on the island, here out at sea, but this dramatic alteration still seems to me unnaturally swift. A blade of light cuts the sky, followed shortly after by a loud crash of thunder. Then Crevan is at my side, pulling on my arm.

"Come on. Inside." His voice is low and urgent. He's half-dragged me across the greenhouse before my senses catch up with me. I hurry then, struggling to keep up. Of the two of us, he always is the faster.

I am only just at the greenhouse door when the hail begins. It comes in violent fists of white, beating down on the glass roof. One catches Crevan on the shoulder as he darts across the courtyard and he curses loudly. In the next moment, he gains the shelter of the stairwell that leads to the catacombs. He stands in the archway, turns, and calls back to me.

"You have to run."

I nod to show that I've heard, but that seems to be the full extent of my bodily control. Apart from that one brief incline of the neck,

I cannot move. I am stuck, frozen in place, a specimen pinned down in a lepidopterist's display cabinet. The hailstones ricochet off the roof in wild battery, and the sound of it clatters in my ears and across my skull as though there is no protection between me and the hammering ice. There's a threatening crack above as a large hailstone strikes and glances away. Spider-fine fracture lines splinter through the glass. *The roof is going to shatter*, I think. *It's going to break into a thousand shards and kill me where I stand.*

It's Crevan who gets me to safety. Swearing and snarling all the way, he tears back across the courtyard and—grabbing me forcefully—half-drags, half-carries me through the hail. There's another crash of thunder as we hurtle into the catacombs but Crevan ignores it, slamming the wicket gate shut and hauling me down the stairs.

"The greenhouse—"

"Come on," he says firmly. "Nothing we can do about it now."

Although we could want no better shelter, it's hard to remember that we are perfectly safe where we stand, not when the storm rumbles thunderously after us through the catacombs. Crevan inspects the bruises forming across his arms and shoulders from where the hail caught him. I have several as well; stinging patches of red that, in the dimness of the catacombs, already seem to be turning indigo-violet.

"It's *her*, isn't it?" I say. "I know it is. Somehow, this is *her* fault."

Crevan shakes his head, but I see the doubt in his eyes, I'm sure I do. We never did have hail before he pulled the drowned woman out of the water. We've upset the natural order of things, that's what. We've upset the natural order of things and now we're being punished. The hail is the storm that wanted Jonah. We won't get any peace until we throw her back overboard, over the wall, return her to the sea from whence she ought never to have been claimed.

"It's just hail," he says. I can't tell if he believes it or not.

We make our way to the den. The fear builds as we go—or mine does, at any rate—realizing for the first time how foolish we were to leave a stranger unattended in our home, half-expecting that we will find the blast door closed, the way barred, our one sanctuary overthrown and a madwoman waiting to slit our throats. But reality does not bear me out. The den is just as we left it, the floor still smelling of pine from when I swabbed it clean the night before, just after taking the woman's bacteria-infested clothes and dumping them in the wilderness beyond the courtyard walls so they can fester and mulch among the tree roots without encroaching upon the safety of our sterile cell. I kept the hairband, though, couldn't not, couldn't stand to say goodbye to so pretty a bow, couldn't bear to drop it on the pile. It's filthy now, of course. Crevan hasn't noticed the navy elastic around my wrist, and I'm not sure what he'd say if he did. Of the two sins, keeping the trinket is nowhere near as bad as bringing a stranger into our home. But hush, I won't tell him. No point. He's got enough to worry about as it is. Not that the hairband is anything to worry about. It'll be fine, like as not. Bound to be.

The woman herself has not so much as stirred in our absence, lying across the bottom bunk in precisely the same manner in which we left her. Still alive, then. Bully for her.

"How are her injuries?" I ask, determining—for the moment, at least—to be as polite and considerate as so ever I can.

Crevan casts an appraising eye over the welts on her ankle and the bruise on her forehead. "The swelling's going down." Then he presses his fingers to the inside of her wrist. It takes him longer than before to find her pulse.

"Well?"

"Slower," he says. "Fainter."

Her breath seems feebler as well, the rise and fall of her chest barely perceptible. She is beginning, I think, to die. Shame.

"I *tried* to tell you, I really did. Three days without water. It's over, really over. We've done all we can."

"No," he says. "Not yet."

Before I can pin him down as to what he means, he disappears to the storeroom and comes back with his arms laden. There are boxes packed with pouches of saline solution along with some tubing and a variety of needles and plastic cannulas: the makings of an IV drip. He sets the lot down on the floor by the bunk. So this is what he intended, all melodrama and occluded resolve.

"A drip?"

"Yes," he says.

"Is that enough to save her?"

"Maybe. But there's a lot that could go wrong."

Now we're talking. "Like what could go wrong? How bad could go wrong?"

"Well, quite apart from the risk of infection, she could have an adverse reaction to the saline," he says evenly. "It could give her a rash or a fever. She might have trouble breathing. Bad swelling can cause the throat to close up. And I'm out of practice. If the needle isn't correctly inserted, it might pierce both walls of the vein and let blood leak out into the tissue. Or an air bubble in the tubing could give her an embolism. She might end up worse off. But we should still try."

My resolve dissolves to nothing in the face of his certainty, of his confidence in determining what is right and what is wrong. I cannot persuade him otherwise, cannot convince him that he has already done enough, that resuscitation is not necessarily a good in and of itself, that fate can be a kindlier master when accepted rather than rallied against. But if I cannot stop him, then I shall be no aid to him either. Not if I can help it. And already I am pain, already I am problem; standing between him and where the woman lies unconscious upon the bunk.

"Come on," he says. "Get out of the way."

"En-oh no. Shan't. Don't want to."

"Please."

It is real, this plea of his, I can hear it in his voice. But still I cannot bring myself to stand aside, cannot quite tear myself away—though I make sweet, insincere promise to the contrary. "I will if you really and truly want me to. But first—*first*—you have to answer a little teeny-tiny question. All right?"

"All right."

"Would you have done the same if it was me?" I ask. "Dived into the sea, I mean. If I was the one drowning, if I was the one drifting in the waves like a cut-loose, no-use hank of bladderwrack. Would you have saved me too?"

He does not hesitate. Not even for a second, not even for a *centi*second. "Yes," he says. "Of course," he says. "But you're a strong swimmer, Kit. And you know better than to be careless with the sea."

And then, and then. I give way, step aside. It comes as much of a surprise to me as it does to him. But she is only a poor, helpless thing after all. What is it to me if Crevan sticks her full of pins and pumps her veins with saline? It cannot change what she is, what she will always be: flotsam—washed-up, worthless—and nothing more.

For the shortest of spells, I am perfectly content, charmed into complacency. Crevan is doing only what needs to be done, attempting decency, performing a ritual of goodwill in service of his own fragile conscience. His actions are no more in defiance of me than they are in honor of the woman, for she is nothing and means nothing; at least, nothing more than a gull with a broken wing or a stranded fish that gasps and thrashes upon the shore. Crevan is like all those others who cannot help but intervene, who act in defer-ence to a misplaced compassion and believe without question that a short-term good can bring no larger ill, that there is no virtue in leaving well enough alone. He is, in short, doing only what he feels he must: grasping for order in the chaos by taking care of the living—whether the living wish to be taken care of or not.

So of course I am content, of course I do not begrudge him his efforts. There's no reason to believe, after all, that they or he will succeed, not when the woman is so far gone—as good as

dead already, if you ask me, about to tip from ripe to rotten. No
amount of industry on Crevan's part can right her, I am sure of
it, sure that something has happened to her brain—to her lungs,
her heart—something irrevocable, brutal, and horrid: a bleed that
won't clot, a laceration that won't scar over. And yet, and yet. Within
half a day or less, it seems that perhaps I am wrong, that perhaps
I have misjudged, for though our sleeping beauty wakes not, she
worsens neither; the sweet drip, drip, drip of the IV seemingly all
the nectar she requires to keep her humming away, a little queenling
larva suckled on royal jelly. Crevan has her hooked up good and
proper, cannula to line, line to saline pouch. Her breathing—which
had, oh-so happily, been beginning to fail—is becoming steady now,
level and not so rasping thin. Against all odds and the evidence of
her injuries (not to mention my every wish), it seems as though she
is recovering, growing strong as strong can be, and I fear it will not
be long now before she returns to consciousness; damn and double
damn her, damn and double damn Crevan. He never stopped to
think what it would mean for us, the bastard, didn't trouble himself
wondering what will happen when she opens her eyes and quits the
cell of her bunk to freely roam the den, this our two-soul hive.

With bees it is known, with bees it is obvious: the would-be
queen must seek every perceived rival and a murderer become, a
sororicide, catching her sisters one by one and sting-stabbing them
all to death. Only then may she assert her rights, divine and royal,
to become a mated queen and fill the hive anew. But this woman is
no bumbling bee—no, nor honey neither—and I know not what
she'll do, how she'll be(e)have. Such an occurrence is not written
of in any of my books, is not mentioned in a single one of my illustrated encyclopedias. It makes me nervous; it would make anyone
nervous.

Though perhaps if I am lucky, if I am good—if I clean my plate
and say the magic word and remember not to slouch—she'll want
nothing to do with me or Crevan, at least nothing more than to get
away from us and the island. It's a small and vanishing hope, one that

fares poorly when I try to fix it as certain, assuming her hypothetical departure as future fact by asking whether we will pack her into a boat and push her out to sea or whether we will send her packing down the causeway. When I ask, Crevan just gives me one of his looks, a stare to out-blank a blank-loaded, point-blank pistol. So I try to put it more simply, as though it's plain as bread, as though I can't believe it hasn't occurred to him already.

"She won't want to stick around here with us, silly. Not forever and ever. Not once she's better. She'll have somewhere she's trying to get to, somewhere other than here."

"We don't know that. She might need to stay."

He doesn't even have the good grace to sound uneasy about it, not for a second as though he dreads the prospect of having to live with a stranger. And maybe he doesn't dread it, maybe he knows already that it will be all right for him, that the pair of them will get along famously, that they'll be as thick as thieves, as arsonists; every burning house a testament to their affinity, fiery and flaming. Because probably they will. Probably she will see Crevan and love him at once, probably his grace and beauty will seem to her like a homecoming—for she is beautiful too. They are kindred, the pair of them, and it matters not where her tastes and preferences lie, she will still seek to claim him for her own. He's too great a prize to refuse: this man sublime of look and limb, who plucked her from the waves, to whom she owes a debt of gratitude, of life—her life— to whom she is indebted for all the years that will now be hers to draw down, all thanks to Crevan and all he has done. And so she will fall—become enthralled—and seek to spend those gifted years in his service, locked up here with us inside the den. Forever.

But she has no right to it, none at all; no right to continue sleeping in a single one of these bunks. Besides, she is too big—too much a grown-up—to stay out here with me, and too close in age to Crevan to be satisfied by so childish an arrangement. I know how it goes, which way the Kitty Kat gets skinned. She will insinuate herself into the master bedroom, either to displace Crevan from

it or—more likely—to share his bed. And that is a foul thought
indeed; all vaporous, spreading sulphur, noxious and suffocating.
I can just see them now, playing together at being mummies and
daddies, smugly satisfied with themselves and oh-so pleased, keeping me a world apart beyond the door, making me the outsider in
my own and only home, pushing me to be baby for always, even if I
don't want to, even if it's not my turn.

　　She is malign, I know it, malign as slander; a malediction delivered
by the roaring surf, a curse sent by some minor god in retribution
for some perceived slight—and for which the punishment is nothing
more or less than ruin. Already Crevan and I are straining against one
another and she is not even awake. Our division is already wrought,
already writ large by virtue of nothing more than her being here
and alive—and once she's hale and whole, there'll be nothing to
stop her from going about it properly, from cutting us apart like a
knife, from biting through the knotted cord that binds us together;
me and dear Crevan, dear Crevan and me. It will no longer be us
two but us three, and nothing can come of that but imbalance and
hurt. Sides will be taken, you mark my words, allegiances forged
and broken. She'll wheedle her way into Crevan's heart and turn
it against me, while he—dull-witted fool that he is—will be none
the wiser, flattered by the attention and pleased to find himself well
liked. He'll hardly know he's doing it. She'll trust him with confi-
dences and he'll respond in kind, pouring out all those little secrets
that I've never yet been able to trick him into sharing. Maybe he'll
even show her what's behind the left-most door of the wardrobe.
Then she'll laugh at me for not knowing—for not being allowed to
look, for not being trusted—and Crevan will laugh too and be even
more glad that she is there so he doesn't have to bother himself as
much with me, silly little good-for-nothing that I am.

　　Even then, it will be only the beginning of my end—of my trou-
bles, of my worries and woe—for her expertise will not be bound
merely to all matters Crevan, no, not forever so, not when she has
an entire life lived out in the world to draw upon. She will know

a great many things, will have seen plants and creatures of which I have never even read; will know their names and habits, their prac- tices and peccadilloes, their whys and whats and wherefores. It is a prospect terrible to behold, to be beholden to; the thought of being corrected time and again, of having her prise apart every fissuring fracture of my pieced-together knowledge, of having my every failure of understanding splayed wide and inspected, dissected, marveled at. She will contradict me, see if she doesn't; she will take her worldly wisdom and dangle it enticing before me, teasing, pretending to share when her only wish is to crow, to mock, to mark my wanting and lack. And I can't bear it, can't stand the thought of it, of how she will take my peace of mind and shiver it into dust and splinters, of how—before long—I might not be able to assert with even a passing confidence which way is up or what it is that makes the sky seem blue in daylight. She will render me alien—even to myself, even here where I have prior claim—and I will lose everything.

And there is Crevan, paying no thought to me or to all our possible futures—each one more disquieting than the next—only come to check on the woman again and never mind what's eating me, never mind the thousand, thousand implications of what he's done. When he summons me over with an excited click of his tongue, I do as I am bidden, putting on an act that is docile and deferential, feigning an interest that I hope will be enough to mask my fear, my discontent. It takes my every effort not to slip, for I see at once what is the source and cause of all his delight: the woman's eyes are fluttering, beating from closed to barely open, each flicker revealing a gaping slice of white. She is—it seems—trying to wake, but it's a task to which she is not yet equal, for which she is not yet ready. In another moment, she is lost to sleep once more—though surely, now, she will not remain so for long.

"See that?" says Crevan. "She'll be up and about in no time."

I pretend that these tidings are good rather than ill, forcing my mouth into a smile that it does not want to give, that makes me feel worse the moment my lips curve and stretch. Not that there's any point. Crevan isn't looking at me, his focus bent entire on the woman, his fingers fumbling with the line from her drip, straightening it as he inspects the pouch of saline that hangs from the railing of the bunk above.

"Better get this changed."

Because of course one saline pouch alone would not be enough to quench the woman's thirst, would be nowhere near enough to satiate her. When she does wake, it will be worse; she will be all hunger, all appetite, too ravenous for this intravenous diet of saline and additives to suffice. She will want food, real food, and we shall have no choice but to provide, to sacrifice to her a tithe or more from our stores. And so our supplies shall slowly, surely diminish, and in time we will learn the cost of all that we did, feel it in the pangs of a hunger that we will not be able to satisfy, lost as we shall be to the ravages of starvation. In all likelihood, anyway. That's how it goes when there are suddenly too many mouths to feed, that's how the cookie crumbles—or would if there were any cookies left and there won't be, not so much as a single crumb to be found and split between us.

"Well, Kit?"

He is all expectation and so, with an effort, I turn my thoughts from our slow-impending doom. In a moment, I understand what he is suggesting, that—even though I don't want to, even though he could do it easily himself—he would like my assistance to change the saline pouch.

"Surely you don't need me, daddy? Not for that, not at all, not silly old me."

"You're always welcome to lend a hand." He pauses and then presses on, not meeting my eye. "When she wakes up, you can tell her you helped. She'll be grateful."

So that's his design, his little game, the way he's decided to toy with me today. I can hardly believe his audacity, his brass-bold presumption. Against my every protest, he brought home this washed-up stray and now he's trying to win me over by giving me a role in her care, trying to trick me into believing that she's as much my responsibility as his. He wants me to be involved, for pity's sake, for me and this woman to both get along. It would be nearly funny if it didn't hurt so much, this compounding insult of his, a piece of nothing that somehow wounds like the back-breaking straw of proverb or a single stalk lodged in the throat; sharp-ended and dry as dust, all that's required to choke, to painfully asphyxiate. That he would do this to me now—insist on my pre-emptively smoothing things over and making nice—makes me sick, makes my skin crawl, makes me see red. It comes in flashes at first, sharp cuts of color that carve through sight and sense. And in their wake comes a sudden recollection of fabric festering, disintegrating. It is an omen, a guide. The image fades and I make a split-second decision. If Crevan wants my help so badly then that's what he'll get—and he'll regret it in the end, just see if he doesn't.

"All right, daddy," I say. "Whatever you like, daddy."

He looks relieved. "Go wash your hands, then."

In the bathroom I peel away the grubby Band-Aids from my palms. The grazes underneath are healing as they should, protected now by a thin layer of new skin. I take the hairband from off my wrist and press it into the pus-steeped pads of my used bandages. Then, for good measure, I run the bow of the hairband under the rim of the toilet bowl, scrubbing it against the scale and grime. Given the circumstances, it's the best I can manage. Pray-praying it will be enough, I lay the hairband carefully on a corner of the sink, using a few squares of toilet roll to protect the enamel from the filthy elastic. Then I pick up the soap and work up a lather under the running tap, massaging the foam into every cranny and crevice of my skin, every fold and crease, from my fingertips up to my elbows. I think about the task that lies before me, about what I'm going to do. Then I turn off the tap and dry my hands. Hairband back on wrist, dirty paper in the bin. I return to Crevan and then it's his turn. He treks off the way I came, off to the bathroom.

I stare hard at the hairband on my wrist as I wait, kidding myself that I can see the wriggling microbial nasties that must surely now be laced among the threads of its elastic. It's certainly looking worse for wear, the pretty ribbon bow sadly stained and limp. And little wonder—it's already been doused with excrement, fertilizer, dirt, mulching plant matter. And now it has been further befouled; besmirched with tainted Band-Aids, steeped in whatever poisonous residues lie lurking beneath lavatorial rim. Yum, yum. Best of all, Crevan hasn't even noticed I'm wearing it. So if my plan works and the woman takes a turn for the worse, he won't understand how it came about, won't have the faintest idea why. He'll have no choice but to put it down to misfortune. Maybe then he will learn he cannot control everything he wants, that chaos does and must ever reign supreme, that this woman was always meant to die, that he should have let her drown. I have nothing to lose—leastways, nothing more than my conscience, nothing more than my soul to sin.

And what is a soul anyway, when it's at home? For that matter, where *is* its home? Where does it reside? The head? The heart? The spinal cord? Preposterous. I've never heard of anything so ridiculous, never contemplated anything so absurd as a human convinced of its own ineffable importance, a survival instinct mumming as divine difference, as some sort of holy mystery. If there are souls, I have no reason to believe that I have one. I've certainly never seen it and it isn't in any of the diagrams of split-open bodies that I have pored over on occasion. I am me, blood and sinew, guts and brains, just like any other beastie. Profoundly mortal, thoroughly mortal; every little bit of me, from top to toe and back again. There is no soul, no brightness to tarnish, no flame to snuff out.

And yet, and yet. My heart is going in all the ways that a clock doesn't; hammering hard, loud, irregular. Perhaps I will not do it, however much I want to, perhaps my courage will fail me. But then Crevan returns, clean-handed and looking oh-so pleased with himself, and I know I will not falter.

"It's straightforward enough," he says, taking a fresh pouch of saline from one of the storeroom boxes. I listen all attentive as he explains what needs to be done, how the cannula and needle in the woman's arm do not need to be touched, how he'll close the line and tell me when I can pull the spiked end of it out of the old pouch and insert it into the new. I nod to show that I have understood and hope I have not blanched, that my lip does not quiver—when it comes, my chance will be brief, briefer even than I had imagined. I shall have to be fast, fast as anything; as instinct, prejudice, reflex.

First hanging the fresh pouch beside the old, Crevan douses a piece of cotton with disinfectant. The date on the bottle is from years back and—quite apart from the effects of age—I guess that the contents are completely ineffective by now, a feeble protection against the rampant bacterial evolution that has wreaked so much havoc, laid so much waste. But it's all we've got. He swabs the base of the new pouch and then closes the line before getting well and truly out of the way, letting me step forward to the woman's bunk.

"Ready?" he asks.

And I am, as ready as ready can be. Working swiftly, I do what I have been instructed and pull out the spiked end of the line from the nearly sucked-dry pouch of saline. Crevan told me I must not touch the spike, that this is the best way to protect it from contamination, and so it is for his benefit that I hold it up to the light, fingers pinched around the drip chamber below, as though looking for signs of damage or chalking on the plastic. There's nothing to see, it's fine as anything, the spike as clean as when it was first taken out; uncorrupted, undecaying, untouched by any plastic-eating bacteria. Seemingly satisfied, I turn back toward the bunk and—for the fleetest of moments, for half a breath—my hands are blocked from Crevan's eyeline, hidden from view by the light-eating hulk of my torso. Then I do it. I really do it. I take the spike and, quickly as I can, press it into the folds of the ribbon bow, smearing the filthy elastic along the plastic shaft. Pray, pray. It might not work. Then again, it might.

Lifting up the dirty, doctored spike, I use it to pierce the fresh pouch of saline. Behind me, Crevan—evidently unaware of my tampering—murmurs his approval and then steps in to open the line once more. The fluid travels the tubing from pouch to vein. I watch. Crevan watches.

"Looks good," he says. "All she needs now is time."

We shall see. If my intervention has succeeded, she won't have much time left, not much time at all. If it *is* working, it's already irreversible—leastways it is with our ineffectual supplies and limited know-how. We can't fight a serious infection. If it's done, it's done. She's already dead.

There's still one more thing left to do, of course. Crevan hasn't noticed the hairband on my wrist, but I can't risk carrying it much longer, can't risk him finally noticing and putting two and two together, can't risk giving him cause to step out into the light of certainty. This only works if he stays ignorant, bless him. But that's OK. I know just what to do. I've got boy-o well trained.

And now—ladies and gentlemen, boys and girls—a star turn from the one, the only, the siren of the silver screen, the heart-throb of a generation. Watch and wonder, watch and learn.

I stagger back dramatically, as though suddenly overcome by the enormity of having completed a task that—however apparently routine—I had nonetheless resisted. I'd try for a ragged sob, but I'm not quite ready for that, not for it to be properly convincing. Simple alarm will have to suffice—though I have to be fast about it, or else he'll strong-arm me into the little panic room beneath the trapdoor like he usually does, and that's not going to be much good to me.

"Kit? What's wrong?"

I shoot him a wild, panicked look. Then I flee, racing out of the den and through the catacombs, up the twisty, windy stair and out into the courtyard. The storm has passed and the dusk is drawing in. Lumps of ice litter the paving stones, some the size of rocks and only just beginning to melt. The greenhouse still stands, but over half of the glass roof panels have been destroyed, shattered into pieces. I can see that the trees within are in a sorry state: branches bare or broken, leaves tattered, fruit bruised. But there's no time to worry about that now. Quick as you like, as you please—in a wink, jiffy, flash—and, most critically of all, before Crevan can catch up with me, I dart to the edge of the courtyard, snap the hairband from my wrist, and throw it over the wall. Then I am back by the wicket gate that leads down to the catacombs, where I drop to all fours on the ground and start panting, working myself up into these flurried runs of shallow breaths so as to make myself dizzy. A do-it-your-self panic attack, or as good as, because I'm not panicked, not really. A little excited, yes, a little flushed with the nervy-anxious fear that Crevan will find me out, but not properly overwhelmed like I get sometimes. I might just have killed someone and I don't feel a thing. How's that for my no-soul theory? Maybe it will hit when she actually dies. *If* she actually dies. But despite my sluggish sympathies, despite this anathema of sentiment, my heart picks up the pace nonetheless, starts to race, starts to hammer, and, by the time Crevan reaches me, I am in a sorry state, visibly struggling, practically dying by the looks of things, choking for breath where I crouch. But he knows just what to do, first laying a steady palm on the curve of my spine and then kneeling close beside me on the flagstones, head bowed soft next to mine, mouth at my ear.

"Sorry, Kit. Sorry for everything."

I can hear the trembling of his heart in the cascade and break of his vowels, his consonants, but I'm wheeze-gasping too hard to reply, to say anything at all. Seeing this, Crevan switches into prac-tical manner; all concern, all helpful, trying to talk me down from what must look like the bleeding edge of fear.

"It's going to be all right," he says and then eases into his habit-ual paternalism as easy as a favorite sweater, soft with age. It's a masterstroke, if you ask me, letting him baby me so he can't tell that *I'm* really the one babying him, the one teaching him his lessons. I should take a bow, a curtain call. If anyone's watching, if there's any applause out there, it's all for me, I guarantee.

"Can you try sitting up?" says Crevan. "Yes, just like that. Put your hands on your head. Can you feel that, how it opens up your lungs? Good. Now breathe. In through your nose and out through your mouth. In for three, out for three. Come on. You can do it. One . . . two . . . three . . ."

I breathe in like I'm told and then I breathe out again, a good dog, following the orders I'm given. I make a show of it, collapsing into him a little, letting him support my weight, making an effort to match the pace of my breath to his count. I don't stop. I lean hard on him and he keeps going, measuring out slow counts of three over and over. For as long as we stay here like this, I am sure that Crevan's thoughts are of nothing but me; me and the incredible pressure he has piled on to my poor, silly, fragile nerves. Eager though I am not to overdo it, I take my time. He doesn't hurry me. The sweet, sweet fool.

"I think that maybe perhaps I am right-all right now," I say when it seems that enough time has gone by. "Thank you."

"No, it was my fault. I should never—"

He lapses into silence, tongue-tied, tongue-torn, forlorn, worn out—properly conflicted, for once seeing how I must feel, what he has been asking of me, what he has been putting me through ever since he dived into the sea the night before when I expressly asked him not to.

"It's OK," I say weakly. "I know you were just doing what you thought was right, what you thought was best. You have a good heart, a good soul. Good as gold, good as anything."

He gives a bitter laugh at that but does not contradict me. Straightening, he helps me to my feet. I am unsteady after my forced hyperventilation and grateful for the assistance.

"Do you think you're ready to go back inside?"

"In a moment, in a breath, in a beat." And then, because I want to and because I can, I slip my hand into his and grip tight. "Look at our poor, poor trees," I say and point to where they stand, sad silhouettes behind the glass.

Crevan squints in the dusk. "They've taken a battering," he says. "But they'll be all right. Just need to prune off the damaged parts and thin out the ruined fruit. So long as there's no infection . . . They should recover in no time. You'll see."

I ought to leave it at that. I ought to nod wisely and approve of this most sensible of plans. Instead, the words bubble out of me before I can think. "Strange, isn't it? The one littlest thing we prize, the one littlest thing we love best on this whole wide island, and it's the thing that gets decimated, beat, the thing that takes the brunt of the damage."

But Crevan is still being obtuse and he doesn't take my point. "Doubt it," he says. "The wild plants will have been worse off. No glass to protect *them*."

I look up at the broken roof of the greenhouse. It didn't provide much protection, as it turns out. Not much protection at all. And if the drowned woman is our Jonah, then she's what brought the storm. I'm sure of it. The devastation of the greenhouse is a punishment for us, for me. The hail that wrought it is a command, a warning, an omen of worse to come if we don't act, if we don't try to put things right, right, ship tight. Well, I've done my best. I may not have a great fish to hand or a whale to which I could throw her, which would be sure to swallow her up, but I've made do. Now it's all down to the little microbes that even now must be swarming through her defenseless flesh, taxing her white blood cells, her antibodies, probing the walls of her immunity—such as it is—for weaknesses. *Let the rot set in*, I think, wish, pray. *Set us free. Deliver us. Please, god, deliver us.* And better make it snappy. I've had about enough excitement for now. I can hardly take any more. Not without a proper rest anyway, and I'm not likely to get much of that sleeping one bunk over from a soon-to-be corpse, am I? The sooner she gives up the ghost, the sooner we can remove her—commit her flesh to the earth, see she's good and buried—and the sooner everything will go back to ordinary. What I wouldn't give for that.

ALL THOSE IRRISIONS,
AND VIOLENCES

The broader consequence—the inheritance, the gift—of bacterial resistance is nothing more or less than this: the most critical of our averages shift, slip out to their extremes and there send down roots, set up shop, turning their sometime-anomalies into plain regularities. Diseases, once carefully managed and controlled—your cholera and syphilis, your TB and your tetanus—are prolific again and more deadly than ever they were. Favorites that are older still have also made a hellish comeback. I am speaking of leprosy, you understand; I am speaking of plagues bubonic, septicemic, and pneumonic. Sketch the rates on a graph and marvel at how they skyrocket, at how they soar. So too amputations, so too deaths maternal and infant. So too mortalities of all kinds—saving, of course, old age. It's just the way of it: we die often, we die young, we die in pain. So it was once, so it is now and forever shall be. World without end, that's what they used to sing. But this is the world beyond end, this is the world ended.

This is the world where—more often than not, more often than is fair—we die of starvation, for famine has remembered where we live and has taken to visiting those parts of the world that it had, for long stretches, previously left untouched. Crops fail and fail regularly, whenever soil and seed become infested with bacteria phytopathogenic and brazen. Livestock sicken and die. What food does get produced goes quickly bad, quickly spoils, for it can no longer be sealed in the plastic that is, itself, prone to spoiling, and can no longer be reliably preserved in refrigerator or freezer, not with their myriad plastic parts, not with their reliance upon plastic cables and flexes to supply them with electricity. And so we are hungry. We are hungry because the bacteria are hungry, because they have eaten everything else, infected everything else.

The cities—breeding grounds all—are empty, denuded. The old-world powers, fumbling their grasp upon their once tightly held monopolies of violence, have now crumbled entire and so acts of individual brutality now go entirely unchecked. More than that; such incidences are on the rise, on the up, on the way to being the standard MO. Scarcity breeds contempt and the mood everywhere has become distinctly medieval. Or so I am told, so I have been led to believe. But perhaps it has changed since I came to the island. Perhaps it was never even quite as I have described, perhaps the brute horde from which I fled was an entirely uncommon occurrence, signifying nothing. Perhaps Crevan's scars were all merely gifts of ill luck and accident. There is no way to tell for sure—leastways not by staying put, leastways not without venturing across to the mainland. And I won't; won't risk life and limb, will not try my chances. No. I am staying here. Here where I can be forgotten, here where I can stay lost and no one will come looking. It's not safe, not exactly, but in my here and my now, it's as close as I can get. Of that much—and how pitifully little it is—I am absolutely certain.

FOR WE COME TO SEEK A GRAVE

Are you familiar with septic shock? I hope not, for your sake, and for the sake of those who love you—if, indeed, you are lucky enough to have such people in your life, if there is anyone in your life at all apart from your lonesome-yearnsome self. But let us never mind your solitude for the time being and concentrate on what really matters: the manner of your eventual death. For when it comes, as it so assuredly will (assuming you are neither the lucky descendant of gods, nor the unlucky descendant of vampires), I'll warrant that you'll be hoping for a good one. Not that you *get* to choose, of course. But if you did, if you got to choose the way that you will die—or worse, if you had to choose a way for your mother to die, your sister, your daughter, your lover—you wouldn't pick septic shock. At least, *I* wouldn't. Perhaps you would: perhaps you are a glutton for punishment, perhaps you welcome suffering as your lot in life, perhaps you are simply depraved. I don't know. All I can say is that, of all the means and modes and methods that a typical human might select as their preferred way of exiting the universe, septic shock is not one of them. It's no carbon monoxide poisoning. It's no orange juice and barbiturates. (You should be so lucky.) No, septic shock is a real thug, a prize bruiser. It's not interested in giving you a quick, painless death. It will draw things out for as long as possible, colonizing your body so comprehensively that it prompts your immune system to mount a massive and untenable response. Soon, blood pressure drops too low to be tracked or recorded. Internal organs begin to fail. The body shuts down. And this would all be quite enough to endure, quite enough to be getting on with, but of course sepsis can be exceptionally grisly as well. A body can become mottled and bloated. The flesh necrotizes as the nerves die; it begins to disintegrate, begins to rot like a corpse, begins to fragment and dissolve like a corroding, burning scrap of red fabric.

There was a time when sepsis was treatable, when the right combination of antibiotics could save a person—if delivered within the first hour of infection, at any rate. But that was oh-so very long ago now, long ago enough to be a myth, to be something you might only half-believe. The antibiotics can still be made—in theory, anyway—but there's no point. They are entirely ineffective. So there's nothing we—I—can do for the drowned woman once the infection takes hold. And take hold it surely does, for all my worries that it might not, that my efforts might have been futile, the introduction of bacteria into her veins itself a vain attempt.

I watch her close after Crevan goes through to his own room to sleep, shutting his door behind him with a sharp click like he's desperate to pretend that there's no one here but him; no me, no her. So let him, let him slip from this universe for a short space, let his door be a boundary wall, let my mind turn away from him for now. I shall not hold him in my thoughts, I shall not wonder whether he has any ability to exist outside of them and of his own accord. I shall allow him his peace, to be and be not, and make no demands of him—for a while anyway, for the passing of this night at least. If it is indeed night. It was dusk when we came in from outside, so I suppose it really must be night now. But perhaps it is already morning, perhaps the hours have already slipped away from me. It's hard to keep track down here, down below the ground, down where night and day have no particular or special dominion. So let us call it night and let me sit at the woman's bedside and keep vigil through the small hours, the long hours. Let me bear witness to the final breaths that pass her lips, to the last minutes and seconds of her life. For she is not herself conscious to register them and really someone ought to be or how will anyone know that she's alive at all? I would sing a lullaby to bring her peace and keep her company but it doesn't feel right somehow. The only thing that fits is silence and this much I can deliver. Externally, anyway. It's never quiet here inside this skull. I wonder what it's like inside hers, whether she is dreaming, whether there's a part of her brain that's still whirring away beneath the bone, remembering, fretting, making lists and lists and lists. Does she know she's dying? Already she is clammy to the touch, already her breath is coming shallow and rapid again. The crook of her arm is swollen and red, the veins inky beneath the skin. On the cellular level at least, her body knows it's in trouble now, more trouble than it was in any position to take on, weakened as it was after being borne on wave and tide to the island. *Hurry up, hurry up.* No sense dragging this out any longer than we have to.

When the woman starts to shiver, I climb into the bunk beside her and wrap my arms around her shoulders, drawing her near, pulling the woolen blanket over us both. It's like when we come out of the ice water; the dropping blood pressure, the body trying to protect the critical core of internal organs. She is cold. Does she feel it? Does she know? No matter, I know, I can feel it in her skin. I press the length of my body against the length of hers, cradling her, rocking her gently back and forth, to and fro, to and fro. Perhaps it feels like the waves that brought her to the island.

"You should never have come here," I say, voice quiet, quiet, lips barely moving. "You should have known better than to give your body over to the sea. The sea can't be trusted. It's too big and too everywhere to care for little individual lives like yours."

It is true, you know. To the sea, you are no more or less precious than a single piece of algae. An alga, I suppose. It doesn't matter. The sea does not distinguish. It is too big. The sea is a macrocosm and cares nothing for the micro. And if you don't think you're part of the micro, then you need to stop taking yourself so seriously and take a proper look at where you fit into the scale of things. Really. You just look out to the horizon the next time you stand on the shore and see if I'm wrong, see how the water stretches out farther than your sight and remember how it covers nearly the whole of the Earth, how it is all one water—separated only in our imaginations, only because we humans like to think in distinct territories delimited by trails of blood and urine. But there is only one sea. The waters of the Pacific are no different from those of the Atlantic, whatever you might think. The dust mites might regard the skin on the sole of your foot as a kingdom distinct from the skin of your scalp, but both patches are equally, irrevocably you. As the dust mite is to you, so you are to the sea: invisible and not worth sparing a second thought—not worth sparing at all, as a matter of fact.

"No," I whisper again into her ear. "You should never have entrusted yourself to the sea. And, having made that mistake, it really was very foolish to float along with the waves, to let the current take you just anywhere it wanted. I mean, you could have drowned. It certainly would have saved us all this hassle, all this heartbreak and agonizing. Crevan wouldn't have slipped into this oh-so-serious mode, wouldn't have proven that he's more than capable of acting against my wishes whenever the fancy takes him. He dived into the water, lady. He dived in just when I said not to. It was really quite brazen. Bold like you wouldn't believe. I wish I didn't know he had it in him, wish I didn't know that he could sideline me like that. If he hadn't seen you floating out there in the moonlight, it would never have happened."

I let my hands slide into her hair, winding fistfuls of it through my fingers and then pulling gently against the roots, like I do for Crevan when he sporadically works up the fear that he will soon go bald. I tease and tug until I have tested the strength of every follicle. Then I stroke and caress, calm-calming, and lift one hand away to instead trace the contours of her profile, the tip of my index finger skiing down the slope of her nose. "It doesn't matter now. You will soon be gone, finished." My finger jumps the curve of her split lip and then stops, hanging in the air. I stare at the narrow gully that stretches from her nose to mouth. It looks different to me now; not so much a difference of anatomy as the beginning of the end—a mid-word ellipsis where an eraser has passed across the graphite trail of a penciled note, the snagged thread in a knitted sweater that is starting to unravel. It is as though she is already coming undone. I imagine the edges of that gulch eroding back and back, dissolving away until there is nothing left but cavity, until there is nothing there at all but a wide void, the edges of which are discernible only by the knowledge that once a body of flesh and blood did lay here, did breathe and sweat and shiver here. It would be beautiful, wouldn't it? To simply evaporate like that. But it's not what will happen—at least, not so quickly. Decay will come fast enough upon the heels of death, but it will take an age for her to decompose, an age for her to return to dust. Even viewed at speed—the whole compressed down into the ragged gasp of a few brief seconds—it will have nothing to do with beauty. Though I bet it would be bewitching in its own way to see a body caving in on itself; putrefying, liquifying. I bet you wouldn't be able to tear your eyes away from the sight of it, I bet you'd be hooked, I bet you'd watch it over and over on a loop if you could, devouring the minutes and seconds of your own life, swallowing them whole until it is your go, at last, your turn to lie down in the ground and rot.

She is slipping away now. Whatever consciousness still lurks behind those eyelids is fading. I lay my ear to her breastbone to hear the scraping of her thin breaths. Below is a beat as fast and faint as the fluttering of the light-bound codling moth. Flit, flit, flit. If every heart is born with a set capacity, able to beat only a fixed and finite number of times, hers must now be tearing toward the upper limit. Each flit comes quick and feeble-thin. When I check her wrists and throat, I cannot find her pulse. But though I cannot see it, I know the poison is there in her veins—must be—thick and terrible, like crude oil in seawater.

"There, there," I say. "Not long now."

Something flicks in the corner of my eye, the hem of a grubby cloak that the wearer hitches deftly out of sight. I do not turn around, for I do not want to see the creature my mind has wrought in its exhaustion, am not ready to meet the reaper with his smiling scythe, even if I'm not the one he's come for. I stay very still, my gaze hooked into the weave of the blankets swaddled about the woman's body, my limbs braced, locked in place around her. "Go quick," I counsel. "Go fast, go now. Go before the bad man can take you, before he can make you. This should be yours and yours alone—it's the last thing that can be. Do what needs be done and go of your own will. Follow this final inclination. I am right here behind you, willing you on, rooting for you."

The spectral figure advances, all the more dreadful for having come at my summons. I was expecting joy, I was expecting the exultation of the righteous, of the benevolent. And there is nothing but this foul approaching mulch and my fear of it. Because it is fear, as much as I'd like to pretend otherwise, as much as I'd like my heart to stop trying to break its way out of the cage of my ribs. It is so loud now, a violent alarm, a thump, thump, thump that gives me away, that makes it seem like mine is the only heart in the room, that says *here I am, pick me*. Only I don't want him to pick me. I'm not ready, not yet, it's not my turn, it's not fair. Idiot Kit, fool Kit, feckless Kit, bad Kit, bad Kit, bad. I'm sorry. My vision kit-cataracts with tears, the weave of the blanket blurs and distorts. I'm sorry, I'm sorry. I grip tight, close my eyes and bury my face in the hollow of the woman's neck. She is cold and does not bend to comfort me.

———

Later, when I am calmer again and more myself, when the spectral reaper has been and gone, Crevan comes to see the drowned woman. I don't say anything, don't explain—I can see that he knows, that it's obvious just from looking at her. She is dead. He sees how I am coiled around her, how my eyes are puffy red from crying, and tells me how sorry he is, how it's not my fault, how there was only a slim

chance that the IV would work, how I did my very best, and how
he's proud of me. The sweet, sweet fool. He reaches toward me.

"Come on, Kit. You have to let her go."

How can he be so unfeeling? Not so long ago, I saw him risk life
and limb for this woman. Now he doesn't seem to care at all that she
is dead. But stop, I am being unfair, unkind, uncharitable. Perhaps
he knows not how to express himself in accordance with the full
breadth and force of his emotions. Perhaps rest has brought him
the distance and clarity I have so often urged him to seek. Perhaps
I have provoked him into this level-headed sensibility by appearing
so pathetic before him. Let it be so, if it will shore him up, if it will
help him to face the death he has wrought, the death he has brought
into our home and so sullied. I shrink in on myself, allowing him
to think me small and frangible. With a piteous sniff, I grasp his
outstretched hands and let him assist me from the bunk. When I am
untangled from the woman and once more on my feet, I cry croco-
dile tears until Crevan slips an arm around my shoulder, sturdy and
supportive. We stare for a moment at the corpse lying recumbent
on the mattress. After clinging on to her through the night, it is
strange to see her like this, her whole body in view. I can't put my
finger on what particular aspect of her appearance marks her as one
of the dead rather than one of the sleeping, but there's no mistaking
it. Her atoms are all there still, every single one of them, but *she* is
not. She has passed from being to non-being. The difference is at
once imperceptible and extreme. I understand it exactly. I do not
understand it at all.

"Are you hungry?" Crevan asks.

"I suppose."

"Come on, then."

We slide gratefully beyond the dividing screen and out into
the living room. The simple furnishings have never looked more
absurd, the slack cushions of the sofa seem inappropriate; their
patterned upholstering offensively bright, the suggestion of comfort
grotesque. The books and CDs shy away from the edge of their

shelves, trying not to be noticed, knowing that the distraction they offer is not yet welcome. We ought to take bolts of drab cloth and drape it over everything, let our home show its respect for the dead, let it become what it is now: a mausoleum. If Crevan feels the same abhorrence, the same disconcertion, he does not say and only drags me through to the galley kitchen. This corner of our den at least seems more appropriately fitted for the occasion, the granite counters somber, the dull grain of the cupboard doors entirely unreproachable. Even the sleek chrome handles cut a severe appearance of which I can only approve.

Although it does not seem right to eat, I find that I am starving. Nothing has passed my lips since I ate that fig from Crevan's hand in the greenhouse. I am hazy on the time, but many hours must have gone by since then. Crevan must be hungry too. He opens one of the cupboards and pulls two silvered packets from off the shelf. These he rips open, tipping the contents into the empty belly of the multicooker that sits squat and abstruse on the counter, no glass pane to see inside, no manual, no way of knowing how it works unless you've been previously introduced. I move to help, my body ruled by some instinct, some habitual familiarity. We've done this a thousand times before. I take a glass measuring cup and fill it with water up to the red line and then pour it into the multicooker. Crevan puts the lid in place, checking the seal before flicking the switch. "Two minutes."

He sets the table as though this is any other day, as though there is not a corpse here with us, lying just out of sight. There are place mats, coasters, enamel bowls, silver dessert spoons, and nested measuring cups. There is salt and pepper, a range of condiments in ceramic jars. There are cloth napkins folded into neat triangles. I make no comment as he works nor any move to help. Perhaps he needs to be busy, perhaps he has let his mind migrate to his fingertips and the action of his hands is sufficient to push out all thoughts of the drowned woman. But I cannot shake her. She is everywhere around us, must be. As surely as the air we breathe is heavy with the

dust of our own constantly shedding skins, so it too must be heavy
with her ferment. She films my skin, she coats my teeth and tongue,
she circulates through my lungs and dissolves into the stream of
my blood. From flesh to flesh. With every inhalation I am become
a cannibal. And Crevan too, for all his studious efforts to avoid the
very thought of it, for all his pretense that it is only us now, that it
was only ever us, that this is just another ordinary day. It does not
escape me that Crevan has set both places side by side, so that we
may sit with our backs to the room and our eyes turned from the
dividing screen.

The table laid, Crevan stands staring into an open cupboard. The
shelves are packed, choking with food—and this is only a fraction of
what we have, a mean tithe taken from the magnificent munificence
of the storeroom. The opulence is overwhelming; even after he has
been here for so long, the sight of it is still enough to make Crevan's
eyes fix wide, to throw him into the turbulent stasis of indecision. I
take pity upon him.

"Cheese?" I ask, coming to his side and reaching up to take down
a truckle wrapped in red wax.

Crevan starts to life. "Yes. And pemmican."

"Good idea," I say, grabbing the airtight box and glancing down
through the lid at the bars it contains, each one wrapped in grease-
proof paper.

"What else?"

"Saltines."

"Melba toast and raspberry jam."

"Canned pears."

"Halva."

"Chocolate."

We put everything onto the table. When the timer beeps on
the multicooker, Crevan ladles out the porridge. It steams and
gloops, wet and grainy all at once, a strange off-gray that makes
me think of brains, even though I know from the diagrams in my
encyclopedias that this is not what brains look like. I make two

cups of coffee, hot and unadulterated. Then we are seated side by side, two kings at a harvest feast with all the riches of our dominion laid out before us. There should really be flesh: pink hams, fat-lined pig bellies, white-boned racks of juvenile lamb, entire fowl plucked and broiled, thin slices of beef that droop like loose jowls and weep blood, inch-thick medallions of venison. But we make do with our porridge, our oatmeal, our gruel. We pass jars and tubs between ourselves in silent ritual. A tablespoon each of tahini and honey. An eighth of a cup of raisins. A level teaspoon of ground cinnamon. A sprinkling of salt and chopped nuts. I mix mine together and eat slowly, biting away at the cooler edges with the tip of my spoon. The gluey mixture is rich and fragrant. Every so often, I stop to take a sip of coffee, enjoying how the bitterness of it makes the porridge taste all the sweeter. When my bowl is empty, I lick my index finger and run it along the tacky residue stuck to the enamel. In a few moments more the bowl is clean as when it was first set down.

"Food of the gods."

"Do you want anything else?"

"Maybe, maybe. In another moment or two," I say. But we both know we can't manage another bite. Everything we set out will be put back away again, untouched. Like always. A feeling of warmth spreads through my body. It's delicious to sit there with Crevan, my stomach full, a bounty still laid out before us. I lean into him, resting my head on his shoulder. He molds to me without a word, his shoulder dropped, his arm around my waist, his head tipped against mine. What would he do if I told him? What would he say? I try to imagine it, try to hear the confession sliding from my tongue. *I killed her, Crevan.* The temptation is unbearable. I have seen much of Crevan but I have not seen this, have not seen how he would react at such unexpected and unwelcome news, and I am greedy to know how he would behave. A thousand Crevans spin out around me, each one differently disapproving: one sullenly silent, one chastising, one interrogating—*How could you*—one vengeful. The curiosity is acute, enough to make me deeply jealous of Crevan for having such complete knowledge of himself, knowledge that I—poor, floundering fool that I am—can only hope to obtain piecemeal and through provocation. All I want is everything of him—is that really so much to ask, too much to hope for? I almost do it, almost say it, almost admit to what I have done. In the end I decide I cannot risk driving him away—though perhaps I can excavate what I require by another means.

"It's our fault, isn't it?" I ask. "You and em-ce me. Our fault that the woman died. We're the guilty, the culpable."

There is no change in his posture, no stiffening or alarm. He gently strokes my hair, all concern, all sympathy. "There was nothing more we could have done, Kit." His voice is soft, confiding. I cannot pretend not to be delighted; his tone speaks of concern, of affection—and it's all for me, me, me. I stay quiet, let the silence shape itself into whatever Crevan wants most. After a moment, he continues, seeming oh-so eager to console me, to reassure, to give me the benefit of his hard-won experience. Be still, my beating heart.

"It's natural to feel helpless. Or somehow to blame. But try to remember you aren't. That this was completely outside of your control."

I cannot tell whether he genuinely believes this to be true or whether he knows in his heart what I have done and simply cannot face it. Whether it is real or feigned, I make no bid to correct his ignorance.

"Don't worry," he continues. "I'm here. I'll help you deal with it. I'll look after you."

And there it is, the blood clouding bright in the water, clear as breadcrumbs upon a woodland trail, as golden thread strung through the corridors of the labyrinth. I dive, follow, seize.

"Who looked after *you*, daddy bear?" I ask, pitching my voice high and infantile. "When you really, truly were to blame? Who looked after you when you killed all those people? All those nasty little girls who came into your house and sat in your chair and slept in your bed and ate your porridge?"

There is a flicker of unease, a tremor of disquiet that I'm sure would show in his face if I turned to check, but I am playing still and cannot break the illusion, cannot seem anything other than the guiltless, guileless creature he is so desperate for me to be.

"No one," he says.

"And you didn't feel bad? Even though it *was* your fault? Because you killed them, didn't you? So it couldn't have been anyone else's fault but yours, could it?"

"It was self defense." His answer comes too quick, all pat and prepared.

"Oh, I know that, daddy. You're not a killer, not really. I know you didn't kill anyone—leastways, not like that. It must have been hard even so and all the same. How many people was it that you did—sorry, *didn't*—kill?"

His arms fall away from me. For a moment, he hardly seems like my Crevan at all, only a grim, glowering thing wearing his face. And then, just as suddenly, the fury behind his eyes gutters and goes out. "Come on," he says, getting to his feet and picking up both bowls from the table. "Let's clear."

I do not move, but I do not stop him either. I grip the edge of my seat and swing my crossed feet back and forth under the table, sweeping the linoleum with my heels. My mind wanders away from the galley kitchen and toward the dividing screen, where it halts and hovers, not brave enough right now to peer beyond, even within the confines of my own make-believe. What if the woman is not there? What if she is there and bad-man death is with her? What if she is there and dead still but awake all the same? What if her eyes see me coming? What if her mouth gapes open and her tongue worms and whispers of what I've done? Well, she can say what she likes; Crevan will never believe, not for an instant, not for a second, not in a million years. And I'm not sorry. I'm not. I have nothing to be sorry for. She is dead because of herself. She is dead because of the sea and because of Crevan. She is dead because she never woke and was never going to wake. She is dead because of an infection. She is dead because her body gave up. It is nothing to do with me.

It does not take Crevan long to put away the breakfast things, to wash out the bowls and spoons. It is just enough time for him to become calm once more, to forgive my naïve questioning, to remember what is owed, his duty of care. He returns to his seat, sitting half-turned so he can face me—even though that means looking out toward the dividing screen. His eyes track to it and then snap back.

"Sorry for getting angry. You're curious and that's only natural. If you really want to hear what happened, then fine. But you should think about it. You might not like me so well when you know."

"Or I might like you better. Or I might like you just the same."

"You're sure you want the story?"

"Sure as anything, sure as hell."

He is out of his seat again, gone that little bit farther away from me, gone to be alone, gone to be out of reach, gone to lean back against the counter of the galley kitchen. Although he faces out in my direction, when he tells his story—which he does, haltingly and with many fractured indulgences and drawn-out pauses—his chin is raised and his eyes are fixed on the dividing screen. It is the dead woman he is addressing, make no mistake about it. Perhaps it is meant as an explanation, as though he is saying: having entered into the lion's den, what did you expect? But Crevan is no lion, not as far as I can see, not according to the story he tells, the story which, as you have not heard it, I shall now proceed to relate.

So there is Crevan, back in the yesterday, back in the heyday, back on the mainland somewhere, somewhere, it doesn't matter where, doesn't matter as much as knowing that he is alone and hungry and exhausted, doesn't matter as much as knowing that he is walking down a holloway—an ancient path sunk deep into the earth with high banks on either side all knotted with tree roots—doesn't matter as much as knowing that he has only what he wears: the clothes on his back, the boots on his feet, the machete in his belt. Already there are four patches needled on his arm, already he has survived four violent encounters with the backbiters—and he doesn't know if that makes him lucky or unlucky, poor lamb. He's only glad that there's no word of the backbiters moving through this neck of the woods, not right now anyway. That means he can expend his effort worrying about the other creeping-crawling nasties instead, make sure he keeps himself safe. He thinks how fortunate he is to have stumbled across the holloway. It's not on any map he's seen, so probably no one else knows about it (fingers crossed, holding thumbs, spit, spit, spit), and the going is easier than cutting cross-country like he usually does. And then. A scream tears the sky. Crevan knows at once that he is lost.

He stops and stares up at the steep banks looming high as sanctimony on either side, not knowing whether to run or hide, trying to fix the source of the cry. But the next thing he knows, three brutes are leaping down over the lip of the left bank and charging at him, swinging crude weapons of wood and stone about their heads. In my imagining, I make their hair wild and tangled, I make their clothes rotting nylon, the threads suppurating on their bodies, but Crevan doesn't elaborate. He only says how he knows at once they are not backbiters but something worse, how he is so scared he can't move, that they run at him—One, Two, Three—and that they are fast and that, when they are close enough so he can see the yellow of their bared snarling teeth, One raises a cudgel and aims it at Crevan's skull and Crevan knows he is going to die, that it's over, that he is finished. Only you can see as plain as I can that the man lives to tell the tale, so it's hard to take his fear serious-wise, hard not to smirk a little, not to wink or nudge, not to mutter: *Oh yeah, of course, I know how it must have been, but give it a rest all the same.* Instead, I am well behaved, the perfect audience, attentive and tied fast to his every word.

Crevan tells. Crevan tells that he doesn't know what guides him, but in a moment the machete is in his hand. There's a ringing of steel, a heavy wet thump and a strangled cry. The blade is buried in the first of them, One, the one with the cudgel, One, the one who was just on the bleeding edge of battering out Crevan's brains. Crevan wrenches the machete free and the would-be murderer falls to the ground, the life gone pure away, bleeding out into the dirt of the sunken path.

Seeing this, Two and Three stagger short, looking a great deal less sure of themselves than a moment hence. Their companion is dead or dying, and their own weapons seem laughably flimsy against Crevan's steel. Even if these hesitant assailants do outnumber him still, they're reckoning fast that he's more than their match. They've hooked a pike when they were only fishing for minnows. What do you think they do? They turn heel and run, of course, Two scrambling up the steep bank and Three racing down the holloway.

So Crevan is safe, unharmed, unscathed. Not dead, like he thought he would be. But instead of thanking his lucky stars or collapsing to his knees to kiss the good sweet earth, he gives chase. He is on Two in a second, who is struggling still to climb up the bank. Crevan lunges with the machete and the blade pierces flesh and bone, straight through the shoulder. Then Crevan pulls the machete free and Two makes hearty scream, sliding back down the bank, immobilized more or less, in no position to run. Two gurgles for breath and Crevan draws back the machete again to bestow another blow, and this time blade splits open skull and soon Two is silent. Then there is only Three, haring away, fast as fast can be. Will Crevan catch up? No need, instinct still directs his hand and action, and he turns in the road and lets the machete fly. The blade catches Three in the back, right between the shoulders. Crevan pauses, breathes. Then he follows the flight of his blade, follows the trail of blood, a red smear against the dirt track of the holloway that leads him to where Three is now crawling painful slow, like a serpent with its thin belly pressed into the earth, with legs limp as though the machete severed the spine. Even so, the life-wish is strong and poor Three inches forward, away, whimpering and mewling, sweating and weeping. Then Crevan is there, a knee jammed hard into the small of the back, hands grasping both sides of the poor worm's head. In one swift movement, Crevan snaps Three's neck. The whimpering stops and Crevan pulls out the machete like Arthur drawing the goddamn sword from the goddamn stone. The blade is bright with blood and he wipes it clean with a handful of dried grass plucked from the bank. It's a more brutal story by far than I was expecting. One, Two, Three; all dead, all told. I can't pretend I'm not thrilled by it, though I do my best to hide as much from Crevan. I can see he won't think well of my admiration should I venture to express it. Still, I cannot help wanting to know more, cannot help asking.

"So then, daddy bear, was that the first time you killed anybody, anyone?"

"No. But the times before then . . . I was in control. And they were fair fights. Single combat, at least."

"And after? Was it back to single combat from then on? Just mano-a-mano, one on one, all gentlemanly and decent?"

"No."

"So there were times after when you had to fight off and kill as many as three when you were just one. Or am I wrong again? Perhaps you had to defend yourself against even more than that? More than three at once, three in one?"

"Yes."

"At least you knew you could. Kill them, I mean. That must have been some satisfaction, some surety. You were very truly brave."

"It wasn't bravery," he says, looking down at his feet. "That means fighting your fear to do what's right. And that's not what happened. I wasn't thinking. I wasn't in control. It was like . . . like I wasn't conscious. Even standing over their dead bodies, the memory of killing those men felt like it belonged to someone else." He looks askance then, looks away, looks up. Continues. Tells me how it was like his every pulse and move had been driven by some other will, some power beyond his own. *Instinct*, I suggest. *Anger*. But Crevan only shakes his head, only says how all he knows is that he yielded command of his body and he doesn't understand how it happened or why, only says he felt like there was some shadow beast lurking in his chest and that it took charge. He tells me how he had no choice in it, and how he is grateful because it saved his life—more or less—and how he is resentful, because after that it made him act foolishly and hunt down the two men who'd already decided to do a runner. How needless, how reckless, to chase away that which is already gone, already fleeing.

"I couldn't control it, Kit," he says, voice hollow as the black *o* of his mouth.

If he were still a-seated next to me, I'd caress and comfort, but he's keeping his distance even yet, firmly out of reach, back rigid against the wall, determined to be a man apart. If I get up and go to him, he'll think I'm taking him word for word, think I'm taking seriously all this nonsense about him being out of his mind. Well, if he wants to absolve himself of responsibility like that, then it's his business. But I'm not here to indulge him, I'm not here to give credence to his sad-sorry self-pitying tale. He has killed, he has allowed violence to get the better of him—and in so doing he was saved from being got the better of by others, by less scrupulous beings with no concern for his health or welfare, none at all. In a crucial moment, Crevan let the blade in his hand decide, that beast in his chest take over. And now he would rather see this capacity, this characteristic, as somehow other, somehow separate from the core of himself.

But I know the truth. I know there's no difference between a man and his shadow. I would rather see it for what it is: a single aspect of the integral whole that is Crevan, whom I love, whom I hate, who is my one and only companion. I know him better now. I know what he was once capable of and know what he may yet be capable of again. I will neither reprimand him for it nor console him for what he has done, any more than I would seek to reprimand or console the carrion crow when it takes its bill of fermenting flesh. Long, long ago, Crevan drew a blade and killed three people. So what? Perhaps he would not have come to me otherwise, perhaps if he had not been ambushed like that—had not been cornered, had not been driven to such a brutal extreme—then perhaps he would never have grown to fear and despise the mainland. Perhaps he would never have sought to escape. Perhaps he would have died long before now.

A silence falls between us and I sit very still, not wanting to break it before Crevan's had a chance to go first. It's the least I can do for him now. At last he does, at last he obliges; kneading the exhaustion from his eyes and straightening, as though this conversation merely tires him, as though he is bored and keen to move on to some better topic.

"Enough of this," says Crevan. "You've taken a lot of strain these last days. We both have. We need a break. Come on." Before I can think to say or move, he's in the living room, running a thumb along the spines of the CDs that are lined up neat on the shelf. He picks one, takes the disc from its jewel case, slots it into the hi-fi. A melody plays through the den, sung loud and true and tender by the voice lying encoded—trapped in the pits and lands preserved beneath the glassy surface of the disc. I know the tune, know it without thinking, know it as readily as the embrace of my own skin.

Crevan turns, extends his hand to me across the emptiness of the living room. I go to him, place a hand in his. He pulls me close, keeps my hand clasped, circles an arm about my waist. At his encouragement, I climb on to his feet. His boots feel sturdy and sure beneath my thick woolen socks. I let myself melt into him, my head on his chest; let myself be sway-sway-swayed in time to the music, let him lead me in this sweet, slow, shuffling dance. We waver and spin.

"Kit?"

It's different this time, the way my name sounds on Crevan's tongue, his lips; a libation that slides from his mouth to mine in a hundred-thousand breath-borne droplets scattered across the small gap of air that cleaves us, lung to lung.

"Yes, Crevan?"

He does not answer at first. He is in silent argument with himself, I can tell; tell from how every muscle in his body has become suddenly tense—taut and brittle-rigid; tell from how it seems he is trying to both at once pull me closer and push me far away and out of reach. Out of harm, perhaps—though whether mine or his, I cannot say.

Before I can ask or clarify, something in him gives, breaks. I feel his body ease, hear his words soft and low. "We should get away from here," he says. "Leave. A change of scene would do us good."

Is this it? Is this what he was wanting so badly to say? Or is that still to come? I can only play along and see, play along and wait.

I try to imagine it, try to imagine me and Crevan doing what people once did, holidaying like the carefree folk of the long, long ago. I try to see it, try to will it: me and Crevan lying side by side on yellow sand, a blue sea before us, tame and glittering. I decide not to remind Crevan that I've never yet known him to venture out into the midday sun except for in the confines of the castle courtyard, that he's too frightened to explore the rest of the island—let alone to take leave of the protection afforded by its austere, secluded shores.

"But wherever so-ever would we go?"

"Just away." He pauses. And then, and then: "Don't you ever feel like we're trapped here, Kit? Sometimes it's like the entire island is a snare. We should be fighting to get free." He clicks his tongue. "It doesn't matter. We could go anywhere. Anywhere we want."

"You'd take me to see the capital? Even there? Really and truly?"

"If you like."

I think how it would be, there in the heart of the ancient city. We'd be real tourists, proper and ill-behaved. I'd take Crevan's photograph at the gates of the ruined palace, he'd steal me a piece of gold-leafed rubble as a memento, and we'd dance together down the empty streets. Or maybe we'd go to find the wild vineyards of the south; forage grapes in the sun, loot the cellars of the old vintners. We'd build bonfires at night and we'd drink and talk and laugh under the stars. Or maybe instead we'd go walking around the hills and lakes of the north, become explorers on our own expedition. Maybe we'd take the pole, chase the northern lights across the sky. Wonderful, wonderful, wonderful.

I hide my smile in the knit of his sweater. "We should pack now. We can leave as soon as the tide goes out—walk along the causeway and go wherever our fancy takes us." I am teasing. I am deadly serious.

"Now there's an idea, Kit. We could put out to sea."

"In a beautiful pea-green boat?"

"If you like. We'll take some money and plenty of honey." Then, changing tack: "There *are* boats in the northern harbor. I saw them that first day. Wrecks, mostly. But one must be repairable."

"You'll have to evict the limpets and mussels first. I don't think they'll like that much. But I could be wrong, you know, not being a mollusk myself."

"We have plenty of supplies. Enough to last for months on end. And we could fish."

"We could make a seaweed stew. Or shark fin soup, if you think you can land the catch. If there are sharks in these parts and waters."

"There must be atlases here," he says, glancing back at the shelves. "We could find a sheltered place to anchor, somewhere close enough that we can come back if we need."

"But there might be storms," I say, feeling I can no longer responsibly avoid pointing out the inherent dangers of the plan. "We might capsize. We might drown. We might drown to death."

"Or we might not," says Crevan reasonably. "Come on, Kit, can't you see it? We'd be safe. Free. We'd be together."

For a moment, I can. I can see how we'll swim in the day and at night the sea will rock us to sleep. How we'll eat brown shrimp fresh from the waves. How we'll play cards and deck games and

learn all the proper words for nautical things. How we'll befriend
the whales and gannets. How we'll put into distant shores and see
wondrous things.

Then the CD skips and judders, lapsing into a looping mechanical scream of malfunction. The song is broken. I slip from Crevan's
feet, from his arms, and go to rescue the disc from the hi-fi. The
silence is worse somehow than all that clamoring alarum and dissonance. Apart now from one another, Crevan and I come back to
ourselves, come back to the immutable reality of the den, where
we live, where we will always live, where we will die too, probably.
After all, death knows this place now; he has us on his list, he knows
where to find us. The dividing screen looms severely, cutting off
the living room from the bunks. For a moment, I'm almost sure I
can see the silhouette of her corpse through the screen. I flick my
gaze away and stare at the back of the CD instead, see the smudge-
scuff-scratches among the iridescence. There is no saving the song
that lies hidden in that part of the disc, it is marred forever, gone
forever—saving for what I know of it, saving for what I remember. I
am the song now, I am all that is left of it. Can I even remember the
words? I place the CD back in its case and the case back on the shelf.

"Would you like to talk about them?"

This question comes from Crevan's lips when he has only been
on the island a few short months. I know at once who he means,
what he's getting at. But I play dumb, playing for time. "Talk about
who?" I ask.

"Your family."

It is kindness that guides his tongue, I'm sure, kindness that
leads him to this offering of cue and ear, this willingness to give
remembrance. Perhaps he is thinking of his own kith, his own kin.
How many did he lose and how? What were their names, what
were they like? I could ask. I could ask and he would tell and, in

telling, show me more of who he is, lay bare yet more flesh, open further his heart. But I would have to tell him first—story for story, like for like—and the telling will split me in two, the telling will kill me.

"Kit?"

At his prompt, I make the only answer I can. "No," I say. "No, Crevan. No. It does not do to talk ill of the dead. Besides, I don't remember them. Not anymore. Not if I can help it."

Crevan clicks his tongue. Perhaps it is irritation—judgment—but perhaps it is only acceptance, as though this much he had expected. I hope so. What little I have said has to suffice, to satisfy. It must, for it is all that I can offer, the only fixed sentence in the story that I tell of myself: there is only me. I survived. I came to the island and now I am alone. I do not like to think of the world beyond or what it was like before. What I have here is enough. More than enough. It is everything. It is all there is. All there ever was.

"It's time," says the Crevan of the here, of the now. No need to ask what he means, not when I can hear it in the hollowness of his voice, not when I can see it in the fixed way he's staring at the dividing screen. "The spades are in the greenhouse. It's nightfall soon. We'll go then."

"Yessir, whatever you say, sir."

We bury the woman out in the brush. We carry her body from the den, through the winding maze of the catacombs and up the stairs that lead to the island above. We stop at the greenhouse door, briefly setting the corpse down on the flagstones while we go to claim our spades from within, picking carefully through the hail-borne disarray of glass shards and broken branches. The carrion plants hum with decay. Something of their stench seems to latch on to the body; it follows us even beyond the courtyard walls as we make our way through the wilderness, our awkward burden strung out between us. It is pitch night, a spectral sky stretching overhead, the moonlight blue and dim.

We are led by our feet to a place where the briars grow thin, a discreet glade where a sarsen dolmen stands among the tussocks of yellowing grass and nettle. Its vast capstone is paled over with lichen and it rests heavily on two slanting legs that jut up from the ground. What purpose the structure originally served, I do not know. It is not part of the castle. I think it might have been sacred once; I can feel it, an echo of something ancient, from something older than even the long ago, something precious and terrible, something forgotten, something that nevertheless lingers still. Perhaps the power of it will be enough to contain whatever unnatural malevolence lingers still in the dead woman's body. Perhaps it will not.

We drive our spades into the ground and gouge, shifting the dirt piece by piece until we have created both a pit and a crumbling mound of loose soil. The work drives all conscious thought from my mind. We dig deep as we can, deep as seems right. We lower the woman's body in with as much decorum as we can muster and then pack the earth back in place around her. We have no psalms, no sermons, no bells to toll. We do not pray for the dead. Our work is done, our part is played. She is buried, and hopefully whatever evil came with her is now buried too. As we walk back to the castle with our spades over our shoulders, I start to feel a little easier.

"Tell me again how it's going to be," I say, slipping my hand into Crevan's.

Crevan catches my drift, gives a soft breath that clouds the night air. "Not so different from now. We'll find a good boat. Small and fast, with a closed deck. We'll make her comfortable, fill her hold with as much food and water as we can from the storeroom. Plenty of fuel too. Then we'll set out. Pick a spot on the horizon and head directly for it. On clear days, we'll go swimming. We'll fish. There are bass and cod and dab in these waters. And we'll keep a lookout. If we see a single thing that concerns us, we'll weigh anchor. Just think of it, Kit. The wind at our backs. It will be as good as lifting up the entire island and moving it out of danger."

His words echo my imagining exactly, like he saw it written on my heart and read it back out to me. It is bliss, utter bliss. "We'll be all right now, Crevan. Just you wait. Everything's going to be all right. You'll see."

And then I don't know what happens. Crevan slips, perhaps, or catches his foot on a twisted root and falls. All I can say is that he is there beside me and then he is not, his hand gone, no longer clasping mine. It's like when he dives below the surface of the sea and I cannot be entirely sure that I didn't make him up. Now, for a moment, I am certain; certain that I did imagine Crevan, that his sudden absence is brought about by some unasked-for interruption to my personal fantasy. Perhaps I've reached a limit of my mental capacity, perhaps I've forgotten him or forgotten how to imagine things so that they sustain and endure. Perhaps he has fallen out of my head. Perhaps he never was and I'm only seeing it now. Perhaps he was a dream and I'm just this second waking up. It's almost a relief. Because if Crevan isn't real, if Crevan was never here, then that means the drowned woman wasn't here either. And if she wasn't here, then I can't have killed her. Or if she was here and I did kill her, then all it was that I killed was a figment of my own imagination—and there's no harm in that, is there? No crime in throttling your mother and your father, your sisters and your brother, your lover and your friend, strictly provided you do it all within the confines of your own skull. You can even take your own life if you want. No one will mind. No one will know to complain or berate or harangue. Not as far as I can see.

But if Crevan was never here and the drowned woman neither, then what is this grave dirt crusted in my fingernails, the whorls and lines of my palm? What is this shovel rested on my shoulder? Why am I out here in the island wilds, alone in the unfriendly wilderness that no longer cares for my company? Have I been acting out my delusions? Have I been out digging graves for figments? Have I buried nothing so much as the thin air? What's got into me? Ah well, at least all my efforts will have kept the earthworms on their toes. Not that they have them of course, not anymore, not out here beyond the boundaries of Eden where they must be condemned to slither about on their bellies. Or is that serpents? I can never keep it straight. Worms were wyrms were dragons once. Now they're for the birds.

A cry comes from the bush next to which I am stopped and my thoughts snap, break, shatter. It is Crevan's voice, I know it at once, know that he is real, that he simply slipped and fell from sight— rather than from out of my head entirely. Although perhaps he is a figment still and this is merely the resumption of ordinary service after a glitch, after an outage, after a server error. It amounts to the same thing in the end: real or not, invented or not. As far as I'm concerned, Crevan is there in the thicket, somewhere out of sight, somewhere among the dense furling leaves and twisting branches. I peer blindly for some sign of him: a lock of his bright hair, a flash of his pale skin.

I hear a sharp intake of breath and then Crevan crawls out of the bush, his face contorted in silent agony. Snarled around his left thigh is a rusted-crusted tangle of barbed wire. Every move he makes seems to twist it tighter and tighter, the knotted barbs snagging at the weave of his trousers and biting through to his flesh. I do not know what to do, what to say. I'd known, of course, that the wilderness had taken against me, but I never thought it would come to this, I never thought it would lay out mantraps to snag-snare and injure. It could have been me who fell. I bet that's what the wilds wanted, I bet it was really me it was hoping to catch and not Crevan at all. Poor, poor Crevan. He looks almost as appalled as I feel, his face white, white, his eyes wide, wide.

"Help," he croaks. "Help me, Kit. Please."

It's all I can do not to close up my ears. I wish he wouldn't ask.

TO FALL FROM A NEAR HOPE
OF HAPPINESS

Backbiters were doctors once, were medics; though that was just
a phase, a glitch, a happy chance that—for a time, a space—saw
hale order spiral out from chaos. For long before they were but
briefly recast, backbiters were much the same as they are now,
though we called them then by other names, monikers deserved
and damningly insalubrious: sawbones, quack, leech. Come, come,
you cannot have forgotten. Not when there is so much ill to recol-
lect and to wonder at. Not when the chronicles that chart our long
pursuit of health are riddled with remedies far fouler than the sick-
nesses they sought to solve. Not when the years are stained with the
legacy of a hundred, hundred villains—moon-faced all and trussed
in blood-streaked aprons—who never felt any compunction against
enacting crude ignorance upon their patients, who could be relied
upon for little more than bloodletting and vivisection, whose hands
were guided by nothing more or less than guesswork or, worse yet,
brute self-importance. Probably both. You know the type.

So. That's the way it was. Same as the way it is now, really, or
near enough as to make no difference. Perhaps it has been static all
along, perhaps there never was any let-up or relief, never any time
when the sick were not subjected to misdiagnosis and negligence,
to contemptuous dismissal, to treatments careless and insidiously
malign; never any period in which the voiceless were not barbar-
ously coerced into being experimented upon or quietly folded into
trials of which they had no knowledge and so to which they could

not possibly consent. Perhaps. But let us at least pretend, let us make-believe, let us say that there really was a golden era; a time of unprecedented medical progress and untold advance, a time when a doctor could be loved, honored, obeyed. (Or is that something else? I forget. Never mind, never mind, it cannot matter now.)

Well, what of this golden age? No, not golden—plastic. Plastic of all kinds: plastics molded, extruded, and pressed; plastics sterile and disposable. Glorious they were, quite glorious. They changed everything, right down to the scope of what was possible, of what could be dreamt up. Suddenly, medical researchers and practitioners alike could work unhampered by fear of introducing infection and so infections became a matter of supreme unconcern—especially given that those which did occasionally arise could be oh-so-easily dealt with by antibiotics. For a while at least; long enough for us to grow complacent. Infinitely complacent, as it happens. We weren't paying attention, that's the problem. We weren't watching for the cues; we didn't stop a moment to contemplate what we'd long known of the various microorganisms with which we share the Earth: that their lust for life far exceeds our own.

At first, there were only a handful to know about, to be concerned by; a much-feted shortlist of pathogens that started growing more and yet still more resistant to treatment. Stubborn, intractable bastards all: *E. coli*, *K. pneumoniae*, *P. aeruginosa*, *A. baumannii*, *S. aureus*, and *M. tb*. (Say *that* ten times fast.) For a time they were in every paper, on everyone's lips; spoken of in the exact manner with which a parent first broaches the problem of an ill-behaved child: *It's a calamity*, they said. *It's a phase; it's hopeless, it's bound to be all right*. And while we were talking, while we dithered and fluctuated wildly between despair and brash uncon-cern, trying to decide whether or not a problem that had been building for years hence was, in fact, a problem at all, the bacteria pressed on and pressed their advantage. In little time or less, the first six were joined by a further, untreatable two—*N. gonorrhoeae* and *C. difficile*—to make a thoroughly unmagnificent eight. Or *magnificent* if you prefer, if that's your bent, if your allegiance is with the lion over the antelope, the spider over the fly.

The worst of these strains—these un-super superbugs—took the hospitals as their home and hunting ground. It's where they were born, after all, where they learned to survive, where they resurrected themselves out of the half-dead cells left behind in the smeared residues of chemical detergent hastily sprayed on door handles and countertops, on bed railings and carts. It was not as though they needed to go elsewhere, not when their preferred prey came to them willingly and in droves, day after live-long day, delivered there by cruel misadventure or—like as not—a primary infection from some lesser bacterial strain. The sick were brought bound and gagged to the banquet table; immune systems already compromised, skin's barrier soon punctured with catheters and needles, creating inlets by which a ready bacterium could enter the blood—the body—and there incubate, colonize, flourish. Imagine. You could be admitted for a routine hip replacement and end up in the morgue. Not always, not at first. But, before long, more often than not.

And that was merely the start of it, mind, for where those first eight bacteria led, uncountable others followed. And we hadn't a single antibiotic to hold them back. It was the end of the cast spell, more or less, the end of medicine's golden era: our loss the microbes' gain, our hell their earthly paradise. Without antibiotics, we were bereft, we were deprived. We were, quite simply, without. We were without surgery, for there was no surgical procedure that could be performed under such circumstances, leastways not one that didn't incur risk beyond measure. Even tooth extraction could be lethal, never mind your appendectomies and biopsies, your bypasses and your transplants. We were without chemotherapy—not because the treatment was any less effective but because it suppressed the immune system and the jeopardy of that was too dreadful to bear, more dreadful, even, than the cancer itself. We were without catheters, urinary or venous; without ventilators; without grafts;

without implants; without pacemakers; without valves; without needle or syringe. We were, in short, without hope. Infection became the watchword and containment the only possible response. And then the plastiphages came and we were lost entirely, lost for good, for bad, for worse. The hospitals became unsalvageable cesspits and the doctors devolved, finally, into what they once had been and all the more dangerous for believing they were ever anything else. Backbiters. Self-proclaimed messiahs all, would-be saviors kill-killing with kindness, inflicting their noxious cures out of the very goodness of their hearts; each and every one a murderer, a plague doctor, befouled and befouling.

At least, now, we knew them for what they were.

We did our best to fight them off, to battle against them, to burn down the hellmouths from which they swarmed—the hospitals and the clinics, the general practices and the laboratories. But it wasn't enough, never ever enough. Still they marched on, bent upon saving the very souls that by each touch they regardless contaminated, regardless condemned to death. And so we fled. Everywhere it was the same: we scattered like seed from the farmer's hand, some to fly far upon the wind and some to sow themselves deep into the yielding earth. And there we are buried still, out of sight and out of mind—out of *our* minds, out of our pretty little heads—keeping time with the dead and pray-praying that we will not—yet—be counted among their number.

AT NO BREACH OR BATTERY

Night, day, night, day, night. Probably. I lose track. So much to say that time passes. Perhaps a few hours, perhaps a few days. The drowned woman is dead and buried still. Crevan and I are doing what we can, trying our best to reinstate our old routines, our old ways, our old habits, and finding ourselves at odds with one another, coming to a loose end more often than not, playing more than we ought, each one of us breaking out into fits of babyishness, each one of us having our turn to panic and cry. We are unsettled. Everything had been just so and then we were disturbed—the drowned woman deranged us, derailed us, diverted us. We need to get back to normal, back to basics, back to the way things were. Discipline! That is Crevan's business and it's not long before he remembers. He cuts a switch from an ash tree and whittles out two stout canes, one for him and one for little old me. Mine is just right, no longer than the distance between the crook of my arm and the tip of my index finger. It is light in the hand and makes a pleasant whipping sound when I slash it back and forth through the air.

"Time to exercise," says Crevan, dragging me out into the moon-washed courtyard. "We've been neglecting your self-defense training for too long. Come on. You won't always be able to rely on me to protect you."

I work hard to keep the muscles of my face still and composed. I do not say that I have never yet needed Crevan's protection, do not say that a wooden cane will be a poor defense against a hypo-thetical invading party, even in the hands of a skilled fighter—and

I have never been that. If the bad men come, they will come in vast numbers, they will come with real weapons and deadly purpose. There will be no beating them back, not for me, not for Crevan. But I know he is worried that the wound on his thigh will claim him and leave me without a hope, without a chance. So, I am resolved; I will let him teach me. If it gives him peace of mind, if it makes him feel better, there can be no harm in it. Like enough, anyway. And it is welcome, after everything, to be out in the air—even just within the confines of the walled courtyard—welcome to have a chance to stretch and scrap and skip. I can feel days of unspent energy fizzing in my nerves, tendons, muscles, crackling up and down my calves, my thighs. I am ready to jump; as high as the sky, as high as the stars. But first, a lesson, a recap of classes past and only hazily recalled. Crevan crouches down and uses the point of his cane to scrape out a pattern on one of the flagstones, its lines chalk-pale in the moonlight.

"This is the pentacle," he explains, glancing up at me, like I've never seen one before. "Each of the five points represents a critical lesson of combat. We'll go through all of them tonight. OK?"

"OK, sir, whatever you say, sir."

"Good." He pushes himself to standing, swinging the cane up to rest on his shoulder. "Then attack me."

It's not what I'm expecting. I don't want to argue with Crevan—don't want to say that if I was going to tackle him it would not be in plain sight, dead on, not for a million years, not forever so. I suppose I *could* make myself run at him if I really set my mind to it, could put one foot in front of the other, could brandish my cane and do my best to aim. But so too could Canute wade into the sea up to his knees and shout at the incoming tide to retreat. A fat lot of good, basically. And although I'm not so self-regarding as to mind looking the fool, I'd rather do it on my own terms, in the course of trying for something I actually want rather than merely doing as I am told. I hover where I am, not arguing against but not bothering to gear myself up for the demanded assault neither.

For his part, Crevan does not seem put out by my evident reluctance to attack. "It's the best way to learn," he says encouragingly. "Come on."

So this is how it will be. Time to get going, Canute, time to pull on your wetsuit. I make a half-hearted lunge forward, aiming so wide of the mark that Crevan doesn't even have to parry. I let my arm drop uselessly to my side and stick out my bottom lip into a fat pout.

"I can't do this," I say, putting on a thin, plaintive whine. "I *can't*. It's too hard. I'm no good. I won't ever be any good. I can't, I can't."

Crevan becomes grave. "You can, Kit. You're much stronger than you realize. You can do this. You can fight."

God, but he's earnest. Oh-so serious and sincere. To be honest, I sort of love it when he's like this, when he's trying to be all inspiring, when he's make-believing his belief in me. How good it would be to prove him right. He'd be so pleased—with me for doing what he asked, with himself for having the talent, the skill, to bring me along. At this very second and minute, I can tell he desires no such thing more than this; that I should—by virtue of his careful instruction—make a good show and demonstrate myself to be a useful fighter. How I would love to give him this pedagogic triumph, to hand it to him on a plate, on a platter, beneath a silver cloche. My heart quivers to think how he would spoil me then, how he would smile at me and confirm his devotion.

And yet, for all this, I find my spirit is not entirely willing. For one thing, there is fear. Crevan wouldn't mean to hurt me, of course, not a chance of that; but he's bigger than I am—the great lout—and there's a chance that he will forget himself, that he will misjudge and do me some serious injury. And, contrariwise, I have not forgotten that wound in his thigh, his daisy chain of lesions. It proved impossible to pull away the barbed wire in the dark—any which way I twisted it seemed to risk further damage. So we left it snagged in his flesh. I helped Crevan to his feet and back to the den, he leaning heavily across my shoulders all the while. It was slow

going, with much cursing and whimpering on his part every time
the barbs bit deep. Honestly, I think he was laying it on a bit thick,
but I didn't say anything, just kept my mouth shut and stoically
allowed him to use me as a human crutch. It must have taken us a
full hour to get from grave to home.

There Crevan sat on the floor, back against the sofa and both
legs splayed out before him. I was the one running about to gather
what was needed to cut away the wire, I was the one who found the
pliers and had to snip, snip, snip. It was not a pleasant task, no, not
at all. In places, the barbs were so deeply embedded that I had to
jiggle and wiggle them free. The wound did bleed ever so much and
Crevan did whimper and cry at even the slightest movement. And
his pain was the least of my concerns. The wire had looked nasty
enough half-buried in his muscle and sinew, but it wasn't until I got
it free that I could really see how old it was, how filthy and rusted.
I did what I could for him, making an even greater show of care
than I had when helping him hook the drowned woman up to the
IV. I had to give him a leather strap to bite on in the end, it hurt so
much when I irrigated his wound with disinfectant. But it may be
a lost cause, a losing battle, a total and utter calamity. Already, the
bandages need changing, smeared as they are with sweat, dirt, and
dried blood. But he did insist upon donning trousers and coming
out here. He'll be lucky to keep the leg, and he may be limping
forever. While I wouldn't normally presume that any attack from
me would do him the least bit of harm, I couldn't be so sure now.
Not when he's like this. Not when he's been compromised.

Seeing my hesitancy, Crevan frowns. "What is it?" he asks.

My eyes flick down to his leg, to the bulky malformity of his thigh
where his trousers are pulled tight around the bandages. Crevan
catches the glance just as I intended and gives a short, sharp bark of
laughter. "Frightened you'll unbalance me?" he says. "Perhaps this
will reassure you."

With sudden grace, he steps forward onto his good leg and swings
his cane down to strike me on the chest. The blow is so forceful that

it knocks the wind from my lungs and sends me reeling. I stagger away and fall backward, cracking my head and badly grazing both elbows. The rush is like nothing you'd believe or imagine, and it's a good few moments before I am back to myself, a good few moments before I realize that the impact has jolted the cane from my hand and sent it skittering away across the flagstones. I squint around in the dark, wondering where it got to, where it's hiding. I roll onto my hands and knees, thinking to get a better look, but I'm groggy still from the crack-bang of skull on stone and Crevan is too fast for me.

Before I've finished groaning, before I can move so much as an inch, he is standing over me and aiming the flat part of his cane at every part of my body he can reach, raining heavy blows on my limbs and torso that will later show up on my skin in a stark array of purples and blues. Every time I struggle to stand, he beats me down. *Hit me, hit me, hit me.* Take it out on me, boy, while you have the chance, while I'm a-letting you. All that pain and hurt, visit some of it on me. Pretend like every bite of the cane is a lesson, believe that you're beating the knowledge—the discipline, the talent—right into my skin.

For as long as I keep trying to stand, Crevan keeps knocking me back down. It is some time before I stop trying and collapse in a limp pile at his feet, the very picture of dejection. He falls back then, panting heavy-hard from all the effort of caning me. When at last he regains his breath, he bends forward all gallant-like and offers me his hand. *Oh, my champion, my hero. You'll have to do better than that.* I refuse his help, his chivalry, turning away until I am huddled on my side. I sniff and snuffle, a whimpering mess, shedding a few false tears here and there so Crevan will have no doubt about how miserable I am. But he's playing tough now. With a *tsk* of annoyance, he grabs the sleeves of my shirt and hauls me to my feet with grotesque ease. And there he is. The brute I always knew he was. All must bow before him; all must tremble and admire.

"The first lesson," he says sternly, "is never let pity hold you back. Pity means underestimating your opponent. Pity means death. It has no place in a fight."

I toy with hissing some retort or other, spelling out for him that it sure isn't pity holding me back—at least, not in the way he thinks—but I know that won't help Crevan, won't make him feel any better, won't help him earn the triumph of schooling me. He loosens his grip and goes to retrieve my cane from where it fell. When he hands it back, I take it warily and quickly retreat beyond the reach of his arm. He nods, curt and approving. "Good," he says. "You're learning. Now attack me again."

This time, I do not pause, do not hesitate, do not make a show of reluctance. I run at him, swinging the cane wildly about my head, putting the full force of my weight behind a blow that I aim at his ribs. But he steps aside and my cane whistles through the empty air where his torso was the moment before. The momentum throws me off balance and soon I am down on hands and knees again. The landing is harder than I anticipated. For a moment, everything is still. My eyes fall on a few tufts of sea thrift growing between the flagstones, every petal a pale tongue curled to taste the brine-misted night air. *How pleasant it would be to lie here awhile*, I think. I wait for Crevan to come and beat at me again, but I do not hear the uneven shuffle of his feet on the flagstones, do not sense his shadow falling over me, do not feel the thwack of his cane on my back. I suppose he must think that particular lesson learned, what-ever it was. Perhaps he's simply grown tired of kicking me when I'm down. Or perhaps he has remembered his place with a trill of disquiet and is worrying now that he has pushed me too hard, taken things too far. Well, there's more in me still. We are far from done.

Knowing I must, I push myself up. My hands are screaming at me, the rough grain of the flagstones has reopened the barely healed grazes on the palm of my left, and the knuckles of my right—which was clutched tight around the cane—have been ripped red and raw. That's what you get for trying to do someone a good turn, I suppose. And it's not over yet.

"That is the second lesson," says Crevan, sounding not relieved to see me standing and in one piece but just his plain old sanctimonious self. "Never signal your intention to your opponent," he says. "Never show your hand before it is time. Again."

Raising my cane to waist height, I step tentatively forward. Strike, but don't make it obvious, don't make it look like that's what I'm going to do. Though I understand the principle, though I know what is being asked of me and why, it is too absurd for words. I could appear to be doing a rain dance rather than seeming like I was about to attack and we'd both know it was a farce, a ruse, a pathetic attempt at misdirection. Crevan has commanded me to attack and I am obliging—because I am being very obliging today and no one can say otherwise—so how he expects me to make him believe I'm doing anything else but fixing to attack him, I don't know. I *think* all he means to say is that I shouldn't be so conspicuous, that I shouldn't draw my cane back behind me, shouldn't make any such flourish to indicate where the blow is aimed. But here again I am in bother, for I don't see how I can possibly strike a sufficiently forceful blow without the momentum that comes from drawing the cane back behind me. I have a vague idea that I need to be quick, that speed will help, but I am not sure. Physical brawling is not my forte, not my wheelhouse, not my thing. If Crevan really wanted me to learn, then he would explain this. But tonight that is not the point, not really.

I inch closer toward Crevan, hoping that soon the problem will be resolved for me. Once I am within reach, he will strike out. Then I can react to that rather than have to decide for myself how to attack. That's the plan, anyway. Only Crevan doesn't respond in a way that fits, doesn't go along with what I've secretly mapped out. Instead of lashing out at me, he stands perfectly still, letting me creep nearer and nearer until I am close enough to count the grays stranded through his long red hair. He doesn't even seem to be looking at me, his attention fixed placidly on the night that dances all around. Then he yawns.

It's a cue for me to take a chance, as obvious as if he's hissed at me out the corner of his mouth or painted a sign explaining what I ought to do. If I came at him for real and saw him yawn like that, I would most definitely fall back and reassess my plans. But I go along with it, taking the chance of his all-too-apparent lapse of attention to strike, making a slashing motion with my cane that should catch him on the shoulder. But, of course, he blocks the blow effortlessly, knocking the weapon aside and then clipping me around the ear with his free hand, just how a strict matron may once have disciplined her charges.

"The third lesson is not to trust your opponent. The gullible die quickly, Kit, you know that."

And how. Of course I know it, of course I knew it long before this particular charade. What's more, Crevan is well aware that I do. At least, he should be. I think I've done enough to prove that I am not easily or needlessly led. Still, I do not point this out, content as I am to play the role that has been given me. Crevan cuffs me around the ear again for good measure and this time I don't wait, this time I take it as another command to attack. I know my part and by now I should be feeling like I've had enough, like I'm fed up of being hit, so I pretend as best I can to become angry, rushing at Crevan in a mighty rage, all snarls and hisses, twisting my cane this way and that. The ploy, I think, works a charm, though of course Crevan parries my every blow with ease, swatting me away as a donkey's tail might an irksome fly. Buzz, buzz.

At last, when I have finally exhausted myself, Crevan switches to the offensive, striking my right hand so hard that I am once more forced to drop my cane. Then he advances. I scramble to get out of his reach but there is nowhere to go, not really, only back and back and back as Crevan presses forward. In the next moment, my spine is up against the brick. Crevan is on me, pinning me in place, his cane pressed across my throat.

"The fourth lesson is never give in to anger. If you're relying on anger, you're not in control. It puts you in danger. Do you understand?"

More than you know, kiddo. But now he is starting to take himself too seriously, the filthy hypocrite, starting to take this too far. His cane digs in and in, compressing my windpipe until I am choking for breath. I keep thinking Crevan will notice, stop, ease off. But he doesn't. Too far gone, perhaps, too in-the-moment, too in-character. I scrabble at his hands, trying to push him back, but he's far too strong for me. I don't think Crevan can tell I'm in danger now—can he? Can he possibly? We're too close; I can't see his face, can't look him in the eye, can't tell what madness has taken him, can't know his intent. I do the only thing I can think of and bring my knee up hard, jamming it into his wounded thigh. He swears loudly and lets go of me, hopping ungainly on the spot as his hands fly to clamp over the bandaged part of his leg. I catch my breath, the air rasping raw down my throat, and linger by the wall, uncertain of what Crevan will do when he has recovered from this flash of pain.

I don't have long to wait. He turns on me in the next moment. His face is ghostly in the light of the moon; his bright eyes clouded, his mouth drawn into a savage snarl. Dread takes me. For the first time since we met, since he ever came to the island, I really believe that he could kill me if he wanted. It would be so easy. He could lift me with one hand and smash my head against the wall until my skull caved in. If he attacks me here, now, I'll be lost. There's nothing I can do, there's no way I can fend off a man like Crevan, not when he's like this, not in this brute mode of his. I shouldn't have played along, I should have known him better, should have believed him when he told me before about the shadow-beast lurking in his chest. I never meant to unleash it. Perhaps, if I'm fast enough, I'll be able to slip beyond his reach and make it to the den. If I can lock myself in—well, he'll have a hard time getting at me. And he'll have a harder time being stuck out here, without any food. It would serve him right. He can see how *he* likes it, being thrust to the edge of non-existence by someone he thought a friend. That'll show him, tame him, bring him to heel.

I am just fixing to run when Crevan changes quick and sudden as anything: his brow smooths, his mouth twitches, and his eyes brighten again. He lets out a deep, throaty laugh. "That's more like

it," he says, clapping a hand to my shoulder. I sink back against the
hard brick of the wall then, so overcome with relief that I don't
know whether I want more to laugh or to cry.

"That's four of the lessons," he says, trying to re-engage me. "The
fifth—"

"I don't want it. No. I don't want to play anymore." I mean to be
decisive and commanding, but the words have a life and a will of
their own. They wobble and waver until my voice breaks and I am
choking on tears. My hand flies to my throat, plucking ineffectually
at the bruised skin as though this will help, as though I could grip at
the sobs and the syllables and manually cast them into the air. This
is all Crevan's fault, I'm sure. How could he be so cruel? I thought
he loved me, I thought we were comrades, I thought he meant it
when he said he'd do anything to protect me. I don't think I will
ever move again. I will just stand here huddled against the wall as
night turns to day to night to day, as the weeks roll forward and
the seasons cycle winter to spring to summer to autumn, as the
years bleed and fade into one another. I will cling to the brick, a
hardy limpet or lichen. I will fossilize, I will erode and crumble and
become dust and scatter on the briny air, every tiny particle of me
dismayed still, sobbing still, mourning still the dreadful day when
Crevan and I were so rudely thrown together, grieving for my poor
lonesome self, friendless still even after all this time, after all this
effort, after all this compromise, after all this trying to be nice.

"Kit—"

"I can't, I can't, I can't."

I can't say all the can'ts that there are, bubbling up inside of me,
each one hungry, hungry, each one threatening to consume my every
natural impulse and action. I'm stuck as stuck can be. I can't move,
can't talk. Can't feel anything but the cold night air and the ache
and sting from where Crevan battered me. Can't shake the numb-
null way that I've become in this last second. Can't thaw, can't snap
out of it. I can't anything at all, in fact—and fiction too. Not now,
maybe not ever again. I can't even look at Crevan, can't bring myself

to lift my eyes and see whether the face he wears is concerned or triumphant, rueful or alarmed, confused or angry. And while I'm stuck here with my can'ts, he's over there perhaps as stuck as me, a looming absence made up entirely of does nots. He does not reach out for me, does not place a reassuring hand on my shoulder, does not stroke my hair or tilt my chin, does not fold me into his arms. And I have nothing to shore me up, nothing to take comfort in but the hard, rough sandpaper kisses of the brick at my back.

While I'm busy with all my can'ts, while I'm not looking, Crevan must shift toward me, must take steps and come close, for the next thing I know is his voice, oh-so near in the night, and gentle-soft as downy feathers.

"You thought I was going to kill you." He is telling, not asking. Telling like he's only just worked it out for himself, telling like it's news to him even though he was right there with me, right there all along. "I'm sorry," he says. "It's not what I meant to . . . but I don't blame you for being scared. Not after . . . not after everything that's happened. Not when I'm . . . not when I've . . ." He chokes, stumbles, stops. Then, tongue click-clicking, gathers and tries again, the words coming gruff, broken, true. "I'm a murderer, Kit. But I'm your murderer. I'll keep you safe for as long as I live. Don't you know that yet?"

And then I am in Crevan's arms. I don't remember how it happens, don't remember being peeled away from the wall. Perhaps I melted and he scooped me up. He is solid and warm. I trace my fingers along the contours of his collarbone where it lies rigid beneath his woolen sweater. When I stop and flatten my hand, I can feel the slow rhythmic bucking of his heart against my palm.

"Kit, I—"

But then his eye catches something high above and he cuts himself short. One arm still about my shoulders, he throws up a hand to shade his eyes from the casting light of the moon and bends back at the hips to stare at the solar-paneled keep. Curious, I follow his gaze and see at once what drew his attention. A flagpole rises up from the top of the keep like a mast, bare but for a steel cable halyard that sometimes rattles loudly in the wind. Now it is still, but the tip of the pole crackles with a bright blue light that dances like fire. A natural phenomenon, as I vaguely recall, though not one I've seen before. Something to do with electric charge and the atmosphere. St. Elmo's fire, I believe it's called. Wild and strange as the northern lights, but just as harmless too. I think. I'm not sure.

Crevan looks serious. "There must be another storm coming. Come on, let's get inside," he says. Seemingly with no concern at all for his injured leg, he lifts me in his arms and braces me across his chest, carrying me just like a damsel in distress from some long-forgotten classic. I do not fuss or complain, I do not protest that he cannot possibly take my weight in his condition, do not insist on walking. Crevan starts back across the courtyard, swaying unevenly with each limp but still surprisingly sure-footed, surprisingly swift. We gain the wicket gate that leads to the winding stair and he bears me down into the ground, down into the catacombs, down into the safety of the den.

———

There are times when it seems to me that the den is an ark, times when I am hounded by the sense that, despite being buried in the earth, subterranean and static, its true counterparts are nevertheless nautical, celestial: the ship and the rocket. Each bears life through that which is inhospitable to it, by necessity incarcerating those within even as they seek the freedom of such lands—planets, stars—that may yet lie beyond. So too the den. It protects, it preserves. It imprisons us that we might be delivered (from evil, from the flood, from the damn backbiters).

One thing I know for sure is that the den dreams, just like any ark would. It dreams of dry land and better days to come, it dreams of when the world will be made pure once more and we'll be allowed out. Properly out, I mean, properly outside-out. By ourselves. No chaperone or nothing. And we won't drown, no; nor suffocate neither. We'll just live, same as now in all regards apart from the horizon, which will shift out from concrete wall to island's shore and farther still, out to the very limits of the atmosphere, to the stars themselves if we so choose, if we wish to trade one ark for another.

I wonder what I did to deserve it, this ark; to deserve being saved when so many were lost, when even our modern-day Noah—or Noahs, our Noah conglomerate, our NBM—must have been claimed by this foulest of floods. Not to mention extraneous family members or the beasts of land and sky that may, under other circumstances, have been granted shelter. There should be lions, there should be tigers. But there is only me. Me, Crevan, and the empty space where others should stand, should sit and wait alongside us. Not that it matters. It's not as though salvation's coming, not as though the flood will abate. This is all there is; only us and the dark earth, only us and our ark, which, lacking any destination or end, becomes what it must: our someday grave and final resting place.

———

Again with the first-aid kit. This time, it's all for me. There's nothing to be done for the bruises of course —they'll violet-green-yellow-go in their own time and of their own accord—but my poor grazed hands could use some attention, some immediate TLC. I douse a wad of cotton with disinfectant and dab at the gritted, ragged skin on my palms, my knuckles. I make little wincing flinching noises, sucking gasp after gasp in through my teeth every time the alcohol stings sharp, which is often. When they are clean as clean can be, I let Crevan help me put on the bandages; he holds my hands still and gently sticks large padded bandages over each palm. Then his eyes flick to the angry marks on my throat, to the blotchy patterns forming across the rest of my body, each one a gift from his cane. "Sorry, Kit. I didn't mean to be so hard on you."

"But you did, daddy. You did." It is the truth and we both know it, though I can tell Crevan doesn't want to acknowledge it as such, doesn't want to admit out loud to having wanted to kill me for a moment there. So he's an ingrate, so what? I've quite forgiven him now, quite forgotten what came to pass, quite prepared myself to accept his penance, which I dare say will amount to several days of being fussed over and cosseted, several days of him not being able to look on me except with rueful, hangdog expression. So I shall be magnanimous. I shall be kind. I shall be good. I shall remind him in the days to come that I didn't take this out on him even though I could have, even though I would have been well within my rights to do so, and he shall be grateful and groveling and beholden to me for ever and ever, amen. "But never mind that now," I say. "Because I don't mind it a bit. How's your poor leg? That's much, much more important. Let me take a look."

It takes very little to coax him into place. At my encouragement, Crevan unbuttons his trousers and lets them fall to his ankles. Then he steps gingerly out of the crumpled pile and settles himself down just like before when he first got snared; his back against the sofa and his pale legs splayed out in front of him. I kneel at his side and carefully pull away the old, graying bandages, unwinding around and around and around. I notice the smell at once, like ammonia. Crevan says nothing, peering at the lesions circling his thigh where the barbed wire cut him, gently pressing his fingertips to the surrounding skin. The wound is weeping incarnadine; too painful even to look at, its brazen color made all the worse by the frail pallidity of his surrounding flesh.

"What do you think?"

He's asking me even though he knows more about this than I do. And I know why. He doesn't want to look. I can hear the edge of fear in his voice, the trembling yearning that I will tell him I think it's fine, that I think the wound is healing well, that I think he's on the mend and everything's going to be all right. But he isn't and I don't. It's plain for anyone to see that his leg is in a frightful state, plain for anyone to smell that he's on the turn, already beginning to rot. Well, I can't say that to him, not without having to spend the next three hours talking him out of his funk, out of his fear, bringing him around to the fact that there's very little we can do.

"I've heard it can be ever so hard to tell with these sorts of things sometimes," I say, as though I know what I'm talking about.

Crevan clicks his tongue. "We should make a record. There are some acetate sheets and things next door. Would you get them?"

I leave him where he is, sitting slack like a dropped ragdoll with parsnip legs, and go to collect what he tells me is needed from the various boxes and containers all neatly stowed away on the shelves in the storeroom. It doesn't take me long to find everything— acetate, cellulose film, a pen. By the time I return, Crevan's finished cleaning out the wound and the smell of ammonia is stronger than ever, bad enough that I have to breathe through my mouth instead of my nose. But I am very good and do not recoil or retch, do not do anything to alarm him. I am as methodical and businesslike as can be. Following his instructions, I bind his thigh with cellulose film and try not to think how much it is like wrapping up leftovers to put away in the fridge and eat later. Concentrate, Kitty Kat. This is for Crevan's sake, remember.

He tells me to layer one of the clear acetate sheets over the top of the cellulose film and then, very slow, very steady-handed, use the pen to trace around the edges of each lesion. When I am done, I unfurl the acetate and hold it up so Crevan can admire my handiwork.

"Is that right, daddy?"

"Yes. Thank you, Kit. That's very helpful. Now we have a record of what the injury looks like. Tomorrow we'll make another tracing— and the next day and so on. Then we can compare what the injury looks like in a week's time with what it looks like now. We'll be able to monitor the progress as the wound heals."

If we're lucky, that is; if it heals at all, that is. I do not say this. Instead, I print the time and date in one corner of the acetate, in my best handwriting, and cross to the galley kitchen to stick the tracing on the fridge door with a magnet. Then I return to Crevan to help him redress the injury, wrapping fresh bandages around his thigh. At last, the smell abates. Crevan gets unsteadily to his feet. I throw him his discarded trousers, which he pulls on a bit at a time and in ungainly fashion, shifting from leg to leg, easing the fabric up over the bandages inch by inch.

Fly buttoned, he groans heavily and then promptly collapses into the sofa, as though he has at last met his match in this final and smallest of tasks, and been utterly defeated. He is perfectly still, head thrown back, eyes closed, one hand gripping the armrest. There is not the faintest of flickering movements in his features; no flinch, no grimace, no shuddering juddering spasm or shiver or twitch. And yet I can see it all the same: the pain crashing over him, through him, the sharp jolts tearing back and forth between brain and thigh, the spreading, burning ache that hungers to devour him entire. How like Crevan to suffer in silence, how like Crevan to think this is what he deserves, how like Crevan not to ask or hope for relief. It's all needless, quite mindlessly, moronically needless. I make loud tut and sigh then fetch him the little that's required: a blister pack of ibuprofen, a glass of water. I thrust both into his hands.

Then, to soothe him further, I step to the galley kitchen once more. Hot, sweet tea; that will set him right. The blend is of my own devising: nutmeg and ginger, cinnamon and cardamom, cloves, star anise, and a few other things besides, all in their right proportions, all designed to clear the head and calm the spirits. I brew it strong and potent, pour it out into two cups and stir them both with amber honey. One for Crevan, one for me. I breathe in the fragrant steam, savor it, feel the spice hit humid on my tongue, on the back of my throat, the soft hum that sets up at the base and pitch of my skull. I stir and stir, the metal spoon clink-clink-clinking like chimes in the wind.

By the time I am done, Crevan has had six little pain pills and all the water. Good boy, all better now. I bring over the tea, press a cup into Crevan's hands. He nods his thanks and nurses the hot ceramic against his stomach. Then I clamber onto the cushions beside him, twisting about so I can tuck my naked, bluing toes into the warm crevice between the seat of Crevan's trousers and the seat of the sofa. How delicious it is to be scooped up here with him, huddled together between the armrests. I watch him, admiring the sharp blade of his nose in profile. Drink up, drink up. I down my tea in greedy gulps, not minding how it scalds the roof of my mouth, the length of my gullet. But Crevan is more cautious. He blows on his tea, and takes only a few slow sips and sups. Even so, I'm sure I see the tension start to ease from behind his brow and fade as the pain begins to ebb, begins to deaden and numb. It will be gone soon, diminished to no more than a faint twinge—if only he is patient, if only he stops dwelling on it. I must distract him, draw him out of himself. I remove a foot from its cubbyhole and thrust it into his lap.

"Play with me," I say.

Crevan indulges on automatic, settling his teacup on the floor and taking my heel in his hand. Then he begins, pinching my big toe between his index finger and thumb. "This little piggy went to market," he says, making my toe wiggle back and forth, just like he's supposed to. After the littlest piggy goes wee-wee-wee all the way home, I too put down my cup and we play "Round and Round the Garden," "Pat-a-Cake, Pat-a-Cake," and "Pease Porridge Hot." For a moment, everything is just as normal, just as it was before, but when I start on "A Sailor Went to Sea, Sea, Sea," Crevan holds up his hands and says he needs to pause and drink the rest of his tea before it gets too cold. And now I'm stuck, because I can't insist that he carry on playing when I already insisted before that he have the tea. So I must just be good and let him drink up and not show that I'm annoyed. I nod and smile and swing around so I can sit with my back straight and my hands tucked beneath me and kick my legs up and down against the side of the sofa.

"Aren't you tired, Kit?"

"Nope. Not at all. Not one little bit."

"It's long past bedtime."

"I don't care. I'm en-oh-tee not tired." I swing my legs quicker and quicker, just to prove it. I'm awake, I'm awake, I'm awake.

"We've let our routine slide these last few days. It's not good."

I stop kicking my legs. It's the first time since we dug her grave that either of us has spoken aloud—however obliquely—of the drowned woman, and I wish Crevan wouldn't, wish he would just leave well enough alone. Because he's invoked her now. Even without a whisper of her name (whatever that may be), she's been summoned—I can practically see her looming over us, a dreadful specter with rictus grin, hair dripping, dirt smeared on her hands, her face, her feet. And we'd been doing so well.

"Is that why you don't want to go to bed, Kit? Been having bad dreams?"

"No. Nuh-uh. Not me." It's not a lie, not exactly. I've had hardly any dreams since Crevan pulled the drowned woman out of the sea, and fewer yet since she died—since I killed her—but then I've hardly slept, so there hasn't been much chance for dreaming, whether sweet or acrid foul. I just lie rigid on my mattress and try not to look down at her empty bunk. But my mind plays tricks on me, sometimes making me think that she is lying there still—no matter how I remind myself that she isn't there anymore, that her body is rotting in the ground out in the island wilds and far from the den—so I have to check, every once in a while, to see what's really true. And then it's worse somehow, the bunk being empty when I was expecting . . . when I was expecting . . . I don't know what. Her body returned, undead. The time erased, unlived. The deed undone.

"No," I say again. "I haven't been having no dreams, not one."

Crevan's look is all disbelief, but there's nothing he can do or say to prove otherwise. He stares into his cup, swirl-swilling the tea around, around, around until it becomes a whirlpool in miniature. "It's important, you know, to keep a structure. There's good reason for it. You have to exercise and take your supplements. You have to get enough sleep. It's easier if you have a routine. That means going to bed at the right time, even if you aren't tired."

I don't argue. I don't point out that he makes us go to bed at just the wrong time, that he's the one who's made everything topsy-turvy, establishing this carnival order whereby we sleep when the sun is out and rise only with the moon. I don't say that routine is for the rat-race, routine is for the before-times. I don't say that if there's any good to come out of the end of the world, it's the sudden redundancy of the alarm clock. What good is keeping time? It will tick by all the same, whether we watch it or not, whether we meas-ure it out or not. And we have no events to attend, no acquaintances to meet, no appointments to be punctual for. There are no demands on our time at all beyond what is required to live: to eat, to cleanse, to sleep. Why then may we not do these as and when we wish, as and when the need arises or grows most acute? Why may we not let our daily instincts and urges dictate our patterns, rather than the other way around? It's topsy-turvy, is what it is. But Crevan always has been insistent upon it. *We are not as the beasts, Kitty Kat*, is what he means to say. *We are not as the fox or the crow. We are not wild things to do as we wish and when.* Which is all well and good—if that's what Crevan needs to believe, then that's his business. If it helps him get through the day, then I'm not going to criticize. But he has no right to project his odd dictums onto me as well. Whatever he may think, I am not under his dominion, not part of his domain. I'll be wild if I want. I'll be as the beasts are. I'll be as the fox and the crow. Caw, caw, caw.

"Do you ever think about what it's really like out there?"

It takes me by surprise, takes me aback, takes me unawares. The question is a paper-cut, is scalding water come sputtering from the cold tap. I can't believe he's asking; can't believe he'd dare when I've been so nice to him. I screw up my eyes and wrinkle my nose, feigning ignorance and playing the dummy. Scratching my head and looking as best I can like I can't tell up from down, left from right, bad from good. I'll get him to clarify, ask questions that carry with them an implication of the limits, an indication of just how far this discussion can go so that he'll know—without me having to say outright and shaming him—that the boundaries are looming.

"Out there in the storm, you mean?" I ask.

"Out on the mainland. Out in the real world." He does not meet my eyes and his voice is quiet. He knows; knows that he's crossed the line, broken the rules. Else he'd be confident with me, else he'd be calm, else he'd be easy as ever and not rigid stiff like a new bristling brush. I must be firm with him now, cut him off before he can go any further, bring him back from the brink, turn him around on the banks of the Rubicon.

"There's nothing to think about."

Crevan pauses at that, holding his tea still for a long moment before finally draining the what-must-now-be-tepid dregs in one big gulp. "You're right. Sorry. Forget it."

If only I could, if only it were so simple. "Consider it done," I say all the same. "Done and over with. Done and dusted."

Silence falls between us. The issue may be closed, the thorny moment sidestepped; but we are not quite out of danger yet, not out of the woods. We cannot leave things like this, cannot let this hairline fracture between us settle and grow and yawn into a gaping chasm. But it is Crevan who must build the bridge, who must stitch the wound together; Crevan who must show his obeisance to me, to me, to me. I shall sit here quietly—not budging, not fidgeting—and wait for his gesture of goodwill, his offering of peace.

"Do you think the storm did come?" he asks at long, long last.

"I don't know," I say, squeezing his arm at the crook so that he will know he is forgiven, that his olive branch—such as it is—has been accepted. "If it has, probably it will blow itself out soon enough. Probably if we go to bed now like you want, then it will all be over by the time we wake up again. How does that sound? Would you like that?"

"Yes, Kit. Very much."

I put Crevan to bed. He comes meekly, slowly, limping-ly, allowing me to lead him by the hand; a frazzled, overtired child reluctantly glad that there is, in the end, an adult in charge, someone else to call the shots, to lay down the law, to enforce the order of the day, to make sure that all the little humdrum necessities do not get missed. So often it is the other way around; Crevan saying what we must do and when. It's only fair that I get a turn now, only right that Crevan should have the chance to prove himself amenable and compliant. He's in a bad way, poor baby. The least I can do is relieve him of the drudge, drear, drab responsibility of being the one to make all of the decisions—for a little while, anyway; until he's more cheered, until he's feeling more like himself, until he's up to playing daddy once more.

Or until . . . No, stop. Don't think of it. Not even for a second, not even for a moment. It doesn't bear contemplation—leastways, I cannot bear contemplating it, not without it settling its gross bulk upon my shoulders to buckle my spine and crumple me down to the ground, clamping clammy hands over my eyes, my nose and mouth . . . no, no, don't think of it, don't dare. We cross the living room and pass the dividing screen. I am careful to make no comment upon the empty bunk, careful not to pause and stop and glance and check, careful not to give any credence to the ghost image my mind's eye casts out onto the mattress, thin and empty, definitely empty, no doubt about it, so no point in looking. Quick, through the door and into the safety of the master bedroom, Crevan's room, somber as ever, save for all the little goblin men who smile out at us from the doors of the cedar wardrobe, frolicking happily among the carved vines and leaves. Crevan climbs into bed, fully clothed, and I pull the covers up over his shoulders. Then I hop up into the space beside him, scooting backward to sit against the headboard. I stroke Crevan's hair, smoothing down the red-gold wisps, soothing the fine furrows in his pale brow.

"I could use a doctor, Kit."

"You're the only doctor here. Or as good as. Leastways, the only one we've got."

He tips his head a fraction to the left, a fraction to the right. *No*, that says. *Not what I meant*, that says. "That's just first aid. A real doctor can do a lot more."

I frown. "There aren't no real doctors. Maybe once. But not anymore. Not here. Not now."

He is silent for a moment, worrying at his beautiful lip with his beautiful teeth; fearful that I am right, fearful that I am wrong. "Backbiters are doctors," he says at last, offering up this morsel as though it is news, as though it might be something I'd never known, never thought of for myself.

"Backbiters are still evil. Nasty dangerous beasties. Everyone knows that. You've said so often enough yourself."

"I never said . . . They aren't evil, Kit. Just trying to help. And there are good backbiters. Ones who understand infection. Ones who are . . . working very hard to get bacterial infections under control."

"It's too, too late for that," I say at once. I know this game, I know how to play. "That horse has long, long gone. Long-ago bolted, long-ago died. They can flog it all they like. Won't do no good, no good at all."

"They could help me, Kit."

I stare. This is not how it's supposed to go. What is he playing at? What does he mean by it? Pushing me like this? "You don't know what you're saying," I venture, when I finally find my tongue once more. "You're too tired for this, silly. Beautiful you need to get your beautiful sleep. When you wake up, everything will be better. You'll see. Because it's all right. I'm here. And I can help take your mind off things. I can . . ." I cast around, trying to think of something halfway useful, halfway helpful. Then I hit upon it. "I can tell you a bedtime story! Would you like that?"

He gives a little snuffling murmur that isn't quite yes and isn't quite no. So I begin as best I can. I tell him about the nail that was lost and the horseshoe and the rider, all the way through to the message, the battle, the kingdom, and then back again to the nail. I don't remember it as well as I should, as well as I ought—it's not a good tale, not really, not a favorite—but it has its own funny rhythm and I can burble along with it even if all the words are wrong and quite unfitting. Crevan hardly seems to notice. Soon his eyes are closed, his breaths coming slow and deep. Seeing that he is drooping, drifting, dropping off to sleep, I stop my muttering, blathering story and press my lips tight shut. But for the brush, brush, brush of my hand, I make myself still and quiet, small and calm. I do not fidget or scratch or click my tongue—nothing that might jolt him fully back to waking. I do not hum, do not mutter or croon. Hush now, hush now; if I don't stir then he won't wake, and if he don't wake then he won't be afraid, won't be pained, won't be able to worry.

———

If any statement purporting to fact may be believed (and I am not convinced there may), then let it be that which follows: we wanted this to happen. By *this* I mean crisis, by *this* I mean so much waste laid, the definite end of our somewhat indefinite civilization. It was desired, longed for: cataclysm the catechism, the craved-for crux and catalyst, the coveted cure-all, corrective, countermeasure. A fix in every sense.

We wanted this to happen. If not necessarily by these particular means, then at least for the purpose of achieving this general end: the cities razed, the social bonds cut, the population of every country decimated quick-quick and from there on continuing to decline and decay, to degrade. That's what we yearned for, what we sought: a little annihilation to wipe clean the slate and give new beginning, as though suffering on any scale could be counted purification, as though the mechanism of those human tragedies—untold and brutal—could be seen as nothing more than the industrial detergent that cuts through the grease of the black-bottomed pan and proves it to be no longer unsalvageable, no longer forsaken.

And what was the wrong to be righted, the malady to be medicated, the transgression to be redressed? Of what had we, really, to complain? Perhaps it was that we had heaped upon ourselves a surfeit of complexity and so longed to simplify, simplify; to refocus, to resolve the thousand knotted problems of our daily lives by replacing them with a single, vital concern: namely, survival— nothing more or less, better or worse. Or perhaps we felt we had fallen into dullness—a rut of routine and responsibility—and needed, desperately, escape; a shot in the arm, an adrenaline rush, an existential threat to liven the heart and quicken the blood. Then again, perhaps it was nothing more than a sense that we had deviated too far from nature, from instinct, and so hungered for return; to release the untameable predator that may or may not lurk in every human heart, to run as the hunter runs, to howl with the wolf, to slake our primal thirst with blood. In any case, catastrophe would be excuse enough to cry havoc and let slip, cut loose, set free. To reclaim ourselves from what we had become, had been made to be.

We wanted this to happen. But it didn't work out like we thought—as just about anyone might have guessed that it wouldn't. An apocalypse does, after all, have a tendency to get out of hand. Definition-wise, you simply cannot rely upon doomsday for a fresh start. It is not a beginning in disguise, not the mere turning of a leaf or a year; it is not a chance to reassess, to improve or to make amends. It is, simply, the end. And our end is unfolding slow and tortuous; the ever-drip of venom onto the face of a sometime god, bound and chained. It is everything you imagined it would be and worse: our lives brief and precarious, our bodies maimed, our dead beyond number, our families destroyed, our morals—such as they were—corrupted. We wanted this to happen. We wished and wished: for a good war to set us to rights and settle old scores, for a nuclear winter to split

the strong from the weak, for an act of god to level the imbal-
ances of overpopulation. And now it has come to pass, and now
we wish that it hadn't.

———

It's becoming harder than ever not to think of the drowned woman,
lying as I am at Crevan's side same as I did hers, the reaper-man
lurking just out of sight, leering at us from the corners, sniff-sniffing
at the rot in Crevan's thigh. No. Stop. Get up, get away.

I am up off the bed in a flash and it makes no difference for all my
fretting that it would; Crevan slumbers on, truly asleep now, though
whether his dreams are sweet or dreadful I cannot tell. I would crawl
into his ear if I could, worm my way through into the soft parts of
his brain, take a look around, do what I can to banish the ill and
enliven the lovely; sharpen the color, turn up the volume. Perhaps
he is dreaming of me. Perhaps he is dreaming of the nail that was
lost and the horse and the rider. Perhaps he is dreaming of that but
in reverse. Perhaps he is dreaming of the drowned woman, perhaps
she is calling to him, perhaps she wanders through his subconscious
even now, trying to suggest through subtle, conning ways what he
should do, to persuade him to give up, to give in, seeking out the
evil creatures festering in his thigh, hoping to encourage them to
venture along his veins and poison the rest of his lovely Crevan flesh.

It's not fair. I don't want him to die. I don't want him to go. I
don't want to be left here alone. Or worse—left here with Crevan's
body, with the husk of a thing that was once Crevan, with a whole
Crevan-sized corpse to carry out and bury in the earth, in the wilds,
out in an island that has already turned its back upon me and will
not look kindly on my choking up its territory with yet more human
flesh. *No, stop, I said. Stop. Come on, Kit, come on.* Time to distract, to
act. Time to stand in the corner and put your nose to the wardrobe
door and not look away again until you've counted every single leaf,
every ornamental berry.

Careful now, easy now. See them hanging there, suspended in the grain of the wood, polished and shining bright. They will be here for ever and ever, as easy and plain as one, two, three. *One, two, three. One, two, three. One, two, three.* It's not helping, it's not helping, it's not—

Quick; open the door and climb into the dark, into the sturdy belly of the wardrobe.

I bury myself in the piles of folded clothes; they burr soft and warm as I shift and flail about, trying to make myself comfortable, trying to make it so that it feels like I'm being held in the secure embrace of the panic room, safe beneath poured concrete and a near-invisible trapdoor. I could go yet, could climb out of the wardrobe and cross to the other end of the den and hide myself away; but the greater reward—the greater security—is far outweighed by the snickering snarling fear, by the many varied creeping nightmares that lurk between me here and the panic room there, just waiting for some poor unfortunate to run on by. I'd never make it in one piece, never make it alive. Better to stay here, better to swaddle myself in sweaters and scarves, better to pull the door of the wardrobe shut and sit perfectly still, breathing in the heady fragrance of the cedar until the fear calms and becomes friendly. *One, two, three. One, two, three.* I am shielded on every side: there are thick wooden panels above and below, to my north, east, south, and west. No one would know I was here, not even Crevan would guess right away. And apart from Crevan, there isn't anybody. There's no one at all. Just him and me. If there was someone else, they'd have to find us first. I'm in a wardrobe, in a bedroom, in a den, in a catacombs, beneath the ruins of a castle, on a spit-of-rock island, in the middle of the sea: the innermost figurine in a set of stacking dolls. I am safe. I am safe, I am safe, I am safe.

Let the eyes close, let the mind root in the now, in the body. Feel the aching knots in every muscle, every place where Crevan sought to school me with his cane, feel the itching beneath my bandages where the skin of my palms is quietly knitting itself back together again. This is real, the lingering pain and the cedarwood, this is all that is real. There was never anything else. My mind slows and stills. Sees differently now it has been so occluded from the light. Sees every fizzing atom that makes up the body of me, the skin of me, sees the atoms in the wood that surrounds and encases. Marvels at the gaps between the atoms, wonders whether the first layer of wood atoms ever slide into the gaps between the skin atoms and vice versa, whether they might not align *just so* by chance and I will slip through the wood entire, or the wood will slip through me, or I'll become one with the wood, melted and merged. I should be falling, I should be dispersing into the air, the ether.

Can't you feel it? How thin and fragile your skin? How each one of your shivering shuddering atoms wishes to escape, to slip its bonds and disband? It's easier in the dark than the light, easier to remember that there is no you, only layer after layer of atoms, no single one of them you any more than your nail cuttings are you, any more than your shed hair is you, any more than the dust that chafes from your skin is you. Atoms and atoms and atoms. That's all there is. You can go through from one side of a body to another and not find anything else. There is no core, no essence hidden within, nothing concealed, nothing fundamental. Only atoms. There is no you. No me. No Crevan. Not if you know how to look, not if you know how to see.

The fear loses interest, the panic slips and fades. They have no choice. I know I don't exist. And if I don't exist, then I cannot be ruled or bullied; I cannot be made afraid. So I am not. I am not frightened, not scared, not quaking where I sit. I am not here, not here at all and neither is anything else. It is only an impression, a passing illusion, a brief and inadvertent collusion of energy and atoms. It is matter pretending, matter playing tricks, matter accidentally taking a shape that—in a certain light perhaps—may be mistaken for a wardrobe, in a bedroom, in a den, in a catacomb, beneath the ruins of a castle, on a spit-of-rock island, in the middle of the sea. But blink and you'll miss it, blink and it will be gone, blink and there will be nothing; only dust dreaming of times past and times yet to come.

I am not here; I do not live and therefore will not die, and therefore cannot die. Or perhaps it is that I am dead already. I do not know; even here in the freedom of no-light I am still too much bound by the limits of this plane of existence. I cannot see exactly as an atom would, cannot feel exactly as an atom might feel. But it doesn't matter in the end, not really. When it comes down to it, there's no difference between eternal life and eternal death, not so far as I can tell. Either we are dead to begin with or we shall never die—whatever the truth, there is nothing to fear, no existential change of state to fear or dread. There is only matter. Sometimes animate, sometimes not. Sometimes solid, sometimes liquid, sometimes gas. Sometimes a thousand other things besides. Each one bound by its own mechanical properties, each one bound by physical laws—some known to us and others not. There is only matter. There is nothing good or bad, nothing right or wrong. That is all. That is everything. That is more than enough.

AS A WASP OR A SERPENT
OUT OF A CARRION

How close the calm to the calamity, the tranquillity to the tragedy, the bliss to the bale, the hope to the hell. They are neighbors,
I think; the dearest of friends, the thickest of thieves—seeming to
each another opposed but in truth only pretending to be rivals.
One distracts and lulls, the other empties your pocket. A fine part-
nership, to be sure: an old reliable. Nice 'em and knife 'em, turn
by turn, all the way to the grave. There is no use complaining or
protesting. It is just the way of things, just how everything works
out over the course of a lifetime. It's swings and roundabouts, ups
and downs, six of one and half a dozen of the other. The fair gives
way to foul. Always has and always will. So I shouldn't be surprised,
really, shouldn't be taken aback each and every time it happens,
each and every time the balm turns to blood.

Perhaps I am not very bright, perhaps I am faulty: the incurious
lab rat who takes the lump of cheese without ever anticipating
the electric shock that always comes next, that has always come
after every single feast. Perhaps I am a romantic; daring to believe
that every brief contentment has the capacity to endure, that peace
can be permanent, that paradise is a real place into which I may
enter and forever reside if only I can find the right door, the right
key. Perhaps I am a logician, perhaps I have carefully surmised
that—in contradistinction to my own personal experience and
history—transience is not an inherent quality of goodness and it
would be therefore foolish to assume that each spell of joy, when

it comes, must pass in the same way as all the others have before. But then, of course, if goodness is not inherently transient, neither too is badness—make of that what you will. The long and short of it is this: me, a wardrobe, a flush of metaphysical calm in among the cashmere. And then, and then. There is a discovery, a disappointment. A surprise, for heaven's sakes, even though I should have seen it coming, even though anyone could have seen it coming. But wait, no, that's not right. Because the truth of the matter is this: the questions were always there to be asked; the doubts to cast, the rat to smell. The discovery was always there to be made, was always waiting for me here where I am now, in the wrong part of the wardrobe—the part that has always been off limits—behind the left-most door, in Crevan's one and only hiding place.

Perhaps I am a fool, an illiterate, a naïf. But in my defense—if any is needed—with regard to this and many other things besides, I do sincerely wish to be ignorant, I do *want* not to know. If I could go back and unmake the discovery, I would. I know it's not the sort of thing I'm supposed to admit to, but there you are. I don't believe it's so strange a position, either. Who has not in their time wished to turn back the clock, who has not fervently prayed that a piece of knowledge learned might yet still be unlearned? Who has not longed to revisit the uncomprehending ignorance of the moment before, of days, weeks past? I am not alone in this, I am sure.

It is the fact of the discovery that stings more than the object discovered, bringing as it does the revelation that Crevan has almost certainly been keeping contact with faceless others— who? survivors on the mainland? I do not dare to guess—that Crevan has the means at least to go behind my back, to seek advice, companionship, conversation elsewhere. Has he been speaking to backbiters? Is that why he was at such pains to tell me they are not all of them evil? Does he plot against me? Does he summon hungry hordes to the island? Does he give away our position? It does not bear thinking about. It is bad enough that it is possible he might—when not a moment before I would never have believed it, never have imagined that he would want or need anyone but me.

I knew what it was—what it meant—the moment I happened upon it, that I had found the burden of Crevan's secret, the one thing he insisted on keeping from me. There is nothing else here, you understand, nothing with which I am sharing wardrobe's darkness that is remotely worth concealing. And either the device works or Crevan believes it capable of working, for elsewise he would never have hidden it, would never have made me promise to keep shut tight the left-most door of the wardrobe. I recognized it at once from the likeness diagrammed in one of my encyclopedias: a satellite phone with a fat antenna, the handset rubberized and ruggedized, built to withstand any and every disaster. What else could it have been? Is there any other single object that can so destabilize the foundations of reality? Is there any other single object that can change everything and still fit into a wardrobe, in a den, on an island, in the sea? It's like finding a body, it's like finding a treasure map. It's like finding a note from a lover; whether it gives you cause to hope or it rejects your affections outright, it changes everything, it rewrites reality around you in ecstasy or in agony and there's nothing you can do, no turning back, no chance of returning once more to the sun-dappled uplands of innocence—not now you know, not now there is no room for wonder or doubt. You just have to continue on, even though the knowledge is suffocating you, even though it's squeezing at your throat with its long-fingered hands— because what's your other option?

Perhaps someone will notice: pat your shoulder in a reassuring way and give you one of those little sympathetic puppy-dog frowns. Perhaps they'll try to buoy you up by saying that what doesn't kill you makes you stronger. And you will nod and smile and say thank you, even though the words are entirely void and empty, even though the sentiment is skewed and suspect, even though there's nothing like a near-death experience to leave you weakened and damaged for the rest of your life. What doesn't kill you makes you stronger. If there were ever a greater leap in logic, I cannot think of it. Imagine: some travesty occurs and passes. In the wake of this mortifying experience, you nevertheless do not die. Your continued existence is observed, noted, and appraised. *There*, they say. There's someone who is still breathing even though one of their lungs has been surgically removed. There's someone who didn't die. They must be fighting fit. Probably they are in better condition now than they were back before when they still had both lungs and no need for the hospital. How wonderful that they have been blessed with this debilitating disease.

And all the while the truth is evident, the truth is obvious for anyone to see: you're still alive because who knows why—some twist of fate that you cannot possibly hope to identify or understand—and, being alive, you have little choice but to continue on in that manner. Little choice, that is, but not none at all. For you may, of course and if you so choose, take your own life. Perhaps it is the not-committing-suicide that inspires the remark. After all, it is only in the absence of having done that—for all that you may be suicidal, for all that you may be right at the goddamn edge—that you may be considered to have not been killed: not only has the event failed to kill you, but you have failed to kill yourself in the aftermath. Is this what is counted as a show of strength? Well, perhaps it is. More like as not you continue on because that is the de facto option, more like as not it is a real struggle. You know in your bones that you are not mightier than before; you know you have been eroded, weakened, permanently damaged—bodily or psychologically or both. What doesn't kill you makes you stronger. And so we lie and lie. But let the lie stand for now, let it remain. If it helps, if it allows even just one struggling soul to battle on, then it is enough, then it is worth the sin. I wish I could claim it for myself, but I cannot. I find the satphone and it kills me not. But neither does it make me stronger. It is an iron splinter in the terracotta brick of my heart—my soul, my self—one deeply lodged, with fracture lines crack-spreading all around. Hell.

I climb out from the left-most part of the wardrobe, the satphone in my hands, intent on showing Crevan that I have him sussed, that I have uncovered his little secret. For I have, haven't I? It can mean nothing else, surely, the act of concealment itself a ready admission of guilt. Yet perhaps Crevan will say otherwise, perhaps he will say only he knew that I would not like the satphone and that he has never used it nor never intended to use it. Well, we shall see. I shall ask and he shall seek to justify himself, lavishing me with explanations that I may choose to believe or not, apologies that will be mine to accept or refuse. Only I cannot make my accusations, not yet, not right away, for Crevan is sleeping and pays me no heed. Thinking to wake him, I bend to kiss his forehead and find his brow is slick with sweat. He tastes like the sea, like a mollusk, like a brine-preserved fish. My touch does not stir him, and my whispered entreaties neither. He is gone, out like a light, dead to everything. I would like to be angry with him, to let the provocation of his discourteous slumber turn my disappointment to fury, but I can see that it will go against me. He is sick, after all, and will think badly of me for waking him when he needs his rest. I'll be put on the back foot then, thrown to the low ground, made to explain why I *had* to wake him—just *had* to—when all I want is to talk about what *he's* done, to find out why *he's* betrayed me—if betrayed me he has. No, the satphone can wait. It will have to.

I put it back behind the left-most door of the wardrobe, hide it among the sweaters and never mind it for now, for the moment, for the time being. I crawl onto the bed beside Crevan and curl up next to him in a tight ball, my knees tucked under my chin. I imagine myself a mummy, embalmed and entombed, a desiccated corpse so tough and leathery that total disintegration remains improbable, instead enduring in the earth like a fossil, a stubborn remnant of an older geological age, a past way of life. I think of the explorers and archaeologists who may come this way one distant, far-off day when the world has righted itself again and civilization is restored. If Crevan and I breathe our last here and now, what will those excavators find in the years after? How much of us will remain? What will be made of the positions of our bodies? Will we be labeled kin, enemies, lovers? Will enough evidence endure to show that I am sleeping on top of the covers and Crevan below? Will our yellowing skulls be examined? Will rough, ponderous sketches be made of the faces we once wore? I would like to see that, would like to see if they can capture anything of Crevan's smile even after it has quite rotted away.

Sleep must come for me, I suppose, because the next thing I am aware of is a burning pain in my left ear as it lies pressed against the pillow. The cartilage got folded over somehow and pinned down beneath the weight of my head, starving the top-most part of the ear from blood, from oxygen. I tilt my head, let the ear unfold. The pain does not ease, only throbs and throbs as the blood makes its slow return. Open eyes, crane neck, massage ear. See the empty space beside me and wonder—what happened to Crevan? Get up, get out. Out of bed, out the door and past the bunks, through to the living room. There he is, there he is; on the floor again, back against the sofa again, trousers around his ankles again, another sheet of acetate wrapped around his thigh. When I approach, he struggles to stand, turning away from me so that I cannot see his leg.

"Bandages needed changing," he says. "I made another tracing." He waves the acetate too fast for me to catch the markings on it and then holds it obliquely against his side. I catch the smell of ammonia. Looking down, I see the old bandages coiled around his feet. They are stained with blood and a thick, pungent discharge. It's getting worse. How sweet that he thinks I wouldn't notice, wouldn't be able to tell. Poor, foolish Crevan. He stoops to pull up his trousers, wobbling undignified on the spot, groaning and wincing. I make no move to help him, only stand and wait. Once he is done, he is so sapped by the effort that he immediately collapses back down to the sofa.

"Sorry, Kit. You must be hungry. I can make you something. Give me a moment."

"This isn't how the routine goes. Not even a little bit. And you said routines were important."

"Sorry, it's this injury. But we'll be back to ordinary in no time, you'll see."

I'll believe that never-ever. But it doesn't matter to me. Routine was always Crevan's concern, not mine.

"Just need another minute. Maybe two. What would you like to eat?"

"I don't know. Nothing. Something. Whatever you're having."

"What's wrong with your ear?"

I have been kneading the cartilage between finger and thumb, but the question stills my hand. The ache has not subsided yet, though it is finally starting to leach and dull. "Slept on it funny," I say.

"Come here."

I dutifully kneel on the sofa beside him and turn my head. He brushes my hair aside, his hands light and gentle, then leans and presses his lips soft against my ear. "There," he says. "All better."

A reassuring hand on my back, his palm smoothing down the length of my spine and then making slow loops and then stops. He seizes and draws away, readies himself to stand again.

"How about macaroni?"

He heaves himself up, limps across the floor to the galley kitchen. Sets some water to boil. Busies himself searching through the cupboards like this is just another ordinary meal. But he has no idea, no way of knowing that I have found what was hidden in the wardrobe, no way of guessing that I've discovered his betrayal.

Clunk, clunk. He places two cans of macaroni and cheese upon the counter. Snaps the ring pulls, rips off the lids. The water is boiled. He pours some into each. Stir, stir, spoon drawing circles through the steam. Leave it to sit. He turns back to me and frowns.

"Is something the matter, Kit? You look troubled."

Honestly. Of course something's the matter, of course I look troubled. Because it seems like you're a traitor, Crevan. I trusted you without question and now I find that I am a fool for doing so, that I should have asked long before now whether you deserve that trust at all. You've made it so that I must now seek redress, remedy, amends—and it's not amends I want, it's blind faith and that's gone now, gone forever. That's what I don't say. Instead, I find myself shying away from the fight, feigning nonchalance. "Do I?"

"You're worried about the injury?"

"I'm not *not* worried."

"—but it's not the only thing concerning you. Come on, Kit. You can say."

"Can I?"

"You know you can."

That was true once. I suppose, in a way, it's still true now. Because of course I *can* tell him. There's nothing preventing me from telling him. It's not like there aren't words, it's not like I've lost my voice or my tongue, it's not like my mouth has been sewn shut. Similarly, it's not like he's been struck deaf, not like his ears have been cut off, not like he's suffered some trauma that would prevent his brain from processing what I tell him. And he is inviting the telling: I have his express permission and reassurance. Of course I *can* tell him. But can is different from should. Always has been, though I struggle sometimes to remember.

When I found the satphone I was set on making my accusations, on having it out with Crevan, probable traitor that he is, on screaming and shouting and stamping my feet, on visiting untold wrath upon his beautiful, treacherous head. I wanted to do all those things. And then I didn't. And then I slept. And now I'm not so sure, not so clear on what to do, what to say, how to behave. So for now perhaps I will delay and defer, asking only what is anodyne, only what can be readily dismissed.

I begin with a lie. "I dreamt about the wardrobe," I say. "That *she* was hiding in it, the woman, hiding behind the left-most door and all ready to jump out at me."

"She isn't in the wardrobe, Kit. She can't hurt you."

"But it was frightening," I say, stubborn as a scorch mark. "I was *frightened*."

"You don't need to be frightened. You're safe here."

"Maybe I'm not. Maybe she hates me, maybe she's angry that she's dead. Maybe she clawed her way up out of the grave and crawled all the way back here to hide in the wardrobe and *get* me."

"Come on, you know that's not possible."

"I don't know anything or anything. I don't even know what's behind that door of the wardrobe."

Crevan stares down into the steam. "There's nothing, Kit. Nothing that matters."

"But there *is* something! I know there is. There must be. Something that matters to you, something that matters so much you have to keep it secret and squirreled away and not tell anyone what it is, not even me, not even after all this time."

Still, he does not look up. "It's never bothered you before."

"Maybe it bothers me now. Maybe it's always bothered me and you never noticed."

"Has it?"

"I *said* maybe."

"Come on, Kit. Stop messing around. What's brought this on?"

And just like that we are at the edge of it; he will not bend even to allay my wildest fears and I can see that he will only continue to evade me if I do not ask him outright, that he will keep putting me off until I confess that I do, after all, know what lies behind the left-most door of the wardrobe, that I know what he has been keeping from me. What will he do if I tell him? Scream back? Accuse me of sneaking just where I said I wouldn't? Deny everything? Claim he has no idea how the satphone came to be in the wardrobe, that he's never seen it before? No, that doesn't sound like Crevan. I can just see it. He will stand there very quiet with his head bowed and say nothing for a long, long time and then probably he won't admit to it or won't apologize neither. No explanation, no argument. He will say only: *I should go*. Then he will gather some few belongings and leave, a self-made pariah. He will hobble down the causeway to the mainland and never come back.

Am I ready for that? To be alone again? He is a hasty man is Crevan, and a proud one too at times—invariably just when it makes matters more difficult—and he will decide quick, he will reckon what is best, he will conclude that my discovery of the satphone— my breaking of his trust as much as his of mine—will make our living arrangements untenable and promptly oust himself; no time to talk and reconsider, no turning back. And what if I am wrong? What if the satphone is brick-dead and useless, nothing more than a souvenir of some long-ago memory, precious and private? Then I will have made him leave for nothing.

But he is sick now, of course. The wound is finally taking its toll and he won't get far, won't be able to move that fast. Perhaps this is the best time to confront him, in that case; when he is captive here, when he is being slowed by laceration and infection and I will have a chance to talk him down (if I want to—do I want to?).

Though, thinking on it, perhaps that makes it worse. Perhaps the pain of the injury will make him more unreasonable, perhaps he will ignore me no matter what I say, perhaps he will insist on going all the same. And that's no good. The causeway is long. In his condition, he might not make it to the other side before the tide draws back in. What if the sea comes and washes him away? Then that will be my fault, I suppose. My burden to bear. Even though *he* is the one in the wrong.

"I'm just hungry, hungry," I say. "I'm just tired."

He nods as though this explanation is perfectly satisfactory. "It's been a strange few days. Let's eat. Get some more rest." He half-turn twists back to the counter, gives each can another stir. Then he takes two forks from the drawer, picks up both cans and limps back to the sofa. "Here," he says, handing one over. "Be careful, it's hot."

Hot is right. Hot metal between my palms, hot steam warming my nose and chin when I bow my head to sniff, uncomfortable hot on my lips, my tongue, the roof of my mouth, my gullet when I scoop up the first macaroni and swallow. The mix is a sicky yolky yellow and roughly the same consistency as glue. My favorite. I take another forkful and another and another. With every bite it seems like my appetite is waking, so though I wasn't feeling hungry before I started, by the time the tines of my fork scrape the base of the can, I am feeling famished, like all I want to do is open up the kitchen cupboards and eat anything and everything I find.

Crevan, beside me, is still only halfway through; eating slow, savoring the meal. The bastard. I stare at him open-mouthed until at last he gives up.

"Finish this," he says, handing me his can. "I'm done."

I don't turn it down, don't remind him he needs to eat, needs to keep his strength up. I gladly swap my empty can for his half-full one and polish it off in greedy, unguarded manner, not hardly even stopping for breath until I am done and there's no macaroni left at all, only a crust of congealing powder-cheese sauce at the bottom. I go to dip my finger in but Crevan snatches my hand.

"You could cut yourself. It's sharp, look."

"All right, all right. I'm not a child, you know." But I hand the can to him all the same and he puts it with the other on the floor, safely out of reach.

"Still hungry?"

"Not me." It's not true yet but in a few minutes it will be; in a few minutes my stomach will register what has been piled into it and let me know that it really is time to stop now, that we'll be all right for a while now and thank you for the dinner.

"Sure? I could go up and get some fruit, if you want. Been a while since we ate anything fresh."

I look at his leg, the bulge of bandages beneath his trousers. *Yes*, I think. *Go on then.* Limp all the way through the catacombs and out into the courtyard. Mind yourself on the stairs. Be sure that you only break a sweat and not your back. It will probably only take you an hour or two. Bring me back a single fig and once I've had that, I'll see whether or not I wouldn't like another. It would serve you right.

"Greenhouse needs inspecting anyway," he continues. "The trees need a bit more attention after that hail."

I shrug. "Knock yourself out. If that's what you want."

"Might help. Good to have something to do."

"If you say so."

"You don't want to come with?"

"Nope." I turn away and inspect the sofa armrest, trailing a finger along the patterns of the upholstery. Crevan's eyes are upon me, I can feel them, can feel his confusion, his uncertainty as to what is wrong. Perhaps, deep down, he is starting to realize that he's done ill, that he's upset me—even if he doesn't yet know how. He watches me a long while but I don't turn back to him, don't say a word. Just wait. At last, he groan-heaves himself up off the sofa.

"You know where to find me."

I make a sound from the throat that is not agreement and not disagreement neither. I keep my gaze fixed on the armrest, though I cannot help how my ears prick and liven to the sound of Crevan limp-dragging himself across the living room. His struggle with the blast door is lengthy and pained, punctuated by grunts and gasps and gurgles of all manner. I do not look. I do not encourage or say stop. I do not get up to help him. But, in the end, he manages it, in the end he gets through, in the end he is gone.

I do not know how much time slips, slides, tears about me. The seconds scrape, the minutes whistle. The pattern on the armrest blurs and clears and blurs once more. I refrain from blinking until my eyes sting, from breathing until my lungs insist. Blink, breathe. Refrain. Blink, breathe. Refrain. Blink, breathe. Re. Frain.

What am I doing here and all alone? Why have I let Crevan leave me behind? Why have I let him go on ahead with that poor wounded leg of his? What if something happens to him? To me?

Then I am gone too, up and on my feet and through the blast door before I can think, before I can stop, before I can question. I look reluctant down every side tunnel and alley I pass, sure that Crevan will have fallen, not wanting to see, not daring to stay blind. But there is no sign of him, good or ill, neither in the catacombs nor on the winding stair. At the last step I pause; catch the breath and cling on to it, gulping at the air until I am ready to open the wicket gate and look out into the night-drenched courtyard. The glass panels and shattered panes of the greenhouse reflect the moon's pitted face in a hundred slivers and angles. Hard though it is to see in, I can sense that Crevan is there. I steal across the flagstones and into the green-house, guided by the moon, by the stench of the carrion plants. I can see better once I'm past the glass, once I'm inside; can see the trees and leaves limned with silver. There is Crevan, an angular silhouette in the midst of the close heat, one hand outstretched to a knot of the fig tree. I can't say what it is, how it can be that I know at once. It is tenebrous in here, it is umbral; too obscure to be sure of anything, too clouded with shadow to be certain. And yet. There is something wrong. Something twisted. Something desperate.

"Kit—"

The word comes harsh and gurgling thin, as though his throat has been ripped out but, by some miracle or dire need, he is still able to speak. I am at his side in an instant, a heartbeat, the bat of an eye, just in time to catch his weight when he collapses, just in time to groan and stagger and awkwardly lower him to the ground. His clothes are drenched through with sweat and he is shivering, trembling, shuddering. When I touch my hand to his forehead, it feels like he is burning. He is sick, the infection is taking him with brutal rapidity. Perhaps it was this final exertion that broke him. Perhaps he was always going to be overwhelmed like this and it was only a matter of time. I do what I can to make him comfortable between the roots of the fig tree, pulling off my sweater to use as a pillow for his head. He needs help. He needs medicine. *He needs*—no, don't say it, don't think it. Focus. He needs to get back inside but he's in no fit state to move and I certainly don't have a hope of carrying him. I stand.

"Don't leave me," he croaks.

"I have to, baby, just for a moment, but I'll be back, back as fast as I can."

It's a wonder that the words don't quaver and judder on my tongue. Somehow they stroll out: calm, confident, assured. And then it's lights, camera, action. In other words: go, go, go. I hot-foot it, racing back the way I came, not stopping once, not glancing to left or right, only speeding ahead (or back?) with all my might and force which, though it is not so great as I might wish, is not so inconsiderable either. When I reach the den, I flit-race around it, darting from place to place like a bee to the flower, gathering what I can: medical supplies, water, clean clothes, a blanket, a flashlight. It's as much as I can carry and will have to do for the time being, for the first attempt. I run back again, slower this time, less sure of my balance, less able to see where I am going what with the bundle in my arms obscuring my own feet from view. If I fall, I will not be able to catch myself. So I must not fall. But I must be fast, must get back to Crevan like I promised I would. He needs me. I've never seen him so weak. I've never seen him weak at all.

He stirs when I return to the greenhouse and then I am kneeling beside him, my arms unburdened, my hand clasping his. I lean forward and kiss his brow. He is still burning. He murmurs something but if there are words in among the breath, I cannot divine or distinguish them.

"I know, I know. I've got you. It's going to be all right."

Can he hear me? Can he understand? Never mind that now, it's not important, not when I have plenty yet to do. I take up flannel and canteen from the pile, twist off cap, tilt bottle, douse the rough fabric so it splutter-spills water all over the greenhouse floor. Then

I lift the sodden flannel to Crevan's mouth. His response is faint but definite, lips parting for more. Very slowly, I twist the flannel so the water trickles into his mouth. He sucks and sucks and does not open his eyes. I douse the flannel again and this time press it to his forehead, hoping its cool touch will help bring down the fever. He murmurs again, mutters something indistinct.

"Don't speak, baby. Just rest. I'm going to take good care of you." There it is again, that coolness, that certainty. I don't sound at all afraid, I don't sound at all mortified that it's suddenly now all down-up to me, that it's my responsibility, that I'm the one who has to coax him back from the edge of death. I don't know what I'm doing. But slow, hush. One step, one bit, one piece at a time. Crevan is sick and needs medicine. No doctors required, no back-biters neither. Just medicine. Anyone can see that. Only what kind? Depends. Let's examine the injury, let's check for clues.

It is no small matter, to wrestle a grown, nearly-unconscious man from his trousers. Or is it the trousers from the man? I do not know, but the task is laborious, unseemly, unpleasant, impolite. I shouldn't mind. I wouldn't mind so much if it wasn't Crevan. But stop, I am fussing, I am proving myself squeamish and silly. He needs to be put into fresh clothes anyway, for his are soaked through with sweat, his are ruined. And I can hardly tend to his wound if I cannot get to the site of it, if I cannot bare his leg.

I manage it, in the end, pull off his trousers and, careful-slow so as not to hurt or aggravate, unwind the bandages from his thigh. I examine the wound by flashlight and have to resist the urge to grimace, to suck air through my teeth, to moan and gag. The rising stench of the carrion plants does not help. But I keep it together, somehow, I keep it in, keep my look level. At least Crevan's eyes are closed. If there is discomfort traced in the lines of my face, he will not see, he will not know. I hold my breath and peer closer at the wound. It is bad as I feared—worse, even. I do not need to compare it to the acetate tracings to see that the lesions are larger than ever they were. And the skin around them is red, inflamed;

hot to the touch. From many of them oozes a thick, malodorous pus. The wound—the wounds—are festering, infected. Hence the fever; hence the shivering feeble mess that once was Crevan. It is the infection, I am sure of it; eating away at his leg, turning him inside out.

What shall I do first? What shall I do next? Think! He is in pain, let me relieve it as best I can. Analgesic will help with that and calm the fever too—there is a bottle, there is a syringe. I have to hold the flashlight in my mouth to draw up a dose. I pull at Crevan's left arm and rub at the crook of his elbow until the vein swells and throbs. I swab his skin with an alcohol wipe. A second slips by. Then ten. Then a minute more passes as I try to summon the courage, telling myself there is no need to worry. It doesn't help. Biting my lip, I breathe in and begin to count. *One, two, three.* I breathe out.

Without another moment's hesitation, I jab the needle into Crevan's raised vein and press down the plunger. Then I yank the syringe away and let it drop to the stone floor of the greenhouse, clamping a piece of cotton onto the inside of his left elbow and pressing hard to stop the blood flowing out to greet the air. I hold it there for a few minutes until I am brave enough again to risk letting go. Then another swab to clean the injection site, and a bandage to keep dirt from getting into it. And all this time, Crevan still hasn't stirred, hasn't so much as gasped at the needle's bite. Well. Nothing more I can do right now to help on that front. In a few minutes, perhaps, the analgesic will start to work. *Please, oh please, oh please.* And in the meantime, I must see to the leg. The injection will help with the pain, with the fever, but it will do very little to combat the infection itself. It is a serious concern and needs to be treated seriously.

There are nightmare stories of how it happens. I've seen them written, I've heard them told. Small cuts and grazes that should heal in a couple of days but end up infected. An entire limb that turns bad, that has to be amputated to stop the spread. And sometimes even that is not enough to stop it if the decay is truly determined, if the infection is sufficiently nocuous. It can claim entire bodies, entire lives. It might already be too late for Crevan and definitely will be if I delay any longer.

No, come now, it's not so bad. I can get this wound properly cleaned out again. And I think I have the seed of an idea, something else I can do, something that might help, that might save him —and the leg too. I read it in a book once.

Saline solution, that comes first. Like seawater but clean, but safe. I take the bottle and pour the sterile brine over and into the wound, doing my best to irrigate it, trying not to think how badly it must sting when, from deep within his delirium, Crevan begins to whimper. I pause, take the flashlight from between my teeth.

"Hush, hush, baby. It's going to be all right."

Flashlight back in mouth. Need to see, can't mess this up. Next is next is next. Zinc oxide, an ointment for the healthy skin that surrounds the wound. Hydrocolloid cut into strips and placed careful around the edges of the lesions. It is a fiddly business, believe you me. There are far too many lesions to be getting on with, and each one different in size and shape. Not to mention how awkward it is to get to the ones on the back of the leg, not to mention the difficulties of doing this all by the light of a mouth-held flashlight. But I manage it all the same. The gel-like hydrocolloid dressing is stiff at first but after I cut it into strips, I warm it between my hands and it becomes more pliable. I peel off the back and stick it into place directly onto the healthy skin at the edges of the wound. Flashlight travels from mouth to hand and I breathe more easily. But now comes the icky part, the grim part, the gross part, the bit where you might want to look away, the bit where you might want to hand in your form, your badge, your notice and say: *This isn't what I expected. I'm out.* Well, perhaps I would do the same, only I have no choice, no option—not if I want Crevan to survive. And I do, of course I do. Even if he is a traitor. The betrayal only hurts because he's mine, because he's all I've got, because I never believed he would.

I pick up gauze, bandages, a knife and go to inspect the carrion plants.

By the light of the flashlight, I see they have been unharmed by the hail. Each one is still perfectly intact, five enormous corpulent stars, each one with a dreadful gaping mouth at its center. I inspect the flowers one by one, clamping a sleeve over my mouth and nose as feeble protection against the stench of rotting flesh that emanates from each. The petals have the unnerving appearance of fleshy cartilage, the pale skin wrinkled with pink and red, the surface fringed with hairs. I peer close; close as I dare. The first three I inspect are clear, but on the first and second gigantic petals of the fourth (there's arithmetic for you), I find them: small colonies of eggs sprinkled across the outer rim of the flower's mouth. The eggs are white and fine like grains of rice. Holding the flashlight in the crook of my arm, I cut off both petals and dart back to Crevan. This time, before I begin, I think to set up the flashlight properly, hanging it from a convenient bough by the looped cord so that the light dangles over Crevan's leg. Then, using the edge of the knife, I scrape a few eggs into each one of the lesions that circle his leg.

Yes, I know, you must think I have gone mad. Mad-der. But consider this: the eggs will hatch, become maggots. And maggots eat dead tissue. They can clean a wound as good as any surgeon—so I've read, so I've been told. It is safe. It can help with infection. No, no, try not to think of the carcasses you may or may not have seen; like the dead sheep that washed up on the shore of my own island a few years prior, its body bloated and maggot infested. Try not to think of the stories you know about people and livestock being blighted with the suppurating sores of parasitic infection. *That* is myiasis. *This* is different, this is good. At least, that's the theory. And it is not all so strange as you might think. It's a kind of symbiosis that has often been observed throughout the animal kingdom, if my books are right. There are (or were) all kinds of fish—like the wrasse and the gobies— that feed (or fed) on the dead skin, ectoparasites and infected tissue they find on the living bodies of fish from other species—usually much larger and often predatory—not to mention sea turtles, whales, octopi. It's a system that works for everyone. The cleaner fish get to eat. The client fish stay healthy. A cooperative relationship and to the advantage of all. It's the same with the maggots. They're cooperating with me. They get a nice meal, Crevan gets his leg back.

In this particular case, you could say that the maggots are getting an *even* better deal than that, because the poor little things would surely have died if I left them on the carrion plant. It's a trickster it is, a cunning operative, as Crevan once explained to me. Normally, you see, the greenbottle blowfly lays its eggs in rotting animal matter. So the carrion plant, which needs the flies for pollination, has several tactics for appearing like a carcass: its extreme size and fleshy appearance, its distinctive smell; all serve to attract the fly to the flower. Thinking it scrumptious-true carrion, the fly lays eggs. But there are no nutrients to feed the eggs, nothing they need to hatch. The maggots would have died. So it's good for them. And good for Crevan. It's been tried before, you know. There are plenty of accounts from battlefield hospitals, of how soldiers with maggoty wounds healed better than those whose injuries were kept free of insects. Swear. Promise.

I keep scraping out the eggs. Then I trap them in with gauze, taping down the edges onto the hydrocolloid. And, last of all, I wrap the thigh around once more with fresh cotton bandages. It is done, it is done. The wound is tended to. I will change Crevan's shirt, put him into something clean and dry. I will make him more comfortable. I will cover his bare legs with the blanket that I brought from the den—better than wrestling him in and out of trousers again. And I will wait. And I will hope. And I will watch the bandages to see when they start to squirm with life, and I will watch Crevan to see when his fever breaks. That is all I can do.

You are not yours, you are barely even you. For every human cell that you possess—that you *are*—count out another ten and know that they belong to those bacteria that call your body home. Do you see, do you see? You are molecularly outnumbered, wonderfully and incontrovertibly. So how, then, can you imagine your life to be yours alone to rule? For it is not yours, not solely. Not enough that you could reasonably be deemed to own it, that you could feasibly pledge it to another. Not enough that you could be judged to exist for your own sake and in your own right.

I know, I know. It's an easy mistake to make. Perhaps that is the human condition, to get it wrong like that, to start off thinking so small. For that is what we do, more often than not: we think of ourselves and there is nothing smaller than that, nothing more diminutive than reducing a human body down to a single, individual life, a soul bearing up a soon-to-be corpse. Because you are not a body, not merely, not unless you mean it in the astronomical sense, not unless—by some glory of chance—you already see yourself for what you truly are: a heavenly body, a celestial body; vast and star-touched. *That* is what you are, don't let anyone say otherwise. You are Mars, you are Venus, you are one-and-only Earth. You are mundane, but not in the way you think that means. You are mundane in the way it ought to mean, in the way it meant once: of the world, worldly, world-like. You are terrestrial, utterly and magnificently. You *are* Terra. For uncountable bacteria, fungi, and archaea, you are fatherland, you are mothership; all that is and all that matters.

So now you know. Whatever you think—whatever you may fear—you are not alone. You were, in fact, never alone. From the moment you were born and possibly even before that, you became host, environment, habitat; a neonate shrouded in the microbiome of the birthing canal, the vagina. Or, alternatively, in that of the abdominal skin and flesh, if your birth was by Caesarean—though these, like so many other once-routine surgeries, are now few and far between (you can thank the bacteria for that, you can thank the no-good antibiotics). Either way, this much is true, verifiable, given: you are born a cosmos, a conjunction of climates and topographies colonized by sprawling microbial communities, each one with its own preferences and peccadilloes; a liking for the crease of your arm over the outside of your elbow, an adaptation that loves the dry epidermis and loathes the sebaceous follicle. Some are pathogens but most are not—or at least not yet, not until they reach some part of you they shouldn't; a cell of staphylococcus from the skin entering the bloodstream through a surgical incision, an accidental burn, a bramble scratch. Then you're dead, likely as not, then you're a goner. There's nothing that can save you now—not from that, not anymore—apart from perhaps your own immune system and that's only if you're lucky (and let's face it, you probably aren't). No, there's nothing that can save you, nothing that can be done.

And what of it? You will die anyway, you will perish. Like every star that came before you and every star that shall follow after. Even now, you are beginning to collapse. It is simply the way of things. You will drop and dim, compound and compress. And it will be astonishing, even so as your birth: a thing to behold. Your many-splendored inhabitants will surge and thrive, will devour and feast, will botulize, will transform you and transmute you into air, into gas, into earth. You will disperse and so shall they; you will become something new, something different. Another planet far, far from here; another star, another universe. You and not you, still, even beyond death and not alone. You are not alone. And nor am I and nor ever was I and nor will I ever be. Even if Crevan dies. Even if, even then.

———

It is still night when Crevan stirs next. Flashlight off, eyes fully adjusted, I have been watching the stars through the broken panes of glass, naming the constellations that I know, making up new names for the ones that I don't. Look, there is the snail. Look, there is the hawk.

"Kit?"

His voice is thin, a faded echo cast by nothing and no one.

"I'm here, baby. Here as here can be." I place a hand to his brow. He is cooler than before, I think. The analgesic must be working. For now, that is enough.

"Am I dying, Kit?"

"We're all dying, Crevan. Every single last one of us. Many of us are dead already." It's not what he means, of course—I know that— but it's all I can answer, all I can dare.

"Were you singing?"

"No. Leastways not now, leastways not tonight."

"I thought I could hear music."

"Of the stars, perhaps. How are you feeling?"

"Don't know. Weak. Head spinning."

"That's because you're sick, baby. That's because your leg's gone nasty infected."

"Kit—"

"But it'll be OK. You'll see. I'm doing everything I can, everything I can think of, to save it. To save you."

He falls very still, his mouth fixing into a grimace. "It's no time for games, Kit."

"No games, no games. You think I'd pretend your leg was at risk if it wasn't?"

"This is serious. Too serious for playing at doctors."

"Who's playing? I've watched you. I've read enough to know what to do—or what to try, at any rate. I'm the best chance we've got, close as we can manage to a real doctor. I can look after you. I can make you better."

"Please, Kit. You know what has to be done."

Of course, I know—at least what he means, at least that he wants me to call the backbiters. But I can't. It's not safe, not safe at all. I can't, I just can't. And it doesn't matter. He doesn't *really* mean it. So there's nothing to really know, no answer to give. I turn my face to the stars. "Actually, I think perhaps I can hear their music too," I say after a moment. "A soft little crooning that twinkle-twinkles

through the night. Is that what it sounds like to you? Is it like this?"
I make a lilting hum that follows no particular melody or rhythm; a
shimmering, uncertain kind of music. Crevan lets out a slow, ragged
breath.

"This is my fault," he says. "If I die--"

"But you won't die. Because I won't allow it. Because I won't let
it happen."

He smiles then. I can see it even through the night, a thing of
bright joy entirely undiminished by his suffering, by his fever, by the
sternness of his last reproach, the desperation of his last unasked
question. I bend on impulse, leaning close to trace his lips with my
fingers, wanting to fix down that smile of his, to paint it in place.
But it fades beneath my touch.

"Am I hurting you?" I ask. "Are you in pain?"

He gives me a long look I cannot read. "No, Kit," he says. "Just
wasn't expecting to have to say goodbye so soon."

And there he goes again, when I've told him expressly that there's
no need, that there will be no dying for him, not today, not on my
watch, not as far as I am implicated, concerned. "If you are feeling
stronger—and you are feeling stronger-er, aren't you?—then we
can try to get you safe and inside, safe and sound, before the day
comes. You'll be more comfortable in your own bed. What do you
think?"

Crevan does not answer, only turns his head among the roots and
peers up at the night sky that lies beyond the branches of the fig,
beyond the broken panes of the greenhouse roof. "I wanted to be an
astronaut, once. Can you imagine what it would be like up there?"

"Staking a flag in the moon? Stamping upon its face?"

"Not like that."

"Floating among the stars? Marveling to see anew what humanity
has watched and measured and mapped for eons past?"

He sighs delight—release--and I am all a-wonder. Crevan has
not talked to me of the stars before. But perhaps it is only fitting.
He is stardust, after all. So am I. So is everyone. Perhaps the little

starry atoms contained in his ribcage—his breastbone, his palate—perhaps they can all sense that a potential end is near, that they have a chance to break free and escape, to return to the heavens from whence they came. Crevan is a thousand, thousand stars netted reluctantly together in human form, and now they are all of them fizzing with excitement, desperate-dying to get free, to go home.

"Perhaps the stars don't enjoy being admired or examined," I say. "Perhaps they resent being seen, being regarded as a mystery to be solved. They are themselves, replete with self-knowledge, with understanding of what it is to be a star. Only our ignorance makes them strange, only our greed makes us want to reach out and devour everything we see."

"Thirst for knowledge, Kit. That's not a sin."

"It's the first sin, the original pattern after which all others are crafted. We never did learn to leave well enough alone." I am fencing, sparring to deflect. Barring the way. Sin was ever a matter of religion, ignorance a virtue extolled by those churches and faiths that have everything to lose and plenty to hide, that rely on believers who ask not, who see not, who accept what they are told and do as they are bid. We are not here religious, Crevan and I, not in that sense at least. We have no just cause to fear knowledge. We should be like the philosophers of old, peering at the shadows on the cave wall and craning around to see what has cast them and how and why and what is that light just beyond, so pale and golden all at once, so like the fire and nothing like it at all? Perhaps, perhaps. Sometimes it is hard to see the harm. Yet I know how dangerous it can be to encourage questions. It wouldn't matter if Crevan would restrain himself to asking only those to which I have no answer, but he is not to be trusted, not anymore. He will ask questions to which I know the answers, answers that I cannot—will not—give. Then we will be stuck. I will have to lie and he will accuse me of it and I will have to deny it and we will argue. And I don't want that now. It is better he does not ask.

"Many of the stars we see are dead already, did you know that? The light takes so long to reach us. We are looking into the past, Crevan. We are watching the history of the galaxy unfold around us."

He soft-clicks his tongue. "Do you think there's someone out there looking back? Seeing the planet as it used to be?"

"Perhaps. Yes. If you want there to be, then there is."

"Do you think they can see us? You and me?"

"If they have a very powerful telescope. Yes, they can see. It's a hundred years from now and they are looking right at us."

"Then we live still, a hundred years from now?"

I hum-hum-trill a three-note laugh. "Yes, if you like. We will be dead here. But the light of this planet travels out for centuries and centuries. We could be seen in it still—if only anyone would care to look—alive in the light, floating on an Earth beam."

Crevan slips his hand into mine and presses. He is weak and the gesture limp, but I hold him firm and squeeze back. "I'm tired, Kit," he says at last.

"Rest. I'll be here."

I keep tight grip of his hand and try not to look as he closes his eyes and surrenders himself once more to sleep. It is not so long before his breathing deepens and slows, before his fingers become slack. He is exhausted from fighting the infection; I should not have let him talk, I should not have encouraged him. Well, he can rest now at any rate—though it's a wonder that he can at all on this hard stone floor, among the tangled roots. I wish I could scoop him up in my arms, carry him back down to bed, make him truly comfortable. But he is too big for me to manage it. I stay with him a little longer, tracking the stars through the sky. Then, certain I will not disturb him, I slide away, stealing from the greenhouse. There are more supplies to fetch, more things I can bring to aid and ease. More water, certainly. More analgesic, syringes, bandages. More alcoholic wipes. As many pillows as I can carry.

Returning, it strikes me how stifling close it is within the green-house, even with a few of the roof panels smashed in. A problem for later, perhaps. For now, I set about tending to Crevan's sleeping body as best I can, moving slow and quiet so as not .to wake him, though he doesn't so much as murmur even when I lift his head to place a pillow underneath.

When the stars are nearly all out and the night is beginning to gray, the fever returns as fiercely as before. I can hear it in the way he is breathing, I can feel it when I touch his skin. Is it that the pain-killers have worn off? Or is the infection getting worse, ready to claim him? I don't know. I give him another shot and hope. I inspect his bandages and see the telltale signs: the bulging, the wriggling, the writhing. The maggots have hatched, the maggots are eating. How long will it take to work? Will it? No, don't ask. It *has* to work. It must. No room for doubters here.

But the hours pass and the sky pales. Crevan's fever isn't abating like it did the last time. It doesn't help that it's so hot in here, so close, so muggy. And only getting worse with every sticky minute. My own clothes are already clinging to me with sweat. It's a prob-lem dealt with easily enough, for our shovels are here, after all, leaning together. Standing, I take one in my grasp and aim the tip of the metal blade at a pane of glass on the far side of the greenhouse from Crevan. The pane smashes easily, noisily, the glass shattering down into the courtyard outside. I break another and another and another, breaking as many as I can to break the hothouse effect of the closed-in greenhouse, to let the air flow and circulate. The glass roof is more of a problem, harder to stove in without danger to all that lies beneath. But a few panes have been hail-broken already and some of those that haven't are on hinges. I get the ladder and climb up to open every panel that can be, then I go back to Crevan and make another flannel compress to place upon his forehead. The air is cooler, certainly, not so close now all that glass-trapped heat has had a chance to dissipate, and it feels a little easier to breathe. But Crevan is sweating as much as ever. And he is no longer asleep, though he is not truly conscious either. His eyes flicker and shut, his head rolls, his mouth gapes open, and every so often nonsense words bubble from his tongue like spittle.

"Crevan? Can you hear me? Crevan?" My one hand grips his chin, my other strokes his hair as I kneel beside him, making my urgent demand. "I need you to stay with me. I need you to hold on. Please, Crevan. Please, please, please."

But he does not respond—leastways, not in any way that is intelligible, not in any way that I can understand or interpret. I don't know what to do. I'm out of options and at the limit of my medical supplies and knowledge. There's nothing to do but wait and hope.

Or that's what I'd like to believe, what I've been telling myself all along. But in truth there is another option still: a last recourse, a final chance to save Crevan's life. To end mine.

The backbiters.

It's not that I owe it to him—he knew the stakes and what he was getting into, what was at risk. It's that he will die if I do nothing. And I can't, I won't. To hell with me and what will happen after— it's the here and now that matters. It's all there is, and not a second nor inch beyond. That's the point. That was always the point. And it's my turn now. I have to be daddy, I have to be mummy. I have to take care of baby.

I croon forward, press my lips to Crevan's cheek, inhale the deep, sweat-musk odor of him. I hover my mouth at his ear. "Hold on, Crevan. It's going to be all right. I promise."

Then I am gone, then I fly. Away again, to the den again. I have come up and down these stairs more times in the last twelve hours than I have in the last week. But I cannot feel the ache of it in my legs, my feet, my back—not separate from the ache of knowing what I must do, what will happen. Cannot tell if my heart is racing from the exertion or the fear. Perhaps I am already too late. Pray that I am, pray that I am not.

All too soon—and not at all soon enough—I am at the wardrobe. My eyes skim over the leering faces of the goblin men carved on the door, my hands reach, open, search among the sweaters. And there it is, just as I knew it would be, just where I left it.

The satellite phone.

Will it work? Will it ring through to who I need? Who I hope, who I fear? Who will come to save Crevan's life and perhaps take my own? I turn it on, pull up the antenna. Notice, for the first time, what I did not see before, what I did not let myself see: the initials—NBM—stamped along the base.

I dial the last number called and hold the phone to my ear. It rings twice. Then a voice I wish I did not know and cannot bring myself to name answers. It is familiar; deep, melodious. It belongs not to a backbiter after all, not at all, but to someone far, far worse—someone I forgot, someone I did not let myself remember. Every syllable it utters hammers on the splinter in my heart, threatening to split me open. It belongs to—no, I cannot say it, do not make me say it.

"Finally. Where have you been? We were expecting your last report more than a week ago."

I search for the words and they come not. Only breath and breath and breath.

"Hello?" says the voice. "Are you there?"

"He's sick. Really sick. I think he might be dying. You have to help."

For a moment, silence. "Nikita?"

"Please. You have to come get him. Now."

"Yes, of course, but—"

"Now!" I am screaming into the receiver. It's as much as I can take, I am at capacity. One word more, one sentence, and I will fizzle, snap, break. I hang up the call and throw the satphone across the room. Protected by its thick rubber case, it bounces off the wall unharmed and falls to the floor. The moment it lands, it starts to ring; a violent mechanic buzz that's impossible to ignore. I don't know more whether I want to stamp on the satphone or to scoop it up and answer the call. But maybe more information is needed, maybe I have not said enough, not done enough to save Crevan. I pick up the satphone and hit the green button.

"He's in the greenhouse," I say hurriedly, speaking before the voice can. "He hurt his leg and the wound got infected. I tried to help but it didn't work. He has a fever. He is delirious. He needs help now, now, now. He needs backbiters."

"Backbiters? Oh—you mean . . . I see. I'm sending a helicopter. It will be there within ten minutes."

"Good."

"And you, Nikita, are you all right? What's happened? Do you need anything?"

"Don't ask me, don't ask me, don't ask me."

"Do you want me to send someone for you?"

"I'm going now. Goodbye." This time when I hang up the satphone, I turn it off as well. No more calls. No more, no more. I stay where I stand, stuck. Half of me desperate to run back to Crevan, the other half intent on dragging me into the wardrobe to wait this out, to hide away until the helicopter has come and gone.

If I stay here, I will not get to say goodbye. If I go, I will have to face the pilot and the invading party. I will have to face being seen. It's different, you see, allowing that a thing will happen and watching it unfold, actually being there. And I have done my part, have I not? I have given Crevan what he is owed: I have suspended my will, my embargo upon the outside world, itself long since resurrected. I have called for help, I have called the gray suits, I have called the backbiters, such as they are. I have admitted that our way of life on the island is not the way of the world beyond, that we are at odds, that Crevan will be better off not here, not now. It's enough. It has to be enough.

Only it's too much, and everything breaks.

ALL THE DAY LONG
WE ARE KILLED

For a slivering space—the breadth of a moment, the depth of a lifetime—I am become nothing; seeing not, feeling not. Just nothing, inside and out. Nothing sensible anyway, nothing rational. Just a snap-crack of static or a gust of wind tracking across grass or the shimmer of heat over unfolding blue. Where there should be thought, only synapse; where there should be spirit, only aorta.

And then, and then. I don't know how it happens. It could be a rebirth. It could be death. Maybe both. I don't know how long it takes, but I start to return to myself. Or, rather, a piece of consciousness that may or may not be mine comes to occupy the body that, in days past, I may or may not have counted as my own. And it is clinging to a single word—choking on it, crying over it—a word that is a name, a name that is Crevan.

He is gone, I remember. He is gone and will not come back; either dead, either free. Both perhaps, depending on your angle. I called. I remember that much. I called and had him taken away. To save his life. To destroy mine.

Again.

———

It had nothing to do with me, you understand; it never did. I was just there, just by chance, just standing by; collateral, cannon fodder. It's not like you can pick your parents, after all, not like you can choose your carers, your mothers, your fathers, your guardians. They just happen to you. You get no say, no second opinion, no backup, no way out. And mine were the worst, mine were the best; the kind that were angels once, the kind that were demons. They blazed bright and then they fell from grace. It's always the way. No matter if the wings are waxed or feathered-real, they always fall, always drop, dive; always pitch down, down and fatally collide, a mess of broken bones and dreams. And mine soared higher than most; mine fell farther, fell harder.

The first of the backbiters.

Not that they were—are—called that, not that they appear or behave in quite the way I have painted them. But perhaps you already know, perhaps you have seen them for yourself; the dull prose to belie the myth. My parents the first, the pattern for all others that followed. The minds that thought, the hands that shaped and crafted.

They were only trying to help.

What I know is simply what they told me. They told me and I listened, they told me and I paid attention, committed it all to memory, to heart; everything they said about bacterial evolution—which itself too happened and happens in a more mundane fashion than I would have it, than I have let on—about the antibiotic of last resort failing and of what had come before, about the drugs in the pig feed, in the water table, about the medications no longer efficacious on those living in densely populated urban centers. I took it on myself to learn. I wanted to know and to understand. I wanted to make them proud. I wanted to carry the truth, because that seemed like something I could do, some way I could help, a responsibility I could take on, a duty I could shoulder. Yet despite my efforts, all I have now are a few shadow-snatches of half-forgotten memories; facts—nothing more. Probably a great deal less.

———

Backbiters. That was the first corruption, a name malformed by truncation and substitution, taking anodyne fact and turning it into coarse slur that even now can be easily exposed, reversed: back-biters stemming from backeaters, and before that backphages, and before that again (at last, at first) bacteriophages. In other words, viruses; parasites that infect and replicate within specific bacteria, pathogenic to their host cells, harmless to us.

That was their intervention, you see, the cure they proffered, their revolutionary contribution to the field of medicine, to the fight against bacterial infection and antimicrobial resistance; their gift to the world developed and developing still: phage therapy. An old technique by all accounts, though overlooked and little understood—at least until my parents decided otherwise. It was they who developed the means of reliably harvesting and harness-ing these microbial allies to fend off our own bacterial adversaries, both prophylactically and therapeutically, to prevent and to cure; they who discovered that phage therapy worked where antibiot-ics had long since ceased to, had long since failed. And the phages proved superior in every sense, for they evolve just as do the bacte-ria they devour, and—each phage being specific and fastidious in its tastes—they none of them lay needless waste to the rest of a body's microbiome. Bacteriophages. They, in their multitudinous variety, were the solution that my parents delivered and for which they were then cursed, for which they were hounded, for which they were so pejoratively named.

The patches, they were just a bonus; devices that could be admin-istered with no training whatsoever and even to the weakest, the smallest, the most fragile with no ill-effect; devices that marked who was safe—protected—and who was not, no databases to be lost or corrupted, no easy way to fake out the system. And it worked. It worked when all else had been lost; when medicine, such as it was once known, had been all but forsaken. It works even yet, even now; however I have been ignoring it, however I have been hiding it from myself, from you.

So there you have it: my parents, the backbiters. I was so amazed by them, so dazzled. I remember that now. The world had collapsed—or was at least swaying wildly upon the edge of so doing—and then it wasn't, and then we were saved. The cities began to be rebuilt and order to be reinstated, reinstituted; our health by piecemeal restored.

For a time—for a spell—we were happy. I was delighted, aflame with pride and eager to be patched myself, just as soon as my turn came. I can still recall that sensation of being overcome, overwhelmed by what my parents had done and were yet striving to do—but what I remember best of them is the unexceptional workaday: my mother swooping me up into her arms and saying with wild affection that she was going to eat me; my father singing to me in gruff but enthusiastic baritone, transmuting his latest earworm into lullaby; the pair of them stooped together over the terrarium—a shared and favorite pastime—pointing out to me the carnivorous sundews and bladderworts. These were the souls who did this remarkable thing, who set themselves to the task with quiet determination and devotion, bent on taking care of everyone and not just themselves, not just me. For a space it was heaven, idyll, bliss. And then fate spun her wheel (as she is wont to do, as she is always wont to do) and we were cast out; out of the garden, black spots all.

———

The first I knew of it—of that sorry turn in our fortune, our lots—were the furrowed brows and whispered conversations; tense-terse debates snatched at strange hours and out of earshot when I was supposed to be busy, when I was supposed to be sleeping. (My father: *It's getting out of hand.* My mother: *It can't last, it can't last—we keep boxing on.*) I would hear their resolve—determination—and parse it wrong, reverse-wise: if they did not seem afraid, it was because there was nothing to fear, *could* be nothing to fear.

I only realized the truth when the slur—*backbiters*—appeared, daubed in dripping letters across the brickwork of our house. I remember a hum dying on my father's lips at the sight, my mother's hands shaking as she scrubbed at the crude graffiti. It wasn't long before it reappeared, of course, the same stale slur scrawled afresh. For a time, it was a near-daily affront—finding new letters glaring down from where the old had only just been cleaned away—but after a while it became merely routine, just another task to add to an ever-growing list of the things my parents did to keep us all decorous and content.

We could have coped if that were the height of it, the worst to come—to fear. Yet no sooner had we found and made our peace than handwritten threats began to worm their way into our home: an infestation of promised violence, precisely worded warnings that ranged from the oblique to the lasciviously detailed and deranged. Most came through the mail. One came through a downstairs window, tied to a brick. Well, you know what they say. Sometimes the old ways are the best.

There were other gifts too. One morning we woke to find the bins upended and their contents scatter-smeared across the lawn, another to find a brace of crows on the front step, poor little corvids, necks wrung and feathers all at horrid angles. And that was before public patching began in earnest. They came not long after that—following in the wake of their foul calling cards—the protesting mob, choleric and snarling, armed with prayers and biblical quotations, with placards and rotten fruit. They screamed, they wept; they bayed for blood, for satisfaction, for sacrifice. Perhaps they feared the resurrected hospitals and surgeries that they had, long ago, learned to distrust and shun. Perhaps they simply feared what they did not know and could not readily understand. They told stories to one another, to the street, to anyone who would listen. Stories that I heard, stories about the bad-evil-nasty backbiters and the bad-evil-nasty things that they did, that they would do to you, that they would do to your children if you let them. Infecting them with actual viruses when everyone knows that viruses kill dead, kill nasty.

It got worse. We got trapped; bounded by a crowd so thick and violent it was impossible to pass through no matter if you were coming or going. They chanted at all hours to stop us from sleeping. They battered the walls with clubs and broke in all our windows lest we forget our lives were in their hands, were in their gift. They shouted threats, sprayed more paint, left feces in brown paper bags on the doorstep.

One day, they got hold of something brightly colored and appealing—a red polyester T-shirt—and laced it with corrosives before neatly folding it into an envelope and pushing it into the mailbox.

And it was addressed to me. To me, to me, to me.

To me, even though I was a child of ten; to me, even though I had done nothing wrong, nothing at all, nothing but exist, nothing but be born to those whom such people deplored, whom such people loathed.

———

The acid burnt my skin, ate holes in the epidermis of my shoulders and chest—and that of my mother's palms when she tore the T-shirt away to save me. I remember seeing the fabric begin to dissolve in her hands, remember it even more clearly than the pain that, ever since, my body will not—cannot—let me fully recall.

So fall the sins of the father.

———

And so we came to the island. My parents must have bought it long before then, must have seen the way the wind was blowing and taken precautions; bought the den from some clear-sighted proven-right prepper who'd used it to see out the world's collapse and eventual restoration. They had the place restocked, refurnished, the defenses reinforced. It's not like they didn't have the money, not like they didn't make a bundle, a fortune, a killing. And it's all there still, tied up in charter and screed, in policy, process, and procedure. Nikita Bio-Medical, latterly NBM. Yes, that one; yes, named after me— their child and pride in one.

It must have made me easy to hate, bearing that name; easy for unsettled, fearful minds to strip me of innocence's protection, to see me not as incidental but ancillary, to set me as the target.

And perhaps, after all, they were right. Perhaps I deserved what I got.

Even if, even so, coming to the island should have been the end of it. That was the plan, anyway. We precious few disappear, go into hiding; we weather the storm, wait for the inclement spell to pass. Then, and only then, do we return to the land of the living; safe, forgotten, invisible. That's how it should have happened, that's how it should have gone. Better still, it should have been adventure, it should have been exploration. We were to become Swallows, Amazons; to become Robinsons Crusoe, marooned on an island of our very own, one that would keep us out of danger, one that would bring us storybook excitement. But fate was not done with us yet. She had other plans, other cards, and could not be stopped from playing them, from triumphant laying down her hand and raking up her winnings, her pound of sorry flesh.

It happened all of a day: a day when it seemed enough time had passed; a day when being cooped up became unbearable, the limit, the end; a day when the mainland beckoned; a day when—still bandaged in hydrocolloid—I was playing scaredy-cat and would not come with; a day when it was deemed—for the very first time—that I was just healed enough and just old enough now to be left behind, left alone, to look after my lonesome self; a day when they wouldn't be long; a day when they went; a day when they didn't come back.

Perhaps there was celebration after, perhaps there was cheer. The land had been purged of evil, the first of the backbiters slain. Rejoice, rejoice. I do not know. There had been attacks before, of course; kidnappings before, killings before. There was fear behind it—fear driving the violence—fear and grief, fear and anger, fear and fantasy. It's always been the way. Backbiters were doctors once, as I have said before. They were nurses, paramedics, midwives. They each of them knew what it meant to risk life and limb, to be asked to do it, to ask it of themselves from day to live-long day; to care for the infected and infectious; to withstand the abuse that drips venomous from the tongues of the sick, the bereaved, the misinformed; to be braced for the coming assault, for fists, for knives, for bricks, bleach, bullets. And still they pressed on, determined, set on saving those who would not save themselves. It's a thing to behold, to praise, to stand in awe of. And yet, and yet. I can't but wish my parents had been weak-willed rather than strong, recreants instead of heroes. Because heroes die, heroes always die.

The first I heard about what happened was when someone in a suit with an NBM pin in the lapel came to explain, came to fetch me. But I would not go, would not anything but stay where I was, alone with my sorrowed anguish, my fear; alone in the emptiness of the den where my parents would never again give breath or laugh or quiet censure.

And so I stayed, and so I was alone; disconsolate, keeping silent vigil for those who had been my entire world and now were only memory. In return, their shadows danced footloose about me: my father standing barefoot on the carpet, pretending for my entertainment to conduct some grand, invisible orchestra as music played about us; my mother peering at me as I asked my hows and whys, saying *Come on, let's look it up* and easing an encyclopedia from the shelf; the two of them sitting together and talking late into the night, the murmuring rhythm of their words gentle and reassuring as I dropped to sleep.

It was too, too much—more than enough to break a child for good (for worse) forever. And yet, and yet. I might have survived, might have coped, if theirs had been the only loss to bear.

———

And I must say it now, at last, coward that I am—I must admit, confess to those lives I've been keeping hidden, keeping from myself: the three bodies that once lay and should still lie in the bunks adjoining mine, the three souls—small and shining—that I once knew and prized more dearly than my own. My two sisters, my baby brother.

Dead, every one.

Only not gone, not entirely, because they are all here, buried inside of me, trapped: their names, their faces, the way they laughed and played and fought. My two sisters, so close in age and look, whispering their secrets to one another in a laughing-lilting patois of their own invention. My brother, the littlest of us, waddling around after our parents like a flightless bird—each arm crooked into a folded wing—just waiting to be noticed, picked up, fussed over. All three piled together into my bunk and growing drowsy as I read to them from our increasingly dog-eared copy of *The Swiss Family Robinson*.

I carry them with me still, their echoing shadow-souls. I'm a perpetual cradle, a walking tomb, a fig heavy with wasps, a CD etched with forgotten melodies. I'm all they've got, all that's left—and they are all I have. I need them. I need them and they are killing me. I need them and they want to get free, but I won't let them escape, won't let them go—not this time. I'll keep them here, keep them safe; their memories untouched, preserved, protected. Leastways that was the plan, leastways that was what I hoped before everything got broken open. Now it's scattered about me like sharded glass—the world I left behind, what happened and what did not, who I was then and who I have come to be.

———

Do you blame me now? Now that you understand, now that you know? Do you call me liar and cry villainy? Do you hold me accused of faking—of posturing, of shamming and being a pretender? I would not wonder if you did; would not be affronted, surprised, dismayed. For I have played inventor, after all, I have played creator. I have played god and now I am slain, as surely as my parents did and were. They pulled a dreaming from their heads and made it real, made it breathe, made it sing, made it corporeal, incorporated; a slavering, hungry beast. Now I have done the same, here in this small corner of the world that I have to shape and maintain, this one place where I thought that everything could make sense, could be *made* to make sense. I dreamt it up—or maybe it dreamt me. It's hard to tell, hard to be sure. It has grown quite beyond the bounds of what I imagined, like it's been working under its own steam, to its own plan; marching to its own obscene beat.

But never mind, never mind. Whether I made it or not, willed it or not, it was what I needed, what I wanted: a dream, dream, fantasy, nightmare; a hell-pit oasis; a counterfactual, an alternative; a rationalization that made sense when real reality failed me, failed my parents, my sisters, my brother.

Oh, but there was beauty in it; there was genius—the true stretched to furnish and explain the false. If a survivor I must be, then a survivor I was but of a better class: one forged and tempered only by general calamity rather than particular tragedy, personal and brutish. If it was only me here, only me on the island, then it was because the world beyond was still destroyed, because the world beyond was eaten, because the world beyond was dead and dying in a manner yet more extreme than that in existence and fact, than that wrought by the certain calamities that had befallen it, from which it had even then begun to recover.

Was it so wrong to embellish, to exaggerate? If a T-shirt could burn and corrode like that, why shouldn't I provide some explanation, some way to make it fit, to make sense? I would rather plastiphages than acid, rather the unthinking hunger of fictional synthetic-devouring microbials than the senseless brutality of real, bad-hearted souls. If the backbiters were hated, spurned, attacked, I would rather it was because they deserved it—deserved the fear, the wrath—deserved it because they were evil like everyone always said; the bogeymen that lurk, the night terrors to run from and flee. And so I turned them into villains that killed and culled, that deployed crumbling, infectious equipment; that used violent means and deserved to be met with the same, deserved to be shunned and stamped out.

A peace descends as I think of it, as I remember how it was—how it should have been—and for a moment I am settled, for a moment I am all right, safe in the still quiet of a world that makes sense, where everything fits together, where I can parse what is written and understand. But then it shifts, but then it falls. It does not last, cannot last, not now everything's been torn and opened. Not now he too is gone. Crevan, my Crevan. The provision that was made for me when it became clear I could not leave, could not face the world beyond, could not find my place within it as it continued to be rebuilt. Someone to watch me, to mind me, to protect me from the shadows, from myself, from what is in my heart, from what I have seen.

But he is gone. Gone as though he never was, gone as though he wasn't ever here in the first place. And it's just like the last time, like the worst time, like the day they none of them came home, even though I tried to fix it, even though I tried to make it right. I did, I swear, I did. The best I could, the only way I knew how. But it didn't work. It didn't work and now I am lost all over again, shattered again, coming apart again. All that I had repaired and rectified, all that I had mended, all that I had carefully pieced back together with wishes and string; it is broken now, quite broken. And here I am in the midst of the destruction, here I am returned once more to the no-good nothing that I am, that I always was: a line sketch; a crude stick figure; an accidental reflection of a face that is not mine, that I do not recognize, whose gaze cannot be met.

CONSIDERED IN
HIS OWN CONTRACT

I do not leave the den again, not for—oh, I don't know how long. I am not counting, not anymore. It is easiest that way. I just stay where I am, where I was put, taking refuge in the knowledge that no one else can get at me here with the blast door shut, no matter who may be roaming the island overhead. And I do not want to see anybody. So here I remain, satphone off, poured concrete demarcating—for the time being at least—the outer limits of my existence. Not only do I remain within the den, but I rarely venture beyond even the edges of the living room. The sofa doubles as my bed, as my reading seat, as my dining table. I stay there for long hours—sometimes sitting upright with a book in my lap, sometimes slouched so low I am practically horizontal and can rest a bowl or a mug level on my stomach. If I stand, it is only briefly—to fetch something from the galley kitchen, from the storeroom, to visit the bathroom. I do not stray past the dividing screen, do not go to my old bunk, do not enter the master bedroom, not even to sit in the wardrobe. I do not wash, I do not brush my teeth. I pay no heed to the ration plan. Some days, no food passes my lips. Others, I cannot stop myself from eating. Probably it all balances out in the end. Anyway, it doesn't matter. Crevan's gone now. They all are. I am alone.

I do not know what is happening out on the island—or if anything is happening there at all. Sometimes I think I hear things, but then that is impossible; buried as I am, sheltered as I am. It must be in my head, all in my head. Apart from that one time when someone does come and knock on the blast door, fist hammering steel, shouting *Nikita, Nikita, Nikita*, like they actually think I'm going to answer. The voice is muffled but booming. It could be the same voice I spoke to on the satphone. It could belong to someone else entirely. I ignore it, making no answer but to put on one of my CDs and turn the volume up, way, way up, until there's nothing but noise. Not so much a tree in a forest as a clamor in a din. It is pandemonium, it is racket, it is LOUD. The kind of beat that you feel first, that you hear in your patella—your spine, your scapula—long, long before it reaches your ears. Which is good. I can't hear my heart over it, I can't hear the sound of my own breath. And even the little phantom whelp that birthed itself in my brain all those years ago and lingers there now scream-weep-howling for Crevan—for my mother, my father, my sisters, my brother—seems muted beneath the music. The melodies flood, Lethean. The rhythms drown.

Only when I turn the music off—when the person on the other side of the blast door has got tired and given up and gone away—the whelp is there still, bedraggled but as wild as ever before. It is hardy: the rat that adapts, the cockroach that endures nuclear Armageddon. Perhaps it will be with me always; a personal curse, my own self-grown hellhound, this suckling vampire that saps my will and replaces it with despair and yet more despair. Perhaps it will grow tired of me—though it never has yet. Only lying used to silence it, only fairy tale and forget. Now there's not much left that makes the grim pup quiet, not much that I can do. Sleep, yes, though he doesn't like letting me do that and sometimes chases me there in dreams and nightmares. Loud, loud, music, yes—though, after a while, it makes my head hurt too and I have to turn it off. Reading doesn't work, though I try often. My eyes simply slip off the page like there are no words there at all, nothing to catch at, nothing to hang on to. Sometimes eating brings silence, but not always and then it's worse—much, much worse—to be shedding tears into a can of rehydrated macaroni than to be simply crying on the sofa.

There are some tricks that are more reliable; mainly, bundling myself up very small and hiding beneath a blanket. Sometimes, if I am lucky, I can stare off into the distance in just the right way, with my eyes unfocused like so, and every thought and sound and whimper will drop out of my head. When that happens, I am careful not to twitch or fidget. I stay like that for hours. Not thinking, not doing, not hearing. It is all the relief I am allowed.

And then, and then. The blast door opens. It has not my say-so nor my permission nor goodwill, and yet it opens all the same; ajar, a crack, a fraction. I stay where I am, half-buried among the cushions of the sofa, too tired now to be afraid, too desperate to hide. There was a master key, I remember now—a skeleton—left in the possession of NBM, left in case of emergencies. Is that what this is? An emergency? Are they coming to get me at last? To take me away?

The door opens wider; admits stale air, the beam of a flashlight, a woman. A woman with short, sensible hair and flat, sensible shoes. Her suit and smile are both neatly pressed, smooth beyond scrutiny, beyond reproach. On her lapel is a small enamel pin bearing the old, familiar logo and the letters you'd expect, sound them out one by one: en-bee-bloody-em.

"Good morning, Nikita." Her voice is deep, melodious, instantly recognizable. She is the woman from the satphone, a creature of boardrooms and brisk efficiency. Our benefactors'—my parents'—earthly representative. My memory unwitting dredges up a name for that round, impassive face of hers. Yes, that was it. Grace. The for-what-we-are-about-to-receive kind, the hail-Mary-full-of kind, the patience-is-a-virtue kind.

"You shouldn't be here," I croak, sad little frog that I am. "You can't, you're not supposed—"

Grace holds up a hand, cutting through my protests and conducting me to silence; a maestro at work. "There is urgent business to attend. Once we have seen to it, I shall leave you in peace." She gives me wary regard, waiting for refusal, for tantrum, for tears. Would that I could give her the satisfaction, that I could perform, that I could so easily invoke these simplest and most selfish of reactions, of sentiments. But I only sit where I am, neither engaging nor ignoring, neither refusing nor allowing. It suffices, it is enough. Grace gives a curt nod of her head and lifts a briefcase I did not realize she is carrying. She unclips it, hinges open the lid, pulls out a thin file.

"Your minder reported a death."

That takes me aback, unawares; enough to make me start where I sit, enough to make my eyes fly wide. *Crevan.* "He's alive?"

"Yes. Hospitalized still but recovering well." She speaks the words as though they mean nothing, as though she is merely commenting on the weather, as though they are not the beginning and ending of everything. Crevan. He lives. My Crevan, oh my Crevan.

"As I was saying," she continues, dogged, determined, "he reported a death." At this point she flicks open her file and scans the first page. "According to his account, he had accompanied you on an excursion to the sea wall when an unknown woman swam ashore and attempted to attack you. He claims to have stepped in at once to fight this assailant off and, in the course of so doing, knocked her to the ground. She badly hit her head, lost consciousness, and, shortly thereafter, her life. Deciding there was nothing more to be done, he states that he left the body there, thinking first to take care of you—his charge—and return you to the safety of the bunker. By the time he came back to the sea wall to retrieve the body, it had been carried away by the tide." Now she looks up, eyes keen, eyes piercing. "Can you confirm that this is what happened?"

I do not think, do not hesitate, not for a moment. "Yes."

The effect is immediate. I see it at once, the tension that leaves the cast of her shoulders, the tightness that slips from her mouth.

"Good," she says. "It'll be hard for anyone to prove otherwise until the body can be found, and there's not much hope of that. The coastal waters are being dredged, of course, but the search will have to be called off soon—the weather won't hold much longer. It never does, these days. Besides, there's not much public appetite for it, not after everything your family's been through. And given the assailant's background——" She breaks off, sees the alarm-surprise-disquiet marked upon my face, adopts a kindlier tone; confiding and intimate. "Of course, we can't be sure that it *was* her, but the description your minder gave is a close match for a missing person. I understand she had one or two key identifying features. A cleft lip, if I'm not mistaken?"

And here there is yet more light in the murk, a term for that which I thought termless.

"Yes, a cleft lip," says Grace again, providing her own confirmation in the face of my silence. "It's easily enough repaired—the surgery was long ago added to the list of procedures that can once more be safely conducted. But just as well for us that she would never have agreed to treatment or we'd have a hard time identifying her. She was a known hostile, Nikita, a member of the same cell responsible for the deaths of your family. The authorities are of the opinion that she intentionally set out for the island with the purpose of, well, finishing the job. I am inclined to agree. How she got past the sea defenses is another matter that we will be investigating in due course. For now, I am only glad that your minder was there to protect you."

So.

So I was right and Crevan was wrong. The woman was dangerous to us—to me—the woman wished me dead, the woman wished to kill me. We should have let her drown, I knew it all along. It was Crevan who should have known better, Crevan who should never have pulled her from the waves, who should never have tried to save her life. Little solace that is to me now, little comfort. Besides, I am being unfair, unkind. He could not have known what she was, not really. All he saw was a body in the water: a human, not a threat. And yet, and yet. Should not he have spied her for what she was? Should not I? She had no patches, after all, not one. That should have been enough to go by, to judge; that deprivation we shared, that telling absence that marked us both for what we were—are—I, who loved my parents, and she, who hated them still.

Grace busily sorts through her file, seemingly unperturbed and unconcerned, untroubled at having had to deliver me this news of all news. But after all, why not; she has brought far fouler tidings before, against which this is nothing, against which this is ordinary dull. And this woman is not the first and will not be the last, you can count on that.

Adjusting her grip on the file, Grace pulls a sheet from the back and holds it out to me along with a pen. "I took the liberty of preparing a statement for you to sign, corroborating your minder's account."

I do not move, do not raise my hands to take the offered page. "What will happen to him?"

"He will be tried for manslaughter. It's somewhat unfortunate that he has previous—although, of course, it's part of what made him so attractive a hire. But given the mitigating circumstances and that he has, so far, been most cooperative, I don't expect he will receive a particularly punitive sentence on this occasion. A few years at most."

"You mean he's not coming back?"

"No, I'm sorry. We shall have to recruit a new minder for you. Again. Not to mention replacing the greenhouse."

"Oh."

"We should perhaps also discuss whether or not you wish to remain on the island."

My response to this is knee-jerk and insistent: the only one I can give, could ever possibly give. "I'm staying here."

She is all indifference. "Very well. Then there is only the matter of your signature." She thrusts forward the paper and pen. I take them both, squinting uncertain at the printed words, the letters typeset close and small. They blur and shift beneath my gaze, unreadable beyond the half-remembered imaginings of Crevan that dance across my mind, before my eyes. A stroke of the pen and I condemn him, a stroke of the pen and he is lost to me forever.

But if I do not sign, what then? Will his story be so readily believed? Will he be blamed for murder rather than manslaughter? Will suspicion turn to me? He is trying to protect me from that, I know it, trying to make amends, trying to undo the terrible wrong that he wrought when he rescued the drowned woman from the waves. This is his fault, after all. He should never have saved her. Failing that, he should never have got himself hurt. If he hadn't, I wouldn't have had to call and save his life and so smash mine own upon the rocks. Yes, this is his fault. Even if he didn't know who she was, even if he didn't know that she wanted to kill me. So I am justified, surely, in holding my tongue, in letting him take the fall, allowing him to take the blame. And yet, and yet. He could walk free. My Crevan. I need only come forward, need only speak the truth, need only explain what happened and point them to her grave.

I sign my name and hand back the paper. Grace slips it into the file and the file into the briefcase. She straightens her collar, tucks a stray hair neatly behind her ear, makes a smart about-turn, clean as any soldier on parade. She's halfway to the blast door when she stops, when she falters.

"Nikita?"

The word comes quiet, comes low, comes tremor-trembling. It means something. Guilt, perhaps. Concern, maybe, or care. I do not know and do not answer. It is not my name, not anymore. Steadying herself on my silence, Grace's level head prevails.

"There are additional supplies in the service tunnel under the keep, should your own stores fall short. Call me on the satellite phone if there's anything you need. Oh, and there is this—"

These last words are an afterthought, as much a surprise to her as they are to me. She reaches into the pocket of her suit jacket and takes out a small envelope. A few steps back across the floor and she awkward drops it in my lap. Then she leaves, then she is gone.

I stare at the envelope, a dull, off-white rectangle with my name written across the front in blue ink; the hand untidy, scrawling. I know it at once.

Crevan.

I don't want to look. I must.

Taking up the envelope—so slight within my grasp—I pinch the sides and tip out that which lies within: a single hairband, navy elastic adorned with a red ribbon bow.

It is not mine—not *hers*—that pristine bow is quite the wrong size, quite the wrong shape. Still. It means Crevan noticed, it means he knew—knows—what I did.

But stay, perhaps this token does not mean blame, does not mean accusation. Not given what he has done, how he has sought to protect me from even beyond the island. Perhaps it is simply a warning to be careful. Better yet, a granting of forgiveness, an admission of collusion, an apology, a promise to keep on keeping me safe. If he were here, I could ask; if he were here, I could explain. But he is not. I am alone, quite alone. Crevan is not coming back, Crevan is gone.

Only he is not. He is not, he is not, he is not. No, I will not have it. Not now, not today. I snap the hairband onto my wrist. He is here, look! Here in this token and here all over the den; in every inch of it a memory, a mark of who and how he was. I am determined now, I am set, animated. I seek them out, one by one—the signs of him—meager scraps that do not touch sides, that cannot hope to fill this glutton's stomach. I look and find him everywhere: among the bandages and medical equipment that has yet to be tidied away; in the red-gold hairs I pick from my sweater's weave; in how the cans are stacked inside the kitchen cupboards; in the space beside me where he ought to sit; in the spines of the books that he liked best; the jewel cases of the CDs that he knew how to sing along to—how to dance along to—with me, with me, with me; in the phantom steps that seem to dog, follow, track my every move through the den. Don't look, it isn't him. It can't be.

The hunger is sudden; severe. I am desperate for Crevan. So compelled, I leave the sanctuary of the sofa and go to his room, bent on examining every part of it, every fraction. I find his scent on the pillow, his fingerprints dulling the polish on the wardrobe doors. He is everywhere, everywhere and I have to slide under the bed to make it stop, to get away from him, from myself, to catch my breath. Only it's no good, no good at all, because Crevan is there as well, even among the dust and shadows. I can see him true—and in furious, frustrated glory—where he has carved out his anger and despair notch by notch into the baseboard. The scrawling of a madman, perhaps, or the testament of a saint. His own name and mine carved a thousand, thousand times, in some places careful painstaking engraved amid a starry field of pentacles, in others jagged and violent scratched out.

I never knew he had done this.

Mind's eye paints him in next to me where I lie, an image of Crevan stretched out beneath the bed, half-cocked and propped up on his elbows, both hands grasped around a penknife, his beautiful features fixed into the hard lines of penitent concentration as he performs the rite of himself, as he tries to keep a hold of what he must and must not do, of who he is, of who he really is.

My throat tightens, constricts. For a space, I try to think of nothing but breathing, of counting. *One, two, three. One, two, three.* Again.

The seconds pass. Nothing worse happens—nothing better, either—but it gets a little easier at least, gets a little quieter in my head, enough that I can look once more at the scritch-scratch scrawling, can reach a hand to touch the lines of his name where it is etched into the wood. Poor, poor baby. I didn't mean for him to take it so hard. I didn't mean for any of this to happen. He was always so good to me, always so careful to watch what he said, to adapt it to fit into the reality I have built. Not that he was much good at telling stories, not that he had the knack; not without my help anyway, not without my flourishes and elaborations. But he cannot be blamed for that, not when he was at such great pains to keep himself in check, to never give breath to a single word that might break this shield I have made, that might bite through this wadding of story I have shrouded about me, that I have wrapped around the island. And all this time it was hurting him; it was pain and burden, pain and woe.

It wounds, it makes my heart light. I am split as ever I was: tormented that he would keep a part of himself hidden from me, overwhelmed that he would bury his cares to keep me safe from shatter-clatter calamity. My sugar-sweet, caustic-cruel Crevan.

And now he is gone, and now he will never come back. And it's no good saying it was his fault, it was his fault, because it was mine all along; my warped reality that pushed him to the edge, that he was trying to defend; my actions and deeds that, even now, he is taking on as burden, that he will atone for, serve time for, be blamed for, forever; forever marked on his record, forever etched into the story of his life. Crevan, Crevan, poor sweet Crevan. Protecting me to the last, to the end—far, far beyond the bounds of what was called for, of what was required. And now I have to learn how to do without him, how to be glad of his absence.

This is too much still, altogether too much. I must get up and out of the dust, out from beneath this empty bed. I slip-slide out and away, go curl myself up tight in a corner, chin capping knees, arms binding shins, holding myself together, dreaming of Crevan.

What would he say if he were here? *Get up, Kit*, or something like that, something muttered abrupt in his habitual gruff grace. Or perhaps *Goodbye*, perhaps *Try not to worry*. Perhaps how he was going to be all right and how he wished he could come and see me again soon. Wouldn't he? I wonder, I wonder; I cannot help but. I close my eyes and imagine; I close my eyes and see. It is easy—easy as breathing, easy as one, two, three—for this is the one thing I know how to do, the one thing in which I am practiced, the one thing in which I am expert.

It happens just like that. I can glimpse, hear, scent him beside me; feel the taut, warm strength of his arms about me; the softness of his lips pressed to my hair; the whispering rush as he murmurs and comforts; pausing now and then to click-click his tongue; telling me how glad he was to come to the island; how he cherished every moment we spent together, just like I did, like I always will; how he doesn't think he's ever known another living soul in the way he's known mine, in the way he's known me; how he wishes he could return; how much he wants to come and get me, how it breaks his heart that he cannot; how nothing matters so long as I am safe; how he'll always be waiting for me, hoping he'll be able to come and find me again one day, one day when he's free; how whether he sees me again or no, he will always, always be mine. Click, click, click.

And then I open my eyes, and then he is gone; as sure as if I made him up, as sure as if he never was, as sure as all the rest.

THAT THE SUN COULD
STAND STILL

The days pass. I slip through them all or they slip through me, neither of us making much mark upon the other. Then it happens. I blink, blink, swallow. Feel the crust of tears and sleep and snot on my face. The fur on my teeth and tongue. The way my clothes are settling fetid against my skin, like they are starting to grow into me. My hair is oily, my skin rough with grime and dust. I gather fresh clothes, go to the bathroom and wash—body and hair in the shower, teeth and face in the sink. For one glorious hour I think of nothing but my ablutions. I scrub and lather, soak and cleanse. I pare my nails; I even take a callous knife and carve the hard skin from my heels. My body is healed now, it seems, or nearly enough at any rate; the grazes gone, the bruises faded yellow. I smother myself over with cream, scented subtle with sandalwood and jasmine. And, just like that, I am done—though I wish I could while away another hour at it, another two. But it can't be helped. I am a human again, or passable at least. I am perfumed. I am fully dressed in clean clothes. My tongue tastes of peppermint.

And I have nowhere to go, no one to see, nothing to do.

I can feel it then, hear it again; the little whelping cry, the tremor of dispirit. As though all my efforts were in vain, for naught. The sofa beckons to me, offers to cradle and rock me in its upholstered arms while I sob, sob, sob and vow to never again be so bold as to clean myself and expect the world to look different. And yet, and yet. I stay where I am, rooted to the spot, resisting as best I can the dangling lure of despair. *No.* I will not weep. I will not sink once more into despondency, tempting though it may be. I can hold off for a few minutes yet. So let me go, let me stride out while the spirit is willing and able. Though what to do, what to do? It is morning, true morning, and the sun will be out. Crevan doesn't like me to go out in the sun.

But stay, wait, listen.

Crevan is gone.

I can do whatever I like or choose. I can light a blazing torch and dance along the walls and never mind who may see the flames from the mainland—it's only my own life I'm risking, only my own neck. I can roam outside with no reproach from him, no reprimand or commands to uphold the precious rules, the precious routine. Yes, oh yes.

My feet know the way, know the rhythm: skip-skipping across the living room. In a wink, in a blink, in a trice I am through the blast door and out of the den, racing through the winding, mazing passages of the catacombs, stopping here and there to greet my old friends, my much-neglected favorites; grave statues and grinning skulls. "And a good day to you and yours. Lovely weather. Can't stop. See you anon and send my love to the missus."

Up the stairs on knees and hands, a giddy scramble to the top, to the wicket gate and through it, out into the courtyard; into the sun. There. Sunlight to warm the skin and blind the eyes. Who'd have thought, believed, imagined? The sun is still here.

I blink and blink until the spreading white resolves and comes into focus. Here is the courtyard, just as I left it—more or less—only puddling water in the dips of the flagstones to show that a storm has come and gone. Probably. I didn't hear it howl or see it rage either. But I suppose the puddles are proof enough that there was rain. Unless the water means something else entirely. Perhaps it is pooling groundwater, swelling up between the cracks. Perhaps it was dropped from a bucket by a passing ghost or traveler. Perhaps a wave of the sea reached over the island in the night and this could-be-brine is all that remains. But the reason does not matter, the reason is beside the point. There was not water before and now there is. All that is salient is this: the sun is up and I am unchaperoned. The whole island is mine and mine alone. Crevan would tremble if he knew, quiver if he saw me even *think* of leaving the safety of the courtyard. He would shout and tell me to come back and behave and how it was only for my own good, how I mustn't tempt fate.

Well, Crevan isn't here now. He can't stop me. I will go down to the sea wall, perhaps, say hello to Mr. Dragon and paddle my feet in the waves. Or I will race up and down the paths on the north face of the island, go to inspect the old boats in the harbor, go to wade along the causeway as the tide comes in, and skim stones if the water is calm enough. I will weave a hammock from vines and hang it to swing between the uppermost branches of the tallest tree. I will complete an entire circuit of the island without ever once touching the ground. I will dig in the castle ruins and see if I can't find buried treasure. I will go into the wilderness and become a hunter, set snares and traps, catch a hare and roast it on a spit. I will make a tent of leaves, I will find the island foxes and befriend them, I will climb up to the roof of the watchtower and rob the gulls' nests of eggs. I will practice at making bird calls until the eagles and the crows come to talk with me. Choices, choices. What is a soul to do? Well there's no reason to go lonely, not when there are the dead to visit.

And why not? We have unfinished business, after all, and my shovel is right there, lying where I dropped it after I smashed in the last glass pane of the greenhouse. I bid hearty good morn to the carrion plants as I pass by. They are all seemingly hale and healthy, all happily luxuriating in their corpulent perfume, all evidently unharmed from my violent attempts at introducing ventilation. "And hello to you and you and you. Oh, don't mind me, I'm just stopping by for a moment, I'm just here on an errand. No, no, I can't stay long. I'm on a promise, you know. Off to see an old friend, an enemy."

It occurs to me then that the smashed glass is gone, missing, swept up and cleaned away. My eyes turn to the fig tree beneath which I left Crevan lying. There is no sign he was ever there; all the medications and bedding that I brought up for him have been cleared away along with the glass. Like he never existed in the first place. It gives me pause and fret, makes me wish he were here still; makes me long to run, to find, to bring him back. Only I cannot, only I never will, however much it wounds. For salve I have nothing but gratitude, nothing but gladness; gladness for the knowledge that he still exists out there in the world and in more-or-less Crevan form and shape. But that is all. He is consigned to the mainland now, to his fate, and is no longer my concern. He's not, he's not, he's not. I must remember that. He has nothing to do with me anymore. He was here and then he wasn't. That's the way it goes. Sometimes people just get up and leave, sometimes they vanish, sometimes they disappear. We will say no more about it. Probably. Not for the moment, anyway, not while I'm still feeling like myself and able to face the day. Now, where was I? I came here with a purpose. Ah yes, I remember now. There it is.

The shovel practically jumps to my outstretched hand. I swing it up and settle the shaft in the crook of my shoulder, as though it is a bayonet and I am a young soldier, just signed up to the draft. Hup! Two, three, four. I march merrily on my way, across the courtyard and through the postern, step and step, out into the bracken and then stop.

Is this my wilderness? Is it really? Is this what it has looked like all along? I thought I remembered but it's been so long now since I've been out here in the day, since I've seen this place lit by sun. It should be a forest of moonlight and shadow. It should be nightmares and strange-shaped silhouettes. It should be everything you ever imagined, everything you ever feared. Not this: not merely fern and bush and tree. Not so small. Not so safe.

I squint and try to see what was there before—or could have been—to conjure the beasts and monsters and bogeymen that

surely once lurked among the branches. I look for outlaws and
fairy gates, for gods and talking animals. But if ever they were here
at all, they all of them have gone now; gone, quite gone. The forest
is empty and tame; a domesticated park, a manicured garden.
Well, that is my cross to bear, my lesson to learn: monsters do
not love the day and I should not seek them there. Crevan was
right to warn me against the sunlit hours, though he was wrong as
wrong as to why. There's nothing to fear here, nothing to startle
or alarm. More's the pity.

In my glancing, I see the bundle of clothes heaped in the shelter of
the courtyard wall. They belong to the drowned woman—I brought
them here to mulch, to keep the den free of plastic-eating bacteria.
How ridiculous that must sound to you now that you know, how
absurd. Of course, the clothes haven't degraded; durable acrylics
and polyesters all. I go to inspect them now, tentatively prodding at
the pile with my toe. The clothes are filthy, but only with ordinary
dirt and muck. There are no plastiphages here in reality; these are
not the festering, corroding red fabrics of my worst dreams, my
nightmares. Proof—if any were needed—of the flimsiness of
my counterfactual against the harder fact of the world: a single sheet
of newspaper lifted against the rain, a lick of wet paint layered over
black mold.

Still, it can't be helped. Half-wondering where fell the ragged
hairband that is the match of the clean one on my wrist and
half-knowing that I will never find it again, I scoop up the clothes
into a bundle that I hang from the end of my shovel, turning my
imagined bayonet into a real-enough bindle. Then I venture in
among the branches, pretending as best I can: I am an explorer, an
adventurer, a run-away from home-rer.

It helps a little, though not quite enough. I know exactly where
I am headed; the course that I must set. But it's all too clear, all too
fixed. I am used to working with rough impressions, with guesses
and hunches, with shadows that do not resolve. Now it is mundane:
the crouched gargoyle merely a tree stump, the gaping mouth a

hollow, the reaching hand a gnarled and thorny briar. I have to keep stopping and checking; retracing, redrawing, making doubly, doubly sure that I am where I think I am. Like having to work in three dimensions after becoming accustomed to only two. I am constantly at a loss, if not lost exactly. It is slow, tedious work. I must crawl where once I flew, decipher what once I knew.

When at last I reach the glade where the stone dolmen stands, I am hot and overtired, wishing I had never set foot outside the den. I throw down my shovel-bindle and crawl gladly into the cool shade beneath the capstone. It is a relief to be shielded from the sun, a relief to feel the damp, disturbed earth against my arms and legs as I recline, lying atop the woman's grave. It's like lounging in bed. It's like a welcoming embrace from a dear, dear friend. In just a few short moments, I feel almost like myself. And it is not so bad as before, glancing out at the forest from this low angle, my vision delimited by the stone edges of the dolmen. The leaves soften and blur, become surreal again, become uncanny again; take up once more their old and ancient menace. Breathe in, breathe out. That's better, that's good. Almost like being at home.

"Hello, dear one," I say, fingers delving into dirt. "Did you miss me? Have you been lonely all this time lying cosseted beneath the ground? Have you been wishing for a friendly face, an exchange of pleasantries with a neighbor? Is being submerged in the soil like drowning in the sea? Are you befriending the maggots and earthworms? Is it everything you thought it would be? Are you more skeleton now than flesh or is there still some time to go? Is it quiet? Does the earth whisper? Can you feel the tremors when it rains, when foxes prowl, when moles burrow? Are there roots that reach this far? Do you talk to the trees and do they talk back? What does it smell like down there, how does it look? Is it too dark to tell? Or have your rotting eyes adjusted, are you seeing things you've never seen before? Are you tasting them with every bud of your disintegrating tongue? Is your hair growing still? Your nails on hand and foot? Do you know where you are? Do you remember what happened? Do you dream at all? Do you wish? Do you hope? Are you content? Are you afraid?"

Silence.

"I know, I know, I should have brought you something. An offering. Flowers. Tribute. A meal for the dead. But I have nothing and it's more than you deserve," I say, tapping the ground with my knuckles. "He claimed your death for his own, you know. Crevan, I mean. I think he wishes he never tried to save you; I think if he had his time again, he would have let you drown. Which is just as well, seeing as you were trying to kill me. That's not very nice, not very kind. But you are dead, so I won't hold it against you. Besides, you're a permanent guest of the island now. We have to try and get along. So no hard feelings, all right? I'll forgive you if you'll forgive me. And you should have your own things back."

I get to my knees, remove the bundle from the end of the shovel and then attack the earth with the blade. When I have made a pit, a sufficient hollow in the ground, I stuff the clothes into the hole and then I cover over the lot with dirt, packing it down tight and fast. That's the evidence gone, stowed away; hidden from myself as much as the powers that be. It's what Crevan would want, for his sacrifice to stand, for it to bring safety, comfort; the kind that endures, the kind that lasts. I seal the mound with a kiss and scramble to my feet, reaching for the capstone with one hand.

"I'll come back when I can," I say, my head inclined to the grave. "When I remember. If I remember. I'll say hello and tell you the news. I expect I'll see you around. If you could steer clear of the den, though, I'd appreciate it. It's strictly invitation only and I'm rescinding yours. But you're part of the island now. One of the family, so to speak—or would be if you didn't hate mine so much. But that doesn't matter now, not now you're all one and the same, not now you're all nothing at all. So you may as well make yourself at home here, enjoy yourself if you can. You're a forest now. You're a tree. You're a fern. Make the most of it."

I give the dolmen a final pat and turn heel, setting my uncertain course back through the wilderness. It's tiring this, being up and about. I should like nothing more than a sandwich and a cup of coffee and a lie-down. Perhaps I will close my eyes for the rest of the afternoon and not venture out again until the proper time, when it is good and night. Then I can say hello to the moon, to the stars. Brave the ice waters and go swimming by the sea wall.

For now, I want only den's surety. But I wrong turn and wrong turn, arriving instead on the north face of the island, where I have not been for so long, where Crevan would not let me come. I hover-halt where the land rises and the trees part, my gaze wandering down to the harbor below and then outward, onward.

The tide is in, the causeway flooded, the sea brine-bright beneath the sun. Beyond lie the distant beaches of the mainland, sand rising to grass-topped dunes. They have changed their shapes since last I looked—taken on new poses and postures to accommodate the wishes of the wave-borne winds that pass this way—and so divertingly that I do not, at first, notice the boat upon the shore, nor the figure stooped beside. Shielding my eyes from the sun, I strain against the light until, at last, silhouette resolves to detail.

A man.

A man, stripped to the waist. He is sun-loved and built to kill, a lithe-limbed hero lifted from a black-figured amphora; an Achilles, an Ajax. He should be clapped in cuirass and greaves, racing fleet-foot to battle with spear in hand. Yet here he is, industrious upon the shore, bailing water from some wreck of a boat he's hauled up onto the sand. My attention keens, piques to fascination. To where is he bound, this more-than-mortal, this demigod? From where was he sent?

An answer flits unprompted to my lips. "Not *sent*, silly. Just fleeing the backbiters like any-everyone does." Yes, that's right. That's how it goes, how I remember. There's a reflexive familiarity to it that soothes, that re-orders in a way that orders *me*; settles, lifts.

Perhaps—yes—perhaps I am ready after all. I can feel it in my gut, my marrow. I have gone and come back, ready to start again, anew, afresh. Ready to invent, forget; to make-believe and make it through the night. After all, this is what I know, this is what I'm best at, this is my oldest of habits; the kind I do not need to practice, the kind I can do standing on my head, in my sleep, with both hands tied behind my back. It is all the same, after all, all of a piece; the object and the nerve, the nerve and the image, the image and the idea. The saint and the sinner just as much as the friend and the foe; the gain and the loss, the flight and the fall, the antidote and the poison, the man and his shadow. All of it the same, all of it alike, all only matter—only dreaming—whichever way you look at it, howsoever you tilt your head.

And so I stand and watch, my attention adhered to the man's every move, as though the flick of his wrist or the stoop of his back might telegraph the truths of him, this fellow survivor, this possible friend, possible foe. Before long, I shall know him better; before long, I shall be able to tell. For if the island harbor is not already his intent, it will be soon. He won't resist tide's pull, not when it shows him the causeway that stretches land from land. His feet shall follow where curiosity is sure to fly and I, I shall be waiting; become myself again, perhaps, unbound again by the once-was and will-be of others—other hearts, other minds. There is only my here, after all, only my now. The improbable is mine to promise, the impossible mine to conceive and make whole—new—in every breath that can shape and bear its burden.

ACKNOWLEDGMENTS

Existential matters first: to my agent, the indefatigable John Ash, whose exacting standards made the manuscript what it is and who played an absolute blinder when it came to going out on submission; my eternal thanks. I am similarly and equally grateful to my commissioning editors—Allegra Le Fanu at Bloomsbury and Chelsea Cutchens at The Overlook Press—for their dedication, enthusiasm, and insight. Consummate professionals, all, and a true delight to work with.

My gratitude, also, goes to everyone at Bloomsbury and Overlook who has been involved in this book, with especial thanks to Francisco Vilhena, my managing editor at Bloomsbury, who made my job ridiculously easy, and to Sarah-Jane Forder, copyeditor extraordinaire.

On a more personal note, although I'm intensely (and perhaps detrimentally) private about my solo work while it's in progress, I'm nevertheless indebted to all those whose understanding, support and general good humor has seen me through, including *ma belle famille*—Mary, Aiden, Catherine, Anne-Marie, and Liam; the Szcwczak-Harris clan—Emma, Andrzej, Hieronim, and Orlando; and various friends near and far—Maia, Graham, Nick and Ellen, Ciarán, Donata, Nassos, EC, and Joss.

In particular, I owe my immediate family more than I can possibly express. Mum, Dad, Alex—thank you for everything.

And then there's Eamonn, ofc. Well and tyvm.

A NOTE ON THE AUTHOR

Natasha Calder earned her degree in English from Trinity College Dublin and her master's in medieval literature from Cambridge University. Her work has appeared in *The Stinging Fly*, *Lackington's*, and *Curiosities*, among others, and she is coauthor of *The Offset* by Calder Szewczak. She is based in the UK. *Whether Violent or Natural* is her first solo novel.

A NOTE ON THE TYPE

The text of this book is set in Perpetua. This typeface is an adaptation of a style of letter that had been popularized for monumental work in stone by Eric Gill. Large-scale drawings by Gill were given to Charles Malin, a Parisian punch-cutter, and his hand-cut punches were the basis for the font issued by Monotype. First used in a private translation called "The Passion of Perpetua and Felicity," the italic was originally called Felicity.